Gilded Age

· · · · · · · · · · ·

CLAIRE McMILLAN

Simon & Schuster

New York London Toronto Sydney New Delhi

Simon & Schuster
1230 Avenue of the Americas
New York, NY 10020

First Simon & Schuster hardcover edition June 2012

For information about special discounts for bulk purchases, please contact Simon & Schuster Special Sales at 1-866-506-1949 or business@simonandschuster.com.

The Simon & Schuster Speakers Bureau can bring authors to your live event. For more information or to book an event, contact the Simon & Schuster Speakers Bureau at 1-866-248-3049 or visit our website at www.simonspeakers.com.

Designed by Jill Putorti

Manufactured in the United States of America

10 9 8 7 6 5 4 3 2 1

Library of Congress Cataloging-in-Publication Data
McMillan, Claire.
Gilded age : a novel / Claire McMillan.—1st Simon & Schuster hardcover ed.
    p.   cm.
1. Rich people—Fiction. 2. Upper class families—Fiction. 3. Cleveland (Ohio)—Fiction.
I. Title.
PS3613.C58539G55   2011
813'.6—dc22   2011009795
ISBN 978-1-4516-4047-2
ISBN 978-1-4516-4049-6 (ebook)

For Sandy

Contents

I declare to you that woman must not depend upon the protection of man, but must be taught to protect herself, and there I take my stand.

—SUSAN B. ANTHONY

· 1 ·

The Orchestra

I'm a native Clevelander. I went east to school, as we do. And I married the loveliest man from Charleston, South Carolina, and convinced him to move back to Cleveland and start a family with me, as Clevelanders do. Nothing is more usual than Clevelanders of a certain ilk leaving, seeing the world, and then dragging a spouse back to settle down. My husband, Jim, calls himself in jest an import—used to vary the breeding stock.

And variety is needed here. I've known most of my Cleveland friends since we were infants, since crawling around together on faded Oriental carpets and cartwheeling in the grass at country club picnics. My parents knew their parents, and my parents' parents knew their grandparents, and so it goes back to the very beginnings when Cleveland was considered the West, and nice families had to stick together. So imports are needed, as few things are less exciting than kissing someone you've known since kindergarten.

I tell you all this so that when I tell you that Eleanor Hart moved back to Cleveland without an import, you have a sense of the problem this presented.

I've known Eleanor since those days when we played while our mothers gossiped over coffee. I call her mother Aunt Hart, though technically we are no relation. Her father died when she was a girl.

It's rumored that my great-grandmother once went on a date with Eleanor's great-grandfather. They say he took her to a speakeasy for some prohibition gin, and great-grandmother never spoke to him again. This only goes to show that Harts are adventurous and my family a bit prudish, yet discreet—a family trait.

Anyway, Eleanor was older than I by a year or two. I always forgot her age, and this coupled with her ridiculous beauty made her seem impossibly glamorous to me. Yet even as a child, she was always friendly to me. She was like an admired older cousin, and I'd known her forever.

My mother told me Eleanor was coming back. Mother talks to Aunt Hart all the time, though Aunt Hart moved down to Florida with a man a few years back. The Harts are a very fine family, but as long as we've known them they've been strapped for cash. My mother says they're lucky the women in their family are so charming, and I suppose that's true.

So I was only a little surprised to see Eleanor at Severance Hall, seated in a family friend's box for the orchestra's opening night of the season. Next to her was William Selden.

Of course I'd known Selden since childhood. He's a little younger than I; the most angelic boy you've ever seen, with a head of wild blond cherubic curls that had darkened only a bit as he'd aged and were now matched by a gruff five o'clock shadow and thick tortoise-shell glasses surrounding his hazel eyes. Those glasses were a stroke of genius. They seemed to say he was a man above caring what he looked like, and it is always most attractive when a man is beautiful enough not to care what he looks like. Now he was a professor of English at Case Western Reserve University, where his classes were packed almost exclusively with girls who had crushes on him. I'd heard rumors of liaisons with students but tended to doubt such stories. Good-looking men always have such whisperings in their wake, don't they?

Good-looking women too, now that I think about it. His specialty was the Romantic poets—a bit surprising, yes, that he'd be interested in those musty old rebels. You'd expect cutting-edge contemporary free verse. But I've since learned that maybe I haven't always had the clearest view of Selden. Anyway, Romantics it was, and he'd been fishing around town for a tenure-track position for a number of years. He probably would have found one long ago had he not insisted on staying in Cleveland.

He and Ellie sat in the box across from ours. To my left, Julia Trenor and Diana Dorset hugged over the waist-high wall separating their families' boxes. The Van Alstyne family's box to my right was filled with people I didn't recognize. The Van Alstynes had likely sold their tickets to opening night. Farther to the right old Jefferson Gryce's nurse pushed his wheelchair into his family's box. In all the boxes around me people rearranged themselves in the heavy velvet chairs so that they could sit closer to one another and hear the latest gossip along with their Mahler. Friday and Saturday nights you might find anyone up there. But Thursday nights the boxes belonged to the same family names that had been sitting there when the concert hall opened in 1931. The Saturday-night opening of the music season was the sole exception.

People were intent on greeting each other. I stood in the front of the box and leaned out, casting a small wave across the way to Ellie. I noted the floor seats were filled, but seats stood empty in the balconies. They hadn't managed a sell-out, but the economy being what it was, I suppose that wasn't unusual. I still felt the general buzz of opening night, heightened by Eleanor being in town, and I enjoyed my prime seat.

Ellie was used to being the most beautiful woman in the room wherever she went, but she carried it lightly. Her thick hair was the color of tobacco, subtly streaked with honey, and hung down her back like a royal mantle. The fretwork in Severance Hall is modeled, so it's said, on the lace of John Severance's wife's wedding veil and the Deco gilt-work glowed on Eleanor's hair like a mantilla. Looking at that hair, I could only think that the upkeep—in cut and color—must be expensive, though that is not the effect it had on men. Men, I felt sure, only wanted to get their hands into it, mess it, feel it, and see what it looked like on the pillow next to them first thing in the morning.

She wore a sleeveless black leather dress of chicly conservative cut that hugged her curves. I don't need to tell you that no one wears a leather dress to the orchestra in Cleveland. She'd tied a wide white ribbon at the waist, and on the knot of the bow she'd pinned a medal awarded to a Hart in World War I by the French. She looked youthful and chic with an alluring edge of danger. I admired her, as I do anyone who dresses well.

The women all forgave her for outshining them—poor Eleanor had returned from Manhattan. Alone. Divorced. And, so rumors said, fresh from thirty days at Sierra Tucson for unspecified indulgences. Though if anyone dared ask my mother if Eleanor had been in rehab, mother insisted Ellie had collapsed from the stress of her divorce. Mother's a bit old-fashioned about addiction and things.

I mean, how many sober ex-classmates and old friends do I have? A bunch. And they'll gladly talk to you about it if you ask, even volunteer the fact if an overeager hostess is pushing booze on them. "No, thanks, I'm in recovery," they'll say. If it's a young hostess, she'll want to know where they went for detox. "Oh, I had a friend go there, too." But if it's someone in my mom's generation, the hostess will turn white as a sheet, smile, nod, and get the hell out of there.

The men in the concert hall all simply enjoyed looking at Ellie.

One man in particular could not keep his eyes off her. He was so obvious that I wasn't the only one who noticed. He sat in the box that the orchestra kept for wooing potential patrons, the box next to Ellie's, and I had a clear view of him staring. The director of development sat next to him keeping up a patter in his ear. He looked to be about my age with a sharply cut suit, the whitest teeth I'd ever seen, and a head full of dark hair—attractive hair, quite glossy, with a heavy sheen of gel in it.

I didn't think about the man again until halfway through the first piece when a cell phone rang during a particularly quiet moment of the performance. Every head in the boxes turned toward it, and I saw it belonged to the same man. The development director turned scarlet. The man reached coolly—I was impressed by his cool—into his jacket and silenced his phone.

"God," mumbled my husband, leaning his shoulder into mine and whispering in my ear. "Typical."

"You know him?" I whispered.

"That's Randall Leforte, the lawyer."

"I should know him?"

"The ambulance chaser. He's sued the Cleveland Clinic for millions. He's as rich as Steve Jobs or those Google guys or something now."

I remembered seeing him on the cover of *Cleveland* magazine as our town's most eligible bachelor; he was photographed leaning up against his Maserati. Charitable and philanthropic boards all over town were vying to get a piece of his money.

At intermission Eleanor slipped into our box, as I knew she would, hugged me, and hugged my husband, Jim.

"Thank God, you're here. I thought you might be." She beamed at us. She'd always liked Jim. Most everyone did. My husband's background of boarding school, Duke, and investment bank on Wall Street made him enough like a good Cleveland son. Yet his southern accent and manners made him an antebellum exotic. There is nothing certain Clevelanders like more than a whiff of a tattered but glorious past hanging about a person. Luckily that particular southern trait rolled off Jim as languidly as his drawl.

William and Jim led us out of the box to the patrons' dining room, talking about the Indians in the playoffs.

"So William Selden . . . ," I breathed behind their backs, fishing.

"You've known Selden as long as I have. He's just a friend."

"Just a friend?" I asked. "An awfully good-looking friend . . ."

"An awfully good-looking old friend," Ellie said with a smile.

We walked into the dark paneled room behind the boxes where

silver samovars of coffee and a bar awaited. I took two gingersnap cookies, their recipe unchanged since 1931, off a Sèvres tray. Ginger is good for nausea and in my condition I'd found a new sweet tooth I hadn't had before. Eleanor eyed me as she drank black coffee.

"Eating for two," I said.

"My mom told me. Congrats." Her tone was flat with disinterest.

"Well, don't jump up and down or anything," I said, joking but feeling stung. Ellie, I knew, was not keen on children. But I thought at least she could muster some enthusiasm for me.

She smiled. "Oh, I'm happy for you. You know how I feel." It was as if she'd said, "That dress looks great on you; I'd never be caught dead in the thing."

It didn't satisfy.

"You and Jim will make wonderful parents," she said listlessly as she scanned the room.

I'd forgotten this part of Ellie in the years since I'd last seen her. She was self-concerned, always had been, in a way that could be annoyingly juvenile. Oddly enough it was also one of the things that made me feel comfortable around her. Ellie made no pretense about who she was or what she thought. Given the Cleveland world I navigated, anyone who was straightforward, even if it was straightforwardly self-centered, was refreshing. You always knew where you stood with her, which is much more than I can say for a good number of people on my contact list. "Tell me about the conductor," she said.

I swallowed a large bite. "You know I'm a musical illiterate. But everyone says he's wonderful. Lovely accent—Austrian or something. I heard him interviewed on the radio once—"

"No, no, you know what I mean," she said in a lowered voice.

I must admit that I laughed in her face. Leave it to Eleanor to be searching out men at the orchestra. Most men in the boxes were married, upwards of sixty, or both. I wondered that she didn't ask about Randall Leforte, given his obvious interest in her. In any case, she'd zeroed in on the man who'd been in front of her for the last hour, the conductor.

"Married," I said. "Happily, I think. There's a child and such."

Eleanor shrugged and resumed scanning the room. "You know what I kept thinking as I sat there?" she asked. "I kept thinking that all these people, their job is to do something they love. Can you even imagine it? The dedication, the discipline, the practice—you couldn't do it if you didn't have passion. And that's what they get to do with their lives. Something they have real passion for. The passionate life. I wish I had that."

"Don't we all," I said.

"Or to have a skill like that. To be one of the best in the world at something."

"You're the best in the world at being fabulous," I said. I meant it truly, and lightly, but it came out as condescending.

"When's the last time you felt passion?" she asked a bit aggressively.

I'd touched a nerve. Her questioning the passion in my life was the old bias that escaped Clevelanders have against the Midwest. The assumption was that you couldn't have passion in Cleveland. It raised my ire a bit, yes. And while I thought this a little provincial, I guess I knew what she was getting at as it related to me. My prospects at the big-five accounting firm where I'd worked before my marriage had never been my life's passion. Recently, I'd started to feel my marriage and a coming child might help me in this area. Not in a Betty Crocker, Phyllis Schlafly type of way, but in the way that I now had someone I could help along in life, a marriage to invest in. This baby, I hoped, might add to that sense. People say nothing else is important once your child is born, and part of me was banking on this. In any case, I wanted to put Ellie at ease. She'd just returned, and it was the first time I'd seen her since her divorce. I pointed to my waist, just ever so slightly showing, and though I knew it was not what she meant I said, "Well, there was at least one night of passion."

Eleanor relaxed and laughed. "It seems like no time has passed since last I saw you."

"That's how Cleveland is," I said, smiling, glad the situation was defused.

"It's good to be back. These last six months have been pretty hard."
She sipped her coffee.

It was then that Jim seemed to materialize at my arm with Randall
Leforte in tow and introduced him to Ellie. Something in Jim's pos-
ture made him seem pleased that he could introduce them. Whether
he was proud of knowing Ellie or glad to be seen with one of the
sharpest litigators in town, I didn't know.

Leforte smiled wide and moved in close as he took Ellie's hand. It
was fascinating to watch—and I'd been watching since we were children—the pull she had over men. I thought he might bend over her
hand and kiss it. He smelled like patchouli, a hippie-ish, slightly dirty
smell that didn't mesh at all with his polished exterior. He clasped her
hand and released it, his eyes wandering up and down her body, as if
he'd like to do so much more than shake her hand.

Ellie was, of course, aware of the effect she had on Leforte. But it
didn't seem to please her. It seemed to bore her. She was looking for
Selden, who was across the room talking to a group of men, each of
them old enough to be his father. I felt sure they were discussing the
financial state of the orchestra, the need for younger patrons.

"Mahler's my favorite," Leforte said, moving in close to Ellie.
"Though I prefer *Titan*."

Ellie rocked back and forth on her feet, looking like she was ready
to spring for an exit, and I couldn't figure out why. Leforte was attractive and certainly some chitchat with him wouldn't hurt.

"You mean his First Symphony?" she asked.

"Yes, I guess I do," he said in a hearty tone as he shifted closer to
her, almost turning his back to me, trying to ease me out of the conversation and gain some privacy until Betsy Dorset interrupted us all.

Betsy Dorset wore trim black pants, a black long-sleeved T-
shirt, and a neon green fleece vest—the type bought at sporting
goods stores. Pinned to the fleece was the immense Dorset diamond
brooch from the turn of the century, valued—so I'd heard—at half
a million dollars. With her kind smile, cropped silver hair, and sensible shoes, she was the very model of a new-millennium Cleveland

dowager. Her son, Dan, and I were the same age and had been at school together.

She hugged Jim and me and then made a great fuss over Eleanor, whom she'd known as a baby. Clevelanders of a certain age love few things more than one of their own returning home, and Ellie had the satisfying air of the prodigal about her.

Just as Randall was quietly trying to slip away unnoticed, Betsy demanded an introduction, and Jim obliged.

"Oh, but I know you from your billboard," Betsy said, shaking his hand.

"Billboard?" Eleanor blurted before she could censor herself.

"Mr. Leforte has a billboard just as you come into downtown on the Innerbelt," Betsy said to Eleanor. "I must admit it doesn't do you justice," she said to Randall. She said it in a flirty, confidential tone, but I knew she'd meant it not at all nicely. She sat on the board of the Cleveland Clinic; I'm sure she'd been forced to deal with Leforte, his clients, and their demands for legal settlements. She knew exactly who he was. "It has your eight-hundred number on it," she added brightly. "Doesn't it, Mr. Leforte?"

The chimes rang, calling us back to our seats for the second half of the music. Leforte made a quick exit.

"That man," Betsy said in a hushed voice as she hugged me good-bye. "Getting rich off hospitals and others' misfortunes. It's the height of poor taste." And she wafted off in a cloud of Joy perfume.

"I'll come see you next week," Eleanor said as Selden took her arm to lead her back to the box.

"Come on Wednesday," I said. "Stay for dinner if you like." Jim clasped my hand and steered me back to the box with my family's name painted in swirling gold script over the door. The box my family has occupied since the hall opened in 1931.

2

The Bungalow

Ellie accepted Selden's invitation back to his house for a drink after the concert. He escorted her to her car, taking her the long way around the reflecting pond in front of the art museum, which was blindingly white under spotlights, marking it as a beacon of culture.

"You didn't have to do this," she said.

"This isn't the greatest area at night."

"You forget I've been living in New York." Though now that Selden mentioned it, she remembered the park nearby had been dicey when she was a girl—rumored to be littered with needles and pipes and other unmentionable trash from furtive liaisons. But earlier this evening, as she'd arrived at Severance Hall, Ellie had seen a bride and groom having their wedding portraits taken right in this very spot. The clean Greek columns of the museum set off the bridal gown perfectly.

As Ellie and Selden rounded on the glowing front of the art museum, passing one of Rodin's thinkers pondering them from his gleaming spotlight, a young couple emerged from under a low-hang-ing willow tree: he in a slim suit, thin tie, and black Converse sneakers, she in cat-eye glasses and a red taffeta dress. The boy was leaning down, intent to hear what the girl was saying, then he whispered in her ear. Lights from the water reflected on his teeth when he smiled, lit up her plump arm as she covered her mouth to laugh.

The gravel paths here were pristinely maintained. The young couple added youthful energy, and what was that feeling Ellie had when she saw them—hope, envy, anticipation? It'd been so long since she'd felt anything; she could hardly remember.

She watched as the boy lifted the girl's hand and kissed it. Was I ever that young? Ellie wondered as Selden handed her into her car.

She drove slowly over to Selden's house, giving him time to get there before her. The Heights were alive with evening strollers, dog walkers, fathers hauling garbage cans to the curb. As she drove past one driveway, a woman unloaded pumpkins, probably from the West Side Market, from her car. A kid in a number 23 jersey rode his bike down the sidewalk. A young guy in scrubs with disheveled hair walked with a cell phone lodged between ear and shoulder, a computer bag slung across his body. The sidewalks were busy and bright under the streetlamps. The Heights' streets didn't have energy like Manhattan. But a cozy warmth emanated from the neighborhood, as if neighbors might still drop in on one another and leave their calling cards during "at-homes" like people did a hundred years ago.

She parked in front of Selden's small prairie-style bungalow. Though she could have had her guard up at his suggestive invitation, she didn't. She'd known Selden from childhood. She knew all the pretty boys. Though she'd spent a few nights comfortably flirting with him in bars or sitting next to him at concerts like the one they'd just attended, she'd never taken him seriously. He was younger and an academic, which only slightly intimidated her and completely deterred her. The academic life was a tough one, almost worse than the military; you never knew where you might have to live. No, Selden had been a pleasant distraction in the pursuit of serious game.

The lawns on Selden's street set the houses back a good way, making everything feel private. The deep porch wrapped around his one-story house like a secluded embrace. Walking up the steps, she felt confident she had made the better choice over staying in New York.

He swung the door wide for her, ushering her inside. Selden's living room had a broad-beamed ceiling and a fireplace tiled in celadon green. He walked here and there, clicking on lamps. He'd furnished the room in what she guessed were thrift store finds—the ratty couch in nubby orange, the white space-age floor lamp arcing over a chrome and glass coffee table—the home of a bohemian and threadbare member of the Rat Pack. A frumpy Queen Anne desk, likely a cast-off from his parents, was littered with a laptop, an iPod, crumpled papers, and a few thick card-stock invitations stuck at random angles under a plastic Magic 8 Ball. Every nice young bachelor had a little untidy stack like that—nice bachelors always being in demand for weddings, birthdays that end in 0, cocktails to meet the new museum curator, and fancy dinner parties.

Selden opened the windows to the crisp night air and the faint scent of burning leaves. Academic books and journals covered the floor near the couch. He took off his jacket and rolled up his sleeves, the dim light catching the fine auburn hair on his arm. On a low table next to a reading lamp was a small bouquet of burnt-orange roses in a dented brass urn. He disappeared into the kitchen.

Ellie appraised it all and then nestled herself into a low chair.

"What a lovely thing to have a place like this," Ellie called to him.

After some banging and clanging, Selden came in the room with a squat glass of tequila with a lime, a pot of tea, and a plate of pears with honey for dipping.

"Women have been known to have their own houses," he said, handing her a cup of mint tea. She noted that he'd not even offered her a real drink. Apparently her stay in Arizona was already public news in Cleveland.

"Everyone says don't buy a house if you want to get married. You'll look too set in your ways, too grounded . . ."

"A lot of bullshit."

"Mmm," Ellie hummed. Selden was typical, she thought, professing not to care if a woman had a life, had a place of her own. But her mother seemed to think that men really did care about that. That a young woman in possession of her own house, her own space in the world, intimidated a man, left him emasculated. Perhaps a man felt he had nothing to offer if he couldn't offer shelter? Absurd. Or did a man want someone with no past of her own?

She sighed and dipped a slice of pear into the honey. "How did you think of this?"

"Enjoying the last of the season."

She held her palm under her hand as she guided the dripping fruit to her mouth, the sweet ooze of honey on the grainy pear. "You'd think it'd be gilding the lily, but it's delicious."

He smiled, and she noticed that he was watching her mouth.

Ellie leaned back in her chair and sipped her tea, sweet and sharpish on her tongue. "Working hard?" she said, gesturing to his desk.

He turned toward the desk as if seeing it for the first time and rumpled a hand through his hair, ending with it resting on the back of his neck. "I'm prepping for a new class I'm teaching next term."

"What's it called?"

"'Decline, Decay, and Death,'" he said with a slow smile.

"Light." She nodded. "That will have them preregistering for sure."

He laughed. "They do. I have wait lists."

"Yes, but it's not because those undergrads want to depress themselves."

"There are some serious students."

"It's the chance to look at you for fifty minutes twice a week, you sweet ding-dong."

"They can find better views than that," Selden said, suddenly turning toward the windows.

Ellie looked out the heavy leaded windows too. "Maybe." So here was William Selden's passion—a lot of old books, descriptions of love, death, and loss. She wondered if he actually had experienced true love or passion in his life, or if he was content to merely read about it. Looking at him now, she couldn't decide.

As she sat there watching him, wondering if he'd ever loved someone more than himself, she wished, not for the first time, that she'd pursued something in her life. She'd gone to a mediocre college and received mediocre grades, and afterward she counted herself lucky to land an internship at a fashion magazine in New York. She remembered those days fondly now, though at the time she'd felt panicked. She'd fetched coffee and copies for mercurial men who wore bronzer and opined about sequins. It had seemed exciting for about six months, and then she'd started to wonder what was next. She was living in a tiny apartment with four other girls. In her life of late nights drinking and exhaustion, of being constantly surrounded by gay men or other women, there were no straight male prospects inhabiting her fashion orbit.

She didn't have the grades or the interest for graduate school. At the time she'd rather have died than return to Cleveland and her mother's house. She started to think about marriage, preferably to a Wall Street type in a bespoke suit with a classic six on the Upper East Side.

"What about you?" Selden asked her.

"What about me?" Ellie started. She'd lost track of what they were talking about.

"Any proposals forthcoming? Any news you'd like to share with me?" His eyes were glinting, back to joking.

She rolled her eyes. "You act like marriage is the only thing on my mind."

"Isn't it?" He smiled.

"No," she said petulantly, though she forgave Selden for saying this. It was what everyone thought of her, wasn't it? Her marriage to her first husband was deemed brilliant by those around her. Alex was the son of an old New York family. Their engagement announcement was written up in the *Times* with ample mention of her husband's background and little mention of her provenance. Their large town house on the Upper East side, all five floors, was a gift from his family. They spent weekends at his family's farm upstate.

All the togetherness, the demands of his family name, used to grate on him. He complained about the expectations. So it seemed natural he would blow off steam. Yes, Alex had enjoyed a good time. What she hadn't understood was that she was not supposed to enjoy herself equally as much. If he dabbled in a few controlled substances here and there, well, so did she.

Ellie had spent so much of her life being attractive, leading up to the ultimate test—catching a husband. Landing Alex had practically been a military campaign complete with complex strategy, precision, and subterfuge. One night, nine months into her marriage, she'd come to bed and found him passed out, his breathing shaky after a forty-eight-hour bender, a wad of blood-streaked tissues on the bed stand next to an orange prescription bottle. She watched him, making sure his breathing steadied, that he was all right. She wondered, for the first time since she'd started dating at fifteen, the first time in her life, really—did she even like this guy? The answer that night was, she wasn't sure.

Over the next weeks as she observed his red eyes, his greasy hair, his complaints about the lazy housekeeper, his constant texts to his source, his bitching about his parents, his manic chattering about politics, she decided she didn't. It wasn't exactly fair; she'd admit that. She'd known what she was getting into. She'd changed, not him.

Anyway, he didn't stop, and she spent nights with either a maniac or a zombie. Could she really be blamed for taking up with a more attentive and lucid young man only tangentially in their New York circle?

Apparently she could.

"You should get a place like mine," Selden was saying.

"If you ever think of selling, call me." She leaned forward and took another piece of pear off the low tray. "What about you?" she asked. "Shouldn't you be settling down by now?"

He tilted his head, looking at her quizzically.

"You're very civilized, William Selden," she said, teasing him. "Very domesticated. You need a wife to complete the picture."

To her surprise he blushed and drained the last of his tequila. "Cigarette?" He opened a wooden inlaid box on the table, and she took one and then took a few more for her purse.

"Ladies buy their own nowadays, yeah?" he said, arching an eyebrow.

"But I like the brand you buy." He lit her cigarette. "They taste better having been with you." She stood up to peruse his bookshelves. "Besides, I shouldn't really be smoking. If I buy a pack, I'll just smoke them all." She felt him observing her, detached and yet interested. Men were always interested. What had it brought her? she wondered. Her wasted ex-husband and other men who wanted to posses her beauty for varying lengths of time. Not that she'd have it any other way, of course. It was much easier to be pretty than not; she knew that.

"Have you actually read all these books?" she asked.

"Course," he answered distractedly.

What did he see in those poems? Did he write any of his own? She didn't want to ask. It'd be rude if he'd been published and she didn't know. Perhaps he'd be embarrassed if he hadn't written anything at all. "Important for being a professor?"

"Important for having a life."

"Life of the mind," she said, nodding.

He shrugged in assent.

She knelt down to look at a book on the low shelf. "What's life for anyway, Selden? That's what I keep wondering."

"Life is for enjoying." He laughed and reached to refresh her tea. But she didn't laugh. "Right?"

She straightened up, eyes still on the bookcases. "Yes, but how?"

"Now, that is a serious question," he replied, moving toward her. "In need of serious consideration." He smiled, his tone light.

"I've already made so many mistakes," she said, cutting him off.

He said nothing but reached for her waist. His hands fumbling there brought a rush of heat to her middle. He tugged at the ribbon, unclasping the pin and worrying the knot like a puzzle until he'd untied her sash. She remembered that as a boy he'd stolen the pink gingham ribbon out of her hair and teased her that her ponytail was as thick as a real pony's. This upset her at the time; now she'd take it as a compliment. He was aware of her past; she knew that. He was aware of the things being said about her. He probably thought her a frivolous gold digger. He took her wrist and wrapped the ribbon around it several times, securing the whole thing with a tight knot, placing the pin in her hand.

"What's that for?" She smiled, but she knew. Men had been marking her since grade school—from the boy who insisted she wear the stickers he gave her, to the college boyfriend who wrote his name in Sharpie on her thigh after each time they'd had sex, to her ex-husband, who'd wanted her wedding band tattooed on her finger, meshing his prep school background with his penchant for the seedy. Fortunately, she'd successfully resisted that last one.

"To remember," Selden said. "That life is for enjoying."

She smiled at that. "Shouldn't it go on my finger for remembering?"

"You'll wear it longer here," he said, leaning close.

"I know I've made mistakes." She turned back to the shelves, mumbling to herself. "I don't want to make any more."

"You won't," he said quietly, moving beside her. "I know it."

He was close enough that she could smell the peppery tequila on his breath, could see the blond scruff next to his ear that he'd missed shaving. Her wrist started to pound where he'd tied the ribbon tightly, almost cutting off her circulation. She walked over to the table and picked up her teacup. "I should go."

"Right," he said, flustered, confused, she knew, by her sudden movements. "Course."

She gathered her coat, her purse, looked at her phone while Selden busied himself with plates and cups. She felt the age difference between them then. An older man, a man her age, would have grabbed her, she thought. An older man wouldn't have picked up on her subtle change of energy or would have ignored it, would have taken what he wanted. But Selden was perceptive, perhaps a bit shy around her. He paid attention. She wondered what it would be like to kiss him.

She gave her head a sharp shake.

"Thank you," she said, smiling at him. "You know there's no one here who understands these sorts of things."

He shoved his hands in his pockets. "You'd be surprised."

She was out the door before he could say more, and she felt him watching her as she walked down the block to her car, blood pounding in her hand below the ribbon, the autumn leaves swirling at her heels.

3

The Coq au Vin

I was nervous when five o'clock rolled around on Wednesday, bringing the expected arrival of Ellie. She sometimes had that effect on me. I always forgot how stunning she was, how alluring to men. Her beauty was rare, based on symmetry and ancient geometry. Her figure was statuesque, buxom I guess you'd call it. She wasn't fat, but her figure wasn't the height of fashion either. Her lush curves seemed to appeal to men though. I'd heard it said she had a nice rack.

Back one day, and she already had the town's most eligible bachelor practically kissing her hand. I wondered, not for the first time, what it would be like to be her and be above the normal rules of how things worked.

Not that I was ugly. I knew that, and I'd had my share of admirers and lovers and a well-remembered few who'd called me beautiful. But if you were Ellie, did your face (and your figure—let's be honest) get you the benefit of the doubt, jump you to the head of the line, deliver absolution for most anything you did?

Then again, a pretty face isn't the thickest armor when returning home to face scandal.

In any case, her lackluster reaction to the news of my pregnancy brought back memories of our childhood in close proximity—both her kindness and her cruelty, as in any long association—and I wondered how it would be having her back in town this time.

She walked through the front door without knocking, as she always had since we were small. She wore slim jeans and a billowy white peasant shirt over a black lace bra. She jingled with jewelry and trinkets of gold and pearl. A messily wrapped white ribbon wound around her left wrist. I was barely showing, but next to her I already felt bulky and hugely pregnant. Ellie wore all her clothes as comfortably as if she were wearing pajamas, with a louche sexiness I'd long ago given up trying to emulate. She brought me a potted calla lily and an enormous box of white chocolates—my favorites. I was touched she remembered.

"You're allowed to eat them all. Eating for two," she said kindly, perhaps making up for her lack of enthusiasm the other night.

"Yes, but one of us is the size of a pea."

She laughed, and I showed her into the kitchen, where I was making coq au vin for Jim, my first effort. I'd finally been able to unpack all the wedding presents that I'd been storing at my mother's, as Jim's and my apartment in New York hadn't had space for an extensive kitchen. Now my French enameled crocks and stainless steel pots gleamed, ready for use, ready to help me turn out the smells and meals of a real home. Unfortunately, my knowledge of cooking was negligible. But never mind, I was ready to learn.

Ellie sat down at my marble café table in the breakfast room and started rooting in her oversized handbag—buttery heavy leather, expensive and scarred from use.

"Drink?" I asked, pointing to a bottle of wine on the counter between the two rooms. I was drinking Pellegrino.

"I'll have what you're having," she said. "Remember?"

"Oh, sorry," I said. Rehab.

I filled an old cut-glass water tumbler that had been my granny's. I enjoyed these little flourishes. So many choices were up to me now that I had my own private world to command—from paint and paper, rugs and light fixtures, to the glass I served a guest in. It was part of why I'd convinced Jim to come back. For just a moment I was proud of what I was starting to form.

"Do you mind?" Ellie asked, pulling out a silver cigarette case engraved with her scrolling monogram and a matching lighter. She must have seen the horrified look on my face because she opened a window, pulled a chair next to it, and sat down. "I'll blow straight out the window. You won't even smell it."

"Ell . . . ," I said.

But she was already lighting up. "You'll see. I'll put it out if it bothers you."

This is how it had been since we were girls. From eating the last cupcake, to borrowing your favorite bracelet without asking, to raiding your parents' liquor cabinet to your certain punishment—there was no stopping Ellie. You could object, but she went right along and did what she liked anyway. It was a trade-off I was used to. Most everyone was. In exchange, when you were around her she gave you a feeling that she'd just come from a party, exciting things were just around the corner, and she'd be taking you with her wherever she was headed next. Ellie was always at the center of things, and when you were with her, you were too.

She lit her smoke and as she exhaled the smell brought the clearest memory of driving with her in her mother's Saab, listening to Morrissey sing, passing red-label Dunhills and lipsticks back and forth between us. I must have been in high school, she in college, as we headed to a party in the woods or a tennis game at the country club with older boys, popular boys, on a crystalline day driving into our limitless futures. She'd exercised a sisterly affection over me as she watched that I didn't drink too much or made sure I was paired with the boy I was interested in for mixed doubles. The smell of her smoke, that faint taste—it flavored my fondest memories of our friendship.

I brought her an old saucer to use as an ashtray and went back to washing mushrooms in the sink. We chatted about our mothers, Jim, and the pregnancy. I avoided the topic of the divorce, figuring she'd bring it up if she wanted to talk about it. She smoked and drank the rest of the Pellegrino before she came to the point of her visit.

"Tell me about Randall Leforte," she said. "I've never seen him before last night."

"Is your divorce final?" I said, moving to a cutting board to start chopping.

I'd meant this lightly, as a joke, but she winced. "Good garden seed," she said, exposing her Cleveland roots with that turn of phrase. "Yes."

"Sorry," I said. "I really am."

"Thanks," she said, waving smoke out the window as if waving the matter away.

"You interested?" I asked. "In Leforte?"

"I might be."

Post-college, when I'd lived in New York, I'd often gone out with Ellie, and I was used to her predatory categorization of men. There was big game; there was fishing; there were game birds; and there were wild animals.

"You want big-game hunting, he's the biggest in town," I said, slicing slowly through my pile of mushrooms and onions.

"Really? That's it? There used to be lots of interesting men around."

"I think he's pretty much it, unless you want to go professional athlete."

She rolled her eyes at this. "You mean become one of Grady's Ladies?"

"Grady Sizemore is adorable," I said.

"He's a baby, and I'm still a good decade away from cougar-dom."

"Over forty, that's the def."

"I'm not there yet." She sat pensive for a moment. "I hate that word."

"Like the older woman is always the predator," I said. "What about the mougar?"

She laughed so hard smoke came out of her nose. "The man cougar?"

"Yeah, like George Clooney."

"No one uses that word."

"I think Sizemore is like twenty-seven, too old for a cougar anyway. Plus he got caught sexting someone."

She raised an eyebrow at that.

"Naked pictures," I said, putting a pile of mushrooms in a bowl and turning back to my recipe for what felt like the hundredth time.

"Well that's more like it," she said, smiling. "Brady Quinn is not bad looking," she offered.

I started picking some thyme. "Definitely cute, but he was traded away."

"That's your flavor, isn't it?" she said.

I blushed.

"Jim kind of looks like him," she said. "Definitely your flavor."

She drew out another cigarette, which annoyed me. "Seriously, what happened to all the interesting men in the Midwest?" she asked, and then lit her smoke.

"They all moved to New York, or Miami—LeBron, you know."

"I'm not going back to New York," she said, exhaling. "Seriously, what happened to Cinco Van Alstyne?"

Cinco was the nickname of Henry Pryce Van Alstyne V. His El Salvadorian nanny had coined the nickname when he was an infant. It'd stuck all through grade school, high school, college, and law school. Now, in a white-shoe downtown law firm where he was a promising associate, he went by Cinco to everyone but the courts.

Calm and reliable, he'd been my first kiss in the sandbox, and we'd remained friends. The Van Alstynes were a founding family of Cleveland. At one point Cinco's great-great-grandfather had been the richest man in Ohio with a huge mansion downtown, long since sold to the state and now a museum. My family has known their family forever. Some called Cinco snobbish, others arrogant, but I knew he was merely shy.

"Married," I said. "Don't you remember the wedding a few years ago? He's just moved back and is living out on that dilapidated country estate. The wife's from New York. You should know her."

I had yet to run into them.

Ellie ran through a list that we'd discussed many times consisting of our ex-boyfriends and the eligible men we'd grown up with. They were all married, married, married with children, and married. One had bought a winery in Napa and was now bankrupt.

"Huh." She ashed her cigarette out the window. "I thought it'd be easier here."

I snorted. "Everyone's settled down here. I'd think it would be easier to find a single man in Manhattan. New York is huge."

I was done prepping my ingredients. It was time to start cooking, and I needed to focus.

"My New York is small," she said, shaking her head. "Alex got the friends in the divorce settlement. Along with all the money." She laughed at the joke, but I frowned, rummaging in the refrigerator for the chicken.

"Oh, they were never my friends anyway. And it was never my money. Ironclad prenup—so my lawyers tell me. Do you know the correct term is 'antenuptial agreement'? I should have known. Anyway, most of his friends bored the hell out of me." She shrugged. "They all think I'm an addict and a cheating whore, which is really unfair considering there's two sides to every story. Nonetheless, they make things unpleasant almost everywhere I go."

"You're staying at your mother's?" I started heating oil in the pot.

"Until I decide."

"If you want to stay?"

"Who I want to marry."

I stopped and looked at her then. "What about a job?"

"What about one?" she asked, keeping my eye.

"I mean are you going to work or anything?" I asked, turning back to the pot. Though of course I thought Ellie should work, she and I both knew that the quickest route to stability for her was to marry it.

Before you hoist a pig's head on a pike and dance around me, let me explain that I think marrying for money is deplorable. But I am a realist, and you cannot deny that even in the twenty-first century a woman can still marry herself out of a precarious situation. No one bats an eye when a woman is broke one day and rich the next through marriage—especially a woman like Ellie. It's not the same for a man though. A man will still be expected to earn a living lest he seem a freeloader on his wife's money or his wife's family money. Whether the double standard is the product of testosterone-fueled pride, evolution, or simply midwestern sensibilities, it is no less real.

"Actually," she said, leaning forward and ashing into the saucer, "I have a friend who's just moved here from New York. He's a designer. He needs some publicity and PR help."

"A designer in Cleveland?"

"He wouldn't mind my telling you that we met in rehab," she said. "He had to get away from New York, from his old connections."

"You always have the most glam jobs." I'd envied Ellie's jobs in fashion—not for her, crunching numbers or sitting through interminable meetings in stuffy conference rooms.

She exhaled out the window, the smoke curling into a rhododendron bush. "It doesn't really pay anything."

I was finishing up sautéing the onions. "If you marry Randall Leforte at least you'll save money on monogramming. I heard he buys Ralph Lauren because the monogram matches his own," I said, adding the chicken and spattering oil.

"People talk about his monogram?"

"Nothing else to talk about in Cleveland," I said with a little laugh.

Ellie rose up out of her chair then to see what I was doing. Worried, I think, that I'd start a grease fire.

"Jim tells me Leforte's well-known downtown," I said. "Not entirely aboveboard—some payoffs, something with politics I guess. I hadn't laid eyes on him before last night."

"Never run into him at parties or benefits?"

"Never."

She nodded and at that moment Jim came through the back door. In his blue suit with the yellow tie unknotted at the neck he looked scrumptiously handsome, the modern warrior returning home. Then again, I was in love with him.

He kissed me, kissed Ellie on the cheek, gave her cigarette a quick second glance, and disappeared upstairs to change his clothes. Any lingering nervousness I'd had about seeing Ellie seemed to evaporate with Jim's arrival. In my cozy house with a baby on the way, I couldn't help but feel a trifle smug—horrible to admit, I know—in front of my old friend who couldn't make her fancy marriage work and had returned home in disarray.

"I should go and leave the happy couple," she said, gathering up her things. "I have to pack."

I felt instantly guilty, as if she'd been reading my mind. "Don't go," I said, ignoring my recipe and quickly pouring a bottle of red wine and the rest of the ingredients into the pot.

"I've been invited leaf-peeping up at the Trenors'. Julia wants me up there early."

"But we're going too. We're invited for the weekend."

We both squealed and then giggled.

The Trenors owned a massive ski chalet in New York state that looked like it belonged on the slopes of Aspen, not Ellicottville, New York. Julia Trenor was our age and famous for her house parties, actually famous for her parties period. The way she and her husband, Gus, entertained took my breath away—that someone my own age should live on such a grand scale. And there were those in Cleveland who hated them. But I'd always liked Julia; we'd been on the high school track team together. Though I didn't count her a close confidant, I relished invitations to her swanky affairs.

"This is perfect. I'm so glad you two will be there," Ellie said. "I was feeling nervous."

"Nervous about the Trenors?"

"Nervous about Percy Gryce."

"Why would you be nervous about him?" The Gryces were one of the oldest and dowdiest families in Cleveland.

"I knew him a bit in high school. And as I understand it, he's never married."

"And he's worth a fortune and his father has a heart condition and will leave him more," I said knowingly.

Ellie ignored this. "I hear he spends no money except for buying dusty old Native American artifacts."

"He lives in Boston now."

"I know," she said with delight. "Can't you see me in Boston? A whole new town. And so much history."

Just then Jim came downstairs in his running clothes. "Is there time for me to go quickly?"

"Let me ask you something," Ellie said, taking his arm and steering him into our little library. Jim lowered his eyebrows at me behind her back, questioning. I turned the stove on low, wiped my hands, and followed them.

Our house was not large, but we did have a small room lined floor to ceiling with bookcases and a cozy mishmash of our books—history for Jim and Russian and French novels for me. Two mohair club chairs and a reading lamp nestled next to a desk littered with invitations and thank-you notes. On the low table sat a pile of fashion magazines, baubles from travels, and a small Capodimonte bowl holding a collection of seashells gathered on our honeymoon.

"I am fascinated by Native American history," Ellie said.

I stifled a laugh.

Jim shot me a questioning look. "Right, sugar," he said to her.

"I am, and I was hoping you might be able to loan me a few books. Just a good overview or primer. My knowledge of history in this area is remedial."

"The hell?" Jim said, turning to me.

"Ellie's coming to the Trenors' next weekend too," I chimed in.

"And you want to know a little more about the history up there," he said, screwing his mouth up in the corner, appraising her. Jim is quite astute at reading people and their motivations, more insightful than I am actually. I think it's his import status that provides him perspective. I could almost hear his mind whirring as he tried to figure out Ellie's angle.

Ellie feigned absorption with the bookshelves.

Jim leaned down and started pulling books off the case. "It's a fascinating area," he said tentatively, going along with her request for the moment. "As far as that goes."

Ellie crouched next to him. "Do you know anything about the artifacts?"

Jim looked at her. "You mean old moccasins and stuff?"

"I guess. Peace pipes, right?"

"I know that stuff is expensive. The real antiques are," Jim said, turning back to his books. "I suppose Percy Gryce has about as good a private collection of that type of thing as anyone." I realized Jim had put the pieces together of why Ellie was suddenly interested in Native American history. "His father, Jefferson Gryce, got him started. I think the natural history museum's been after them both for years trying to secure an agreement that they'll hand it all over at some point." He looked her in the eye. "He'll be at the Trenors'." My charming husband with his southern lockjaw drawl—not a twang, but a drawl—could take the sting out of the shrewdest comment.

Ellie flipped open a book to a page of baby cradles. "Maybe the tribes would want some of it back too? Some of their own heritage?"

"They're easily outbid at auction by the Gryces." I heard something strange in his voice then—almost like a taunt. "And other collectors like them," he finished.

Ellie sighed and snapped the book shut. "Would you mind if I borrowed a few?"

I went back to the kitchen to check my pot. Everything still looked raw.

Jim loaded Ellie down with a depressing-looking pile of books. She happily carried them down the back steps, jingling while she walked, waving and blowing kisses. I found I was actually looking forward to seeing my old friend Ellie in action that upcoming weekend. Ellie on the hunt was always a wonderful spectacle.

4

The Vegan

Jim and I arrived at the Trenors' high-concept contemporary house in the midafternoon. The place was inconspicuous in a multimillion-dollar sort of way, carved right into the side of a mountain so that every room had commanding views of the valley and the national forest beyond. We were greeted at the door by the Trenors' assistant, who took our bags, and their cook, who offered us tea or mulled wine in the enormous entryway that featured a rock-climbing wall, as Gus had lately been taking lessons.

Everyone was out hiking and scheduled to return any minute. I settled things into our room—slate fireplace; rough-hewn furniture that looked like it was made of logs; faded kilims on the floor, each worth a small fortune, I felt sure—and chatted with Jim.

There was a light knock on the door and Ellie came in. She wore a long white cable-knit sweater that gave a clean glow to her face, woolly leggings, and some sort of superior suede moccasin boots that laced up over her knees. The white ribbon from the other day was fraying around her wrist.

"You look amazing," I said.

She flopped down on the bed made up with crisply ironed, but clearly vintage, Irish linen sheets, thickly monogrammed with the initials of relatives long forgotten. Ellie blew a kiss to Jim, who was rustling around in the closet. He nodded his head up once in acknowledgment and continued rummaging through our bags, looking, I think, for his hiking boots.

"You know who looks amazing?" she asked. "P. G. Gryce. That's what he's called now, P. G., not Percy."

What I remembered of Gryce was a lumbering boy of eighteen with a touch of acne and a sweet smile.

Ellie continued. "He's out leading a hike with them all now. Looks like a regular mountain man—beard and everything."

"Beard? I don't see you with a beard guy."

"Oh changeable, changeable," Ellie said, waving a hand. Jim smirked. "Though I kind of like it on him. It's so Grizzly Adams."

"Grizzly Adams was not hot," I said.

"A little beard burn? Frankly I like it rough sometimes."

"Ladies, I'm going to leave," Jim said, making an exaggerated reach for the door.

"Oh stay, I'll behave," Ellie said. "There are some issues though, and I need your help. Both of you." She twinkled at Jim, demanding his attention. "Apparently he's very serious about sustainability, ecology and all that. He's a vegan."

"Lord," Jim said.

"And a teetotaler."

"A what?" I asked.

"Doesn't drink."

"Holy night-night," I said, lying down next to her on the bed and propping up my head with a lace-trimmed pillow.

"What does that have to do with ecology?" Jim asked.

"He explains it as the ecology of his body. His very fine body, I might add. He doesn't put anything into it that alters his mind or deadens him to experiencing life."

"Hence the vegan thing too?" Jim asked.

"That's a very political and ethical choice. Just ask him about it," Ellie said. "If you need to fill a conversational gap for a good forty-five minutes or so."

Jim groaned. My southern husband raised on pork barbecue and country ham had little truck with vegetarians or vegans, whom he viewed as a messianic cult focused on beans. "I'll steer clear."

"And so will I," Ellie said. "Of meat. I won't be eating any meat, and I don't want you to act like this is strange for me." She looked at us both seriously. "I'm not smoking. And please don't bring up rehab."

Jim made a skeptical face. "He's been out living in the world, hasn't he? He's got to know people who've been in rehab."

"He's been a bit sheltered, and it doesn't need to be the first thing he knows about me. Please, now, you two. You're my allies."

We heard people in the foyer below and the excited skittering nails of dogs returning from the hike.

"We should go be social," Jim said, ushering us both through the door and downstairs.

Gus Trenor welcomed us in his effusive, red-faced way. He kissed my cheek gruffly, almost pulling me over, and heartily shook Jim's hand. He was buttoned in tight in his high-tech hiking clothes and held a rough walking stick in his hand, which I noticed had rope burns across the knuckles, presumably from his recent rock climbing lesson. Though he was only in his late twenties, the beginnings of middle age spread across his ample torso. At a word from him the dogs quit skittering and sat silently at his feet while the Trenors' assistant put leashes around their necks to lead them off to the kennel.

P. G. Gryce stood by the door unloading canteens and nature books from a backpack onto a plain Shaker bench. He had indeed changed since high school. His jet-black hair and well-trimmed beard made his blue eyes the more light and startling. His well-muscled form was visible even under the flannel shirt he wore. I had to agree with Ellie; he looked like an appealing modern-day Paul Bunyan.

Julia, clad in tasteful tweeds that enhanced her blond hair, ushered us all into the living room dominated by the cavernous fireplace made of stones from the river running through their property, complete with an elaborate hob grate with shining brass urns. Julia aspired to interior decorating and had recently started a small company, despite the bad economy. As far as I knew she'd only been hired by Gus's relatives. This room, this house in fact, was her showcase. She lit a fire and though there was a cook in the kitchen, Julia brought out a little plate with a few Triscuits, a brick of cheddar cheese, and a small dish of Beer Nuts. I couldn't help but smile. Julia was displaying her midwestern roots. Cocktail hour meant drinks, not spoiling your appetite. No elaborate puffs and piped nibbles here. Everyone but me, Ellie, and P. G. drank Taittinger out of flat water glasses etched with leaves—Julia's nod to being in the country.

I sat on the cracked leather sofa next to Gus's sister Viola—a hearty girl who favored her brother in looks. She wore Birkenstocks with her toenails painted sparkly green, slim ripped jeans, and a T-shirt with 100% RECYCLED FUN printed on the front of it. I thought it a wry commentary on the Cleveland social scene and smiled. I liked Viola, who was as earnest and giving as Gus was sybaritic and egocentric. She'd called me many times trying to get me involved in civic organizations and boards of trustees. She hosted teas for which the invitation suggested you bring a book or a toy or canned food for the poor, as if she felt she must do penance for the indulgence of hosting a tea party. She was such an interesting contrast to her brother, as they both came from serious family money.

She was unmarried, and Gus was constantly setting her up with his business acquaintances. I kissed her on the cheek when I sat down, and she told me of her latest cause, recycling used baby toys and giving them to destitute mothers—hence the T-shirt.

"The Dorsets are coming up after dinner," Julia announced to all. I wasn't surprised; Diana Dorset was one of Julia's best friends. "And I've invited William Selden." I thought I saw Ellie start when Julia mentioned Selden. It surprised me too. I'd heard rumors that Selden and Diana were involved. Only gossip about bankruptcy flew faster and farther than innuendo of adultery in the Cleveland scandal mill.

But given the unreliability inherent in such talk, it could have been anything—a flirtation, a fascination, an unrequited interest on one side. In any event, I'd stopped hearing about it months ago and assumed it was over. Perhaps Julia invited him up for Viola, but that struck me as odd, as he didn't seem the right type for her at all.

When we were called into dinner, Julia stage-whispered to me that the cook had once worked for Oprah.

The dining table, made from salvaged lumber, was set with mismatched transferware plates whose patterns showed fox hunting and carriage riding in England, all of them bought in country junk shops, not costing more than a few dollars apiece. The flatware was mismatched too, but heavy and definitely sterling, giving everything the air of wealthy casualness Julia strove for. Two long benches ran down either side of the table—uncomfortable as hell since all, save those seated on the end, had to climb onto the benches and swing their legs under the table. Two magnificent heavy Irish silver candelabras engraved with scrolling leaves and flourishes held six tapers apiece and came from no junk shop I knew.

The cook brought in an immense bowl of some sort of curry—I believe it was chicken—then another bowl with nutty rice pilaf and a little dish of yogurt *raita*. A huge salad of apple and pear and nuts arrived alongside a platter of roasted fennel, eggplant, and squash with rosemary and thyme, and finally a stack of warm pita bread. Each dish was delicious and well executed, but the combination made me queasy, or perhaps that was the pregnancy again. I suspected Julia had been flummoxed by the presence of P. G. and newly vegan Ellie at the table and had the cook make some unplanned vegetable dishes, which resulted in the off-putting cornucopia.

Ellie and P. G. seemed to be on a private date in the midst of our small group. In a conspiracy of approval, everyone around the table kept up a patter of conversation and ignored Ellie and P. G.'s cozy tête-à-tête.

Ellie, in keeping with her new purity, ate little, just a few vegetables; drank nothing; and her cigarettes were absent. They looked well together,

her lushness adding decadence to his spare good looks. Yes, I thought, perhaps Gryce could keep Ellie on the straight and narrow. Boston is duller than New York and more intellectual than Cleveland. With Gryce's money she'd be at the pinnacle of that town—attending natural history museum benefits, helping her husband with his Native American artifact collection. She'd never worry about money again, that's for sure.

After dinner, we had settled with cognac and coffee around the fire. Abstemious Ellie was seated promisingly close to P. G., when the Dorsets arrived.

Diana Dorset was a tiny birdlike woman with dark hair and glittering dark eyes. She was dressed in her country clothes, cut close to her svelte body. Some women dress to seduce and some women dress for comfort. Diana dressed for competition. Her clothes always had an aggressive edge of style to them—half the time I rolled my eyes at her obvious effort and half the time I wanted to rip off what she had on and wear it myself.

She worked in development for the art museum and mostly planned their parties and benefits, which was a perfect match for her skills. She added a level of energy wherever she went, as if the evening had now been placed in capable hands and we were all about to have a good time.

Her tall and angular husband, Dan, had a reputation for being wild, though dim, and always up for a party. His mother, Betsy Dorset, with her diamonds, was at the center of the elder generation.

"So we were at the Van Alstynes the other night for dinner," Diana said after she'd accepted a cup of coffee and sat down. The Dorsets knew everyone. I thought I saw her look at Ellie. The party collectively leaned forward, knowing a good piece of gossip would follow.

"I didn't know they entertained at all." This from Julia, who was no doubt calculating how many times she'd hosted the Van Alstynes and wondering why she'd never received a reciprocal invitation. She passed a plate of dark chocolates around after the coffee.

"At the house?" I asked. As I've said, I've known the Van Alstynes all my life. Cinco now lived on his family's country estate east of town. They all turned to me. Everyone knew that I'd dated Cinco off and on since we were children—everyone but Jim. Things with Cinco had long settled into friendship by the time I'd met my husband.

"Just wondering how the place looks," I said, reaching for the plate of sweets. The rumor was that his grandfather had spent almost all his money breeding racehorses, and now the family seat was in dire need of repair.

"Like a construction site. Something to do with the foundation," Diana said. "But it was the strangest thing . . ."

"Di," her husband said in a warning tone.

"Given what happened, I don't think they'd care if everyone knew," she said to him. And then she turned to the group. "After dinner, they seated us all in the living room with dessert—"

"Who was there?" Julia interrupted, again trying to keep social tabs on why she hadn't been invited.

Diana paused for a moment.

Ellie surfaced from her cozy conversation with Gryce to toss out to the group, "I was."

"You didn't tell us," I said before I thought about it. It was reflexive. But I suppose it wasn't too strange that she hadn't mentioned it. Cleveland was so small that people were discreet about their invitations, lest feelings get inadvertently hurt. I popped a chocolate caramel in my mouth, crumpled the little fluted cup, and passed the plate to Ellie, who waved them off. I gave her a pointed glance. She loved dark chocolate. But she ignored me, trying to engage P. G. again.

Diana continued. "And the usual. The Rezaees, the Gretters, the Babcocks, and a couple I didn't know."

"I hear Babcock's company's about bankrupt." This from Gus.

"Well, he wasn't talking about it at the Van Alstynes' dinner party," Diana said. She knew Babcock was bankrupt. She probably knew more than Gus, given that her job at the museum made it imperative she know everyone's financial situation. "Anyway, they seated us all and handed coffee and dessert around. Then she gave him this look. He came over to her, took her hand, and they told us all they'd be right back. Then they went upstairs."

We all waited.

"And came back down twenty minutes later," she said with an arched eyebrow.

"Old Cinco looked like he'd been ridden pretty hard," Dan said, laughing. "Hair every which way."

"Sex hair," someone gasped.

Dan laughed, but I noticed that Ellie didn't smile. I wondered that she hadn't shared this bit of gossip with us earlier, or at least told me. She tried to engage P. G. back in their cozy exclusive chatting, but he was as fascinated by the story as any of us.

"They went upstairs in the middle of their own party and had sex?" Gus asked with ill-concealed admiration.

"Like high school?" Viola asked.

"Where did you go to high school, darlin'?" Jim asked, and everyone laughed.

"How can you be sure? Maybe they were fighting or something," I said, embarrassed for Cinco. Jim looked at me with a smile, smug at his witty aside and thinking he'd made me blush. But I realized that the idea of my old friend Cinco Van Alstyne doing something so completely out of character had intrigued me, was maybe even a little exciting.

"I swear they did," Diana said with a huge smile. "Didn't you think so, Ellie?"

Ellie shrugged again. "They're in love."

I passed the plate of chocolates to her again with a smile. This time she took it and turned her attention to it, intent on choosing the right one.

P. G. blinked when she said this and looked away—shocked, I think. But in a moment, after he'd considered what she'd said, I saw him smile at her warmly.

Diana continued. "Ask Sara next time you see her. She thought the same."

"Come on," Dan said. "You can tell when someone's been fooling around."

"Ewwww," Julia breathed, her voice between disgust and awe.

"What? Like it's gross?" her husband asked.

"Not gross, just . . . ," Julia said.

"Ghetto." Dan Dorset finished for her, and I winced at his choice of pejorative.

"She's kind of an eight ball. Thought so when I first met her," Dan continued. Of course the motivation for any questionable action always fell at the feet of the import.

I remembered Cinco's wife from their wedding. She looked like she could be his sister, with reddish-blond hair and cream complexion. I'd had the feeling Cinco liked that about her, as if it confirmed they belonged together. I couldn't picture her doing something so outré.

"Leave it to old-school Cinco Van Alstyne to basically marry himself," Julia said, as if reading my thoughts, but perhaps she was referring to his appetites.

"I thought they might be trying to get pregnant." We all looked at Ellie when she said it. She passed the plate of sweets over to Diana. "Doesn't it require timing and stuff?"

"Not that precisely. They could have waited 'til the end of the party," Diana said, chuckling as she took the plate and passed it on to her husband without a glance. "I mean it was a small party. It's not like they slipped off and no one noticed."

"It was the opposite, and I think that was on purpose," Dan said, receiving the platter of sweets and settling back on the couch to make his choice. "He all but announced, 'I'm going upstairs to screw my wife now.'"

"Don't say 'screw,'" Diana said.

"Well what word would you use in these circumstances?" he asked, then shoved a large chocolate in his mouth.

Diana pursed her lips.

"Jules, what do you say?" Gus said, nodding toward the stairs with a wink.

Everyone laughed then, dissolving any tension between the Dorsets. Julia rolled her eyes before getting up to come around with the coffee again.

. 5 .

The Foraging

The next morning, after having slept later than I felt was polite, and with Jim already up, I crept downstairs feeling rattled. The pregnancy had brought on the most explicit dreams, hormonal nocturnal liaisons starring everyone from Jim, to an old boss, to last night's Cinco Van Alstyne. I hadn't thought of him that way in years. Julia and the cook were in close conversation in the kitchen when I entered.

"What kind of man won't even eat butter?" she complained to the cook. "Is it too much of a bother to make him something special tonight? Hippie gourmet, I guess?" The cook made a face. "You're the best," Julia said to the cook, and noticing me, she turned. "There you are, sleepyhead. They've all gone hiking again. They didn't think you'd want to go." When I started to protest she said, "Enjoy it while you can. They'll be back for lunch. Come have some breakfast."

She seated me at a table laden with crumb cakes and berries. The cook brought me herbal tea.

I'd made decent progress on the berries when Julia finally sat down next to me, having finished dispensing instructions to the cook.

"Things are going along with Ellie and P. G.," I said.

"Don't they look well together? He seems smitten, though I'm not sure she's in for such an easy time of it." Julia reached out and began re-arranging the pitcher of field phlox and asters in the center of the table.

I nodded over my cup.

Julia continued. "She's led this glamorous life in New York, her photograph in *W* magazine every month at parties, bloggers following what she wears. That's so not his scene."

"Which might be good for her," I said.

"It might. And of course there's all that money. Ellie always did like that." I raised an eyebrow at this coming from Gus Trenor's wife. "I mean, who doesn't like money?" she said quickly. "But I just wonder how long she can last. No parties, no drinking, no smoking, no butter for God's sake."

"Perhaps it's a new leaf."

"Mmmmm," Julia said. "I've known Ellie as long as you have and we both know how she is."

"People should be allowed to change, Jules," I said. I don't know why, but I felt the need to stick up for Ellie. Maybe I also recognized the radical change her character would have to undergo to be with Gryce—becoming a vegan, a teetotaler, and adopting his ways of un-derstatement and discretion. Not that Ellie wasn't proper, but I knew sometimes her enthusiasms could verge on the vulgar. She always had the refreshing air about her of not giving a shit—that would have to go or be toned down if she was with Gryce. Maybe I thought she deserved some credit for that. "None of us are who we were in high school, or even college. People should be allowed to evolve past high school views of them."

"Of course you're absolutely right," Julia said. "I'm just saying that it's not often that the leopard changes its spots. Now, have another piece of this cake, would you? You're the only one who can."

I agreed, which brought out the cook's nodding approval. I spent a cozy morning with Julia and her many home decorating magazines in her chintz-covered sunroom asking her advice about decorating the baby's nursery.

At noon, Ellie and P. G. weren't with the group that returned for lunch.

"They're foraging," Gus announced, disgusted.

"You're kidding." It was out before I could stop it.

Diana laughed. "They're searching for berries and there's some sort of mushroom that's in season right now," Diana said, brushing her hands together. "God help her, I hope they're hallucinogenic."

We all laughed. I followed Jim up to our room, where he was changing out of his sweaty clothes before lunch.

"She's eating berries and grubs in the forest?" I asked.

"Not grubs. She was so enthusiastic about it." He smiled, shaking his head. "I've never seen her in action. I've only heard about it from you, but it was impressive. She's memorized all these facts about the Native Americans up here. She even mentioned some nut they used to eat, and she and Gryce are looking for it. She certainly did her homework." He shook his head. "One more day of this and I swear Gryce is going to propose."

"Already! Up here?"

"He's the type. The outdoor extremism and the dietary convictions, he's a big-R Romantic and a real headfirster. I can just hear the story he'll tell his children about meeting their mother and knowing she was the one so he didn't wait even a week before proposing."

"Forever skewing their expectations of a proper romance."

"That's hardly romance," Jim said with a grin. "That's more like filling a job opening with the best candidate."

I smiled at him, wondering at his arch tone. Though he was never sentimental, this was particularly sharp.

He went on. "It seems a waste." I wasn't sure if he was referring to Ellie or to Gryce or what. "He's actually a pretty nice guy. His interest in the plants and everything—it rubs off on you. I can see why Gus likes him. It's like hiking with your own personal naturalist."

"Do you think she'd marry him?" I asked.

He shrugged. "She could do worse than Gryce—rich, outdoorsy, a little dull and puritanical, but she might loosen him up. She'd be good for him." I can forget how clearly my husband sees things sometimes. "How she'll do married to him . . ." He trailed off.

I later learned from Ellie how the foraging went. P. G. suggested it to the group and when Ellie volunteered, everyone else begged off, again in silent solidarity with Ellie. So she'd spent the afternoon following Gryce through the damp forest. It wasn't actually that bad, she'd thought. Gryce was handsome, and he kept up an interesting patter about the plants and their origin. He was certainly passionate about it all. Here might be a new wholesome way of life, Ellie thought—organic essential oils, starting a lavender farm somewhere, an organic skin care line. So chic. She could see her future with him as she followed his trail in the forest, his way of life, his beliefs and prejudices, all with access to the Gryce millions.

Yet when he'd pulled an orange mushroom out from the base of a tree, brushed it on his jeans, and with dirt still clinging to it, popped it in his mouth, the dream of the lavender farm faded just a little. He offered the next one to her and with an inward cringe she ate it, hoping he was correct that it was indeed a chanterelle and not poisonous. It tasted exactly like dirt with a fleshy, squeaky texture. She forced herself to swallow it. She ate one more and then suggested they take some back to the house for the others. They searched for berries but only found a bush with shriveled fruit that looked like birds had already eaten most of it. He ate these heartily. She ate few.

Gryce, on the other hand, had a wonderful time. He'd finally found the woman he'd been waiting for. Smart—she knew a lot about Native Americans from the area. Easygoing—she'd been willing to forage with him. Healthy—she was a nonsmoker, nondrinker, like himself. Attractive—certainly; in fact she was damn sexy. As they descended a hill he grabbed her hand, pulled her close, and kissed her.

She closed her eyes. He tasted like mud, and his beard tickled annoyingly rather than scratched satisfyingly. He started out hesitant but became confident, until she was wrangling with more tongue than she liked. Not a promising first kiss, but not a disqualifying one either.

He had an enormous erection almost immediately and walked quickly down the hill in front of her, talking loudly about invasive trees in the area.

The group who lunched at home went out for a drive in the afternoon to a nearby lake for a walk among the fall foliage. When we came back Viola was scrubbing Gryce's mushrooms in the sink asking about their botany, afraid, I think, that he'd poison us all. The cook hovered with a skeptical look on her face. I was told Ellie was in her bath.

The cook put another cup of chamomile tea in my hand, and I walked into the living room to await the others for the start of cocktail hour. William Selden was leaning against the fireplace, looking splendid in frayed cords that hung off his hips, a faded gray T, and a tweed jacket. He had a gleam in his eye that typically signals a man means business.

I suppose it wasn't all that unusual that Julia should invite him. Cleveland hostesses loved him—a handsome, single poetry professor. I'd spent a few enjoyable evenings seated next to him at dinner parties listening to him quote famous Irishmen.

He hugged me, and we settled in to await the others. Gus came in next and poured drinks for us with a heavy hand. He even brought me some complicated juice mixture in a martini glass.

Diana Dorset came down and sat proprietarily close to Selden. And Viola came and sat by my feet. Though Selden paid polite attention to Viola, it became clear to me that she was not the reason he'd been invited up.

I excused myself to head for the powder room. "Are you stirring the pot?" I whispered to Julia as I passed her, and nodded at Selden and Diana on the other side of the room.

She wrinkled her nose. "Actually he called me up and fished around for an invite."

"I thought everything was over between him and Diana."

"Over on his side, yes. Not hers. Look at her. It's a wonder Dan stands it."

Though looking across the room at Dan and Gus happily opening up a bottle of Gus's Caol Ila, each with an unlit contraband Cohiba hanging out of the side of the mouth, it seemed like Dan stood things just fine.

Gryce had come in and was recounting the foraging, complete with the Latin names of the berries they'd eaten, when Ellie came down dressed in a wheat-colored floor-length cashmere sweater dress that clung just enough to reveal the perfection of her figure, but not enough to be vulgar. She wore no shoes and behind her ear she'd stuck a red maple leaf that matched her lacquered toes.

I watched Gryce's mouth drop in wonder, but Ellie wasn't watching her triumphant effect on him. She was staring quizzically at Selden. She flopped down next to him on the couch in my old place and playfully kissed his cheek.

"What are you doing here?" she asked conspiratorially.

I gave Julia a wondering look, and she shrugged.

He picked up her hand and quickly kissed the wrist where the white tattered ribbon was tied. Selden somehow made it seem a friendly throwaway, but I saw something fierce cross Ellie's face. "Peeping leaves," he said.

Everyone laughed but Diana.

That night at the table, Julia seated her guests with place cards. She put Selden and Diana together, while just this one night separating Gryce and Ellie. Such placement gave Ellie a view of Gryce at one end of the table and Selden at the other. And that, I believe, was the beginning of her undoing. I mean, how else do you explain what happened next?

Gryce was distractedly listening to Viola describe the need for urban gardens for the inner-city youth of Cleveland as Ellie watched. Even from across the table I could read Gryce's face. He frowned into his soup, likely worried that he was unwittingly eating some errant butter or chicken stock. He ever-so-slightly leaned away from Viola on his left, worrying no doubt that she would hit him up for a check any minute now. His wineglass was conspicuously empty.

I had a flash of Ellie's future stretching out before me. I'm sure she did too—the dinners of healthy, flavorless food, the passion for things and plants but not people. What of passion, I thought, or intoxication for that matter—intoxication with life, love, sex, with her?

Gryce turned away from his close conversation with Viola toward the table in general and announced to all in a loud voice, "It's like I was telling Ells today about foraging . . ."

I thought I saw Selden flinch at Gryce's use of a nickname.

"People have to pull themselves up by their bootstraps," Gryce said. "Be self-sufficient. You can't help someone who doesn't want to help themselves. Addicts and things—they're hopeless."

The cook was at Ellie's arm then with a bottle of champagne.

"Just water," she said a little too loudly.

"But the gardens are for children," Viola countered quietly. "In poverty. The plants inspire them so much. The teenagers work for minimum wage. They're dying to, actually. We have five times the number of applicants to spaces for the jobs."

"See, they're helping themselves," Gryce said. He seemed very young to me then, a boy dressed in his mountain-man suit playing Indian with his precious collection of artifacts.

Viola fiddled with her knife on the table. "But they wouldn't have the opportunity if our program didn't exist. They wouldn't be exposed to nature like this."

"A lot of nonsense. No offense, Viola, but you have the cream of the crop there. They'd find something else to do that was worthwhile even if it wasn't your urban gardens. You shouldn't underestimate them."

"Perhaps," Viola said, defeated. I thought then that Gryce should give her gardens some money. He loved plants. What better cause than helping poor children love them too? I made a mental note to send Viola a small check when we got home.

"There aren't that many jobs downtown, P. G.," Selden piped in. "It's decimated right now—especially for teenagers, yeah? And not everyone has a family who can expose them to history, anthropology, conservation, and market auctions like yours has you."

On the one hand this was a rather flattering portrayal of Gryce's family's hoarding artifacts; on the other it implied Gryce had been handed his life on a silver platter. You're a privileged bastard, Selden was saying. Shut it.

But Gryce didn't get it.

"True, not everyone has a family like mine," Gryce said with obvious pride and a complete lack of guile.

I thought I heard Selden groan. Jim rolled his eyes at me across the table.

"Or yours," Gryce said, turning to me.

I was mortified to be implicated in his snobbery. My family may be old and decently well-off, but I detested talking about it. My three options whenever put in this situation depended on how much I liked the speaker. If I really liked the speaker I could 1) make a joke, preferably self-effacing, if I could think of something witty fast enough; if I didn't know the speaker I often 2) changed the subject, which alerted everyone to my discomfort and usually put the topic aside permanently; or if I didn't like the speaker I could 3) say absolutely nothing and let everyone marinate in the weird discomfort of the silence.

I chose option three.

The table was silent for two full beats before Gryce swallowed a bite of vegetable and then turned to Ellie.

"Ells knows what I'm talking about," he said, and smiled adoringly at her. "How foraging makes one feel self-sufficient. Gives you pride in yourself. More people should do it."

Ellie smiled a tight, close-lipped smile at him and nodded.

"These mushrooms are heaven," Julia interrupted then in a forced cheery voice, spearing a mushroom on her fork. "Now, tell me again where you found them, P. G." Excellent hostess that she was, she easily steered us back to calmer waters. "I've found blueberries, but never very many as the birds get them all."

And Gryce was off recommending books and discussing bird nutrition. Dan mentioned his new binoculars, and the table was then on to a safe subject.

Selden got up from his seat and walked to Ellie with the third bottle of Perrier-Jouët to go around the table. He gestured toward her glass, and she shook her head. He frowned and leaned in close to whisper something in her ear.

"Just water," Ellie said, her voice a hoarse whisper.

"Come on. Share a glass with me," I thought I heard him murmur. The voice of Bacchus could not have been more seductive with its promise of pleasure and abandon. For an instant Ellie had a look in her eye that I hadn't seen since we'd been living in New York.

"A taste," I heard her say. Selden, I noticed, poured her glass to the rim. And then he set the bottle down next to her place with a jaunty wink behind his glasses.

I wondered at his forcing champagne on her. Surely he'd heard she'd had struggles. Perhaps it was Gryce's priggishness that brought out the rebel in Selden.

Diana Dorset smiled a bright hateful smile at Ellie.

At first Gryce didn't notice Ellie sipping. But midway through his polenta with special mushrooms, it became clear to everyone at the table that he kept a continual eye on Ellie's diminishing glass.

When dinner was over, we sat in the living room for dessert. Ellie refilled her glass herself. I started to worry. The whole room was tense watching her.

I think Selden wanted to diffuse the tension. Because after Julia had served the apple pie, he left and came back with a polished ebony box.

"Treats?" Diana asked, animated for the first time since Ellie had come downstairs.

Selden opened the dugout to reveal a stash of very green, very fragrant marijuana and a narrow pipe—a one-hitter used for medicinal purposes—the instruments of an adept and tidy pothead. Was it me or had he directly looked at Gryce after he'd opened it?

"Who'll smoke?" he asked.

I saw Viola and Gryce stiffen. The Dorsets were enthusiastic yeas. Gus Trenor eyed the pipe resignedly and Julia laughed. "I haven't been stoned since college. You've got to be out of your mind."

Ellie shook her head no.

"Come on, El," Diana Dorset said loudly to all. "Selden's bound to have better stuff than that ditch weed we smoked at Cinco's the other night."

Gryce's head snapped toward Ellie. She didn't respond.

"After a good roll in the hay," Dan said, "old Cinco likes a little puff as dried out and nasty as hay."

We laughed, and Ellie was off the hook. But I noticed that Gryce was appraising her from the other side of the room. Diana's comment had hit its mark, and I couldn't help but feel a little angry with her for so uncharitably blowing Ellie's cover.

Selden expertly packed a tight little pipe. Though I had smoked a bit here and there, it had been a good decade ago, and now in my pregnant state there was no way I was getting a contact high. I wanted to get out of the room as unobtrusively as possible. As quietly as I could, I got up and headed for the stairs. Jim caught my eye and nodded slightly.

Julia was on her feet at once. "Don't go. We'll make Selden go outside."

"Oh no, I'm exhausted," I said, embarrassed and not wanting to end the party. "Good night." Before she could further protest, I was upstairs and in my room.

I closed the door, glad of the silence, happy to be away from Diana's meanness and from witnessing Selden's corrupting influence on Ellie. Seconds later there was a knock on my door.

"It's me," Ellie said, peeking around the door looking as wary as a child. "I've been sent to tell you it's okay. Jules sent them all downstairs into Gus's man cave."

"I really am tired." The pregnancy had me in bed most nights before Jim. I didn't want to talk. I knew she'd want bolstering, and I wasn't sure I was the person to do it. Ellie could convince herself of most anything, and I didn't want to help convince her she was in love with P. G. Gryce and his prim starchiness after witnessing him and Viola at dinner.

"Come back down," she said. "Julia will fret all night if you don't."

"Tell her I already had my nightgown on," I said, though I was still dressed. I went in the bathroom and started brushing my teeth.

Ellie sat on the edge of the bed, champagne glass in her hand. "What did I tell you about Gryce?"

"A regular Ranger Rick," I said after I'd rinsed out my mouth. "You weren't kidding." Here it comes, I thought. I was used to hashing over men with Ellie. We'd done it regularly when we'd both been living in New York. Truth be told I got a little thrill out of it. My dating life had never been as exciting as hers. And it was touching to me that she seemed to value my opinion, though I'd never understood why. I was less experienced with men than she, and certainly less glamorous.

"But nice," she said. "I'd never have to worry about cheating or other women or anything." It was certainly true that a man like P. G. would never stray sexually.

"Not with him, no," I said. "Definitely a one-woman type if you ask me."

"And smart. Interesting I guess."

I nodded. Though P. G. seemed to have the farthest thing from an original and exploratory mind, I suppose he'd been to the proper schools.

"And rich of course."

And there it was. "Of course," I said, smiling.

She smirked. "Don't think that about me."

"Ellie . . ." I was going to protest, but then again Ellie and I had known each other too long to be coy. But P. G. Gryce, I thought. He was such a prig, such a bore. After seeing him tonight I'd come around to Julia's way of thinking. Could she really do it?

"I know what you think," she said as she finished her glass. Perhaps she was tipsy. "You've never had to worry about these things."

"You don't know what I think."

She paused, waiting for me to tell her.

"You're a realist," I said. "You know what you want." I tried to phrase it as gently as I could.

She nodded deeply. "I do. It's true."

"I think you have perspective on it too, having been married once before."

"Money wasn't the problem there."

"But you know it's important to you."

"To me?" She sounded a little angry. "Like it's not important to every single one of them down there?"

"Except Selden," I said, wanting to know exactly what had been going on between them since I'd seen them at the orchestra. I suspected she was the reason he'd come up here. I didn't know why, but I liked the idea of Ellie and Selden. Perhaps if she found love it would ground her. Ellie, my friend, had always been searching. Didn't true love take care of yearning like that?

When she didn't answer I asked, "Ellie, what are you doing?"

"Nothing."

I went in the bathroom and put on my nightgown. Then I crawled into bed, Ellie seated at the foot. "Selden just makes me a little crazy," she said.

"What brand of crazy?" I asked with my eyes closed. "There's the crazy-in-love crazy, the angry crazy, the actually nuts crazy . . ."

"When I'm around him, he makes everything I want seem tawdry. He lives just fine off his salary. He worries about dusty old books, and he's fine. He judges me, I know."

"Well, you work too."

She snorted. "I'll never make any real money. All my jobs are just time fillers. Do you know what I'd have to do to make the kind of money Gryce has? It'd be impossible."

True, but Gryce had everything handed to him. When you got right down to it, how different was having everything handed to you by your ancestors from having everything handed to you by a husband?

"Gryce didn't make the kind of money he has," I said. "There's a lot of room in between Gryce's money and supporting yourself well. You could do it." Ellie always did have the most ambitious, expensive taste. If she just came down and lived like the rest of us, I was sure she could find happiness.

"But there's no freedom in that. That's the only thing money's really good for anyway. Freedom. It's not meant for cars and diamonds."

"Oh, you might enjoy opening a wing of a hospital or something," I said, yawning.

"Yeah, but Gryce wouldn't," she said in a deadly serious voice.

Of course, she'd noticed at dinner. "He lacks a certain . . ."

"Compassion," she finished for me.

"Ability to take another's perspective," I said.

"Think I could teach him?" she asked. Again, it always flattered me when she asked for my opinion.

"Pull a Mother Teresa and show him by example? Sure."

"I'm not the Dalai Lama."

"No, but he strikes me as pretty malleable," I said, wanting to sound encouraging. If anyone could change a man, it was probably Ellie.

She shook her head then, and I thought I saw a tear, which made me immediately anxious. "Seriously, I don't even have a design degree. I've had all these dead-end jobs in fashion adding up to a résumé filled with nada. Plus, I haven't worked in four years. The economy's shit. I'm lucky to get this gig with my friend as a favor."

I sat up and put an arm around her. "You don't know what's in the future. You don't know where this job could lead." I meant it. Ellie, I felt sure, could conquer the world if she'd just figure out what she wanted to do.

She stood up then. "Which is why I'm going down and sitting with P. G."

There was a knock on the door then and Jim came in. "You better go down," he said to Ellie. "Julia's missing you."

Ellie leaned down and gave me a quick kiss on the cheek. "Sleep tight."

Jim came in and lay down on top of the covers next to me. "You coming to bed already?" I asked.

He kissed me long and lingering. "I could, sugar." His hand snaked under the covers, bunching up my nightgown as he reached for skin.

I kissed him back but then froze.

"Get downstairs," I said, pushing him off me. "They'll all think we're up here . . ."

Jim smirked and rolled toward me. "Up here what? Fucking?"

"That's the word Dan was searching for last night, I think." I smiled.

He kissed me again, quite convincingly.

"God, we can't do this," I said, shoving him aside. "Diana will run all over town talking about us just like the Van Alstynes. Get down there."

"You care what she thinks?" he asked, propping himself up on an elbow. "We're married and you're pregnant; won't they just think it's sweet?"

"No," I said. "Diana thinks nothing's sweet."

He looked at me for a moment, as if weighing his options. "Okay," he said, heaving himself up and out of bed and then leaning back down to give me a quick kiss. "Except Selden," he said to my astonishment.

"You're sharp tonight," I said as he walked toward the door. I regretted then that he'd taken my cue, and I'd managed to turn him off. But really, I thought he should have tried harder. I mean, what good is flouting conventions and scandalizing friends if it's not because your husband has swept you off your feet? It's backward, I know, and unfair to expect Jim to ignore what I say I want. I'm sure somewhere Gloria Steinem's hair is going to spontaneously combust, but since being married I've learned that sometimes, when it comes to sex, what I want and what I say I want can be two very different things.

He paused at the door. "You were right about her being a spectacle," he said, referring now to Ellie. "Can't wait to see what happens." He winked at me and was gone.

I tossed in bed, trying to sleep, thinking about Jim, about Gryce and Ellie, and as I drifted off images of Cinco Van Alstyne came to me again, pushing me with old expectations and assumptions—expectations of how a wife behaved and where she lived and how she acted. Expectations I was intensely familiar with since I'd grown up with them, as had he. Expectations I'd assumed he'd want a wife to fulfill. But the story Diana had told us, the dream I'd had last night . . .

· 6 ·

The Man Cave

I woke the next morning to Jim snoring beside me, gruff with stubble and warm. I snuggled in the crook of his arm, ready to sleep more, only to be met by the undeniable smell of pot.

I leaned back and sniffed—definitely pot.

He woke then, opening one blurry eye and scrubbing his face with his hand. He smiled, didn't say anything, and went in the bathroom and closed the door.

His pillow definitely had the oily, carbon smell of smoke on it. Obviously he'd smoked with Selden and the others last night. I heard the sink turn on, could hear him scrubbing his teeth.

I'd never known him to smoke; we'd never gotten high together. And I was suddenly upset that he'd done this with them, without me, and while I was pregnant too. It seemed oddly selfish.

I heard the shower turn on. Jim never showered first thing. Clearly he wanted to scrub the smell off him too.

I hated using the bathroom when he was in there, but pregnancy being what it was, I went in out of necessity.

I flushed, hoping the water would either freeze him or scald him and he'd get out of the shower and talk to me.

It had the effect I wanted, or maybe he was just done, because he got out and wrapped a towel around his waist. He smiled, shaking water out of his hair, picked up his toothbrush and toothpaste, and started brushing his teeth.

Again.

"So?" I asked.

He raised an eyebrow, standing in his white towel, looking clean and scruffy. He spat and rinsed.

"It was a pretty ugly night," he said.

I kissed him, but he kept his mouth firmly closed when I brushed my tongue against his lips.

"What happened?" I asked, wary.

He led me back to the bed and crawled under the blankets smelling warm and damp and like the Ivory soap that Julia stocked all the bathrooms with—the eighty-cent bar.

"Like I said, ugly." He started his tale.

The lowest level of the Trenors' chateau had been renovated into Gus's private domain. Julia called it his man cave. He called it his den of iniquity. The two flat-screens mounted on the wall were permanently tuned to sports. A computer hooked into some satellite gave instant betting access to Vegas and Atlantic City. The green felt poker table usually hosted Gus and his "boys." There was a bar, huge couches for lounging, and a hot tub on the deck outside of it all. I'd heard rumors that during Gus's boys' weekends hookers were present, though it seemed unlikely Julia would tolerate that. News from the haters, I thought.

The party retired downstairs for cards, Jim told me. Selden, the Dorsets, and the Trenors passed the pipe a little.

I raised an eyebrow when he said this.

"What?"

"You didn't smoke?"

He groaned and leaned back. "A few hits."

I didn't say anything.

"You're mad?" he asked.

I shook my head. I didn't want to seem prim, but I was upset. "No," I said. Somehow I was sure that Ellie had something to do with Jim's smoking pot. As I've said, Ellie had a way of getting you to do things you usually didn't. I just never thought she'd work on him.

He went on with his story. Ellie abstained from the pot but drank more champagne, he said. So maybe I was wrong in my assumptions. Viola went to bed, and Gryce sat in the corner with a glass of soda water. Soon the cards came out and everyone played except Gryce and Ellie, who sat on the couch, their backs to the poker players.

Jim played poker regularly through college and had a weekly game in Cleveland. But he thought it bad form to take all his host's money and so he didn't focus too intently on the play, but watched Ellie out of the corner of his eye as she inched closer to Gryce. Selden was watching her too, he noticed. Jim threw a few hands, and then he saw Gryce reach his arm around Ellie and kiss her.

"She must have been drunker than I thought," Jim told me, laughing. "I haven't seen macking like that since junior high school." This comment annoyed me. He seemed to take delight in Ellie's predicament, or maybe just delight in watching her kiss another man.

"What did you all do?"

They continued playing is what they did, and ignored the make-out scene just a few feet away.

And then Diana called out, "Get a room, you two."

Though Gryce laughed, he turned red and put a good two feet between him and Ellie. Pretty quickly after that he left to go upstairs, saying good night to everyone.

Ellie sat on the couch for a few minutes, straightening her dress, fixing her hair. She sighed, rejected, and then pulled a chair up next to Selden. "Now, where's a tiny puff for me?" she asked.

"Did he give it to her?"

"He'd gone upstairs for the rest of his stash, and he packed the pipe and passed it to her. She was taking a haul off that thing when Gryce came back downstairs. I think he was looking for Ellie. Perhaps he'd been hoping she'd follow him upstairs or maybe he realized that he wanted to continue privately what she'd started publicly. He saw her smoking, turned on his heel, and was gone."

"Poor Ellie."

"She packed that one-hitter like a pro and passed it to me. That's when I started smoking," he said, laughing.

I laughed too, but it jarred me, confirming that Ellie had been the corrupting influence on him.

They played cards for a few more hours. Ellie was dealt in too. She started losing almost right away. Gus's buy-in is a thousand, and she lost it all, maybe even more. Ellie didn't have money to lose, but Gus Trenor didn't play for pennies. He did take IOUs though, which Ellie wrote out to him on cocktail napkins.

I could see it: the play becoming stupider and stupider as the pipe made the rounds and the evening wore on.

Jim continued with his story. By the end of the night Ellie was practically sitting in Selden's lap. His lucky charm, he called her. Diana Dorset was pale with rage.

"So I came up and crawled in next to you. You didn't even notice, you were so out."

I smiled.

But an hour later Jim was woken up by laughing and someone bumping into that fragile satinwood table in the hall. Jim cracked the door and saw Selden and Ellie kiss and then go into Selden's bedroom.

I was scandalized. "Do you think she slept with him?"

"It looked like it was going that way to me."

"Really? She told me they were friends."

"Looked like more than friends to me."

"That's so surprising."

"Why should it be?" Jim kissed me good and long, and I swear I could taste the faint hint of smoke on his breath. "Come here, you," he said, smiling.

I smiled, kissed him back without fervor, but he didn't seem to notice. My mind was on Ellie, her new influence over Jim, her stealing upstairs with Selden. It was all so distracting.

"We'll have to keep it down," he said, hand on my expanding waist, pulling me toward him. "News travels fast in this house."

I rolled toward him feeling awkward, though I was just barely showing and not in a position to put him off if sex was what he wanted from me.

"You okay?" he asked, sensing the disconnect between my thoughts and my actions.

I smiled and nodded and kissed his neck right under his ear. "Never better," I whispered.

After, I left Jim in bed, showered, and went downstairs, embarrassed again at my late rising. Remembering the conversation from the other night, I hoped no one would be able to guess what I'd been up to. I found Julia and Ellie in the sunroom. Julia glanced over at me when I came in and didn't even stop her tirade at Ellie.

"I invited him up here especially for you. Viola, Diana, everyone was hands-off. And then you go and smoke pot. You know how he is."

"You were smoking too," Ellie said.

"A tiny puff—the equivalent of a glass of red wine."

"Same here," Ellie said.

"But he *saw* you." Julia looked as upset as if the defeat were her own. "Why did you go through all this if you weren't serious? None of us imagined you'd put up with Percy Gryce—I mean, foraging berries, for God's sake—if you didn't mean to marry him. Then you act like you've never seen William Selden before in your life. You've known him for years. I mean, why, of all nights, sleep with Selden last night . . ."

Ellie's hair was impeccable and she wore a crisp white shirt with sharp dark jeans. A nearly imperceptible dusting of makeup enhanced her features. She'd had to have been up early to look this pulled together. But I saw the dark circles under her eyes. Her chin was red with beard burn.

"I didn't sleep with him," she said.

"El, we all heard you go into his room," Julia said.

"But I didn't sleep with him. We just smooched." She smiled.

"Gryce thinks you slept with him. Diana made sure of that."

"What?" I asked.

Julia turned to me. "Gryce left this morning after Diana packed his ear full of horrors over breakfast. She told him all about rehab. She told him you were up in Selden's bed at that very moment. She even told him that you'd borrowed money from Ned Hollingsworth when you were in New York. I mean, did you ever?"

"He's my cousin," Ellie said in a low voice.

"She left that out. Diana squirrels things away for later use. I warned you not to piss her off. She was in a foul mood when she arrived and only cheered up when I told her Selden was joining us. And then you jumped him."

"I did not."

The cook stuck her head in the room. "Sorry to interrupt."

Julia followed the cook out, and I took the chance to turn to Ellie. "Are you okay?" She looked at me then, as if she'd just noticed that I was in the room.

"I'll get Gryce back, if that's what you mean," she said dismissively. "This isn't a deal breaker. I can repair it."

"That's not what I mean."

She looked at me.

"I mean should you call your sponsor or something?"

"I'm fine," she said, looking me in the eye.

"You're drinking, then smoking . . ."

"I wasn't in rehab for pot. Or alcohol for that matter."

"I don't know much about this, but doesn't that all compound on itself?"

"I have it under control."

Given that she'd spent the night in Selden's room, I didn't think she had it under control at all. "If I can help in any way—"

"Thanks," she said flatly, cutting me off, which annoyed and worried me.

Julia came back in the room. "I'm sorry to be a bitch about this, El, but I'm just so disappointed. You would have been perfect for P. G." She shrugged. "But I suppose you can't fake things, and you're not nasty." She paused. "Like Diana. And for getting what she wants, give me the nasty woman every time."

I started at this. "I thought you and Diana were good friends," I blurted.

Julia shrugged. "It's easier to be friends with Diana than not." She turned to Ellie. "You should remember that."

Lunch was served, and we all sat down to quiche, fruit, and a sharply acidic salad of greens.

The table was dismal as Gryce was gone as well as Selden, who'd only been able to get away from Cleveland for a night. Jim had gone back to sleep, and Gus was out walking the dogs. Diana came down with her hair wet from the bath and languidly sat down.

"Aren't we a small group? I like it when the men are gone. Gives a girl a chance to chat. No offense, Dan."

Her husband shrugged.

"Did Gryce leave already? I thought he was staying longer. Maybe we shocked him last night. He's so pure, you know. Never smoked, doesn't drink. Do you know he told me he didn't know anyone who'd been to rehab until he met you, Ellie?"

"How did he know I was in rehab?"

"Oh, I didn't think it was a secret." Diana speared a piece of melon. "Such a nice old family. He said he had to go back for an auction. Apparently his father is selling some important antique, and they're donating all the proceeds to poor Indians. Isn't that nice?"

Viola piped up then. "I think it's wonderful that he's trying to make other people comfortable too."

The Rappelling

Comfortable! Ellie thought. The word dragged her into despair. Not so much because rich-girl Viola Trenor categorized a colossal fortune like Gryce's as comfortable, which did make Ellie smile, but at the thought of what Ellie might have done with money like that—comfortable indeed. Diana's barbs didn't hurt her that much. They were nothing compared to the flogging she was giving herself. And the coup de grâce? Selden had left that morning, without waking her.

She ate little at lunch and was looking forward to taking a sleeping pill and napping in her room for the rest of the afternoon, but as they were leaving the dining room Julia took her elbow and steered her into the sitting room.

"Look, can you do me a favor? A decorative mural painter is coming up any minute now from Cleveland with the man who runs up my curtains and the upholsterer, and it drives Gus insane to see them. He hates it when I have people come from Cleveland on business."

Ellie thought once again how different her life was from her friend's. Julia had a business so she would have something to do, not that she'd ever have to support herself doing it. Ellie wondered, as she had as a bridesmaid at the wedding, what the Trenor marriage was made of. How did Julia turn a blind eye to Gus's constant sporting and the fact that he had no real job aside from looking after his money? Did Gus love Julia, or did he love that she performed her role well? Was theirs a singular meeting of souls, a tacit business arrangement, a comfortable similarity of perspective bound by shared social background, true love? Ellie knew it was futile to conjecture about life behind closed doors in anyone's marriage.

Julia went on. "And so I was wondering if you would get Gus out of the house. Ask him to teach you rock climbing or something."

Ellie hesitated. She felt she couldn't refuse her friend's request after she'd disappointed her with P. G. It was her duty as a guest to help her hostess, and Julia's eyes were narrowing the longer Ellie hesitated.

"Sure," Ellie said with a forced bright smile. "Rock climbing—right."

So after lunch she found herself with Gus Trenor hiking the back side of a rock face where Gus's climbing instructor had installed a rappelling rope.

"Are you sure it's safe?" she asked Gus's back as she followed him through the woods.

"I've done it hundreds of times. It's a blast. You'll see."

Ellie continued walking behind him up the steep trail. His broad back was sweaty, and his waist was hooked up with water bottles, ropes, and gear. Gus had seemed flattered when Ellie asked him to teach her a little climbing. She knew it was the type of thing Julia had done when they were dating, when she was trying to win him. Now, Julia felt no need for the façade. Gus admired a sense of adventure in a woman, and Ellie thought his wife ignored this at her peril. An insect buzzed her neck, and she slapped at it. Gus continued bush-whacking in front of her.

"You know who's a great rock climber?" Gus asked over his shoulder, but then answered without waiting for a reply. "Randall Leforte."

Ellie groaned a little.

"I wish you'd convince Julia to be nice to him," Gus said. "I've tried to get her to invite him up, and she refuses."

"I met him at the orchestra on opening night. I heard someone tried bringing him around and took him to some parties, and he was ridiculous."

"Oh, just because he's super-shiny and gets nervous and doesn't know what to say. . . He's smart as hell. His fees are astronomical. He's going to be richer than all of us someday. If we were friends though . . . If he felt a little indebted . . ."

They trudged along in silence till they reached the top of the mountain, where a rappelling rope had been set up. The view of the mountains was alive with the changing fall trees. Ellie sat down.

"Well come on, I'll show you how it's done," Gus said, fidgeting with his gear impatiently.

Ellie sighed but didn't move. "Do you mind if we just sit here for a minute? It's such a gorgeous day, and I've been a little down lately."

Gus Trenor was not used to being taken into the confidence of his wife's attractive friends. He sat down next to her on the warm granite ledge. "Why?"

Ellie waved a hand in front of her face. "It's nothing really. I don't want to bother you."

"What? You're bored with Cleveland shopping and parties compared to New York?"

Ellie winced. "You think I'm an airhead too."

"Sorry, not at all." The truth was, had he been consulted, Trenor would have declared Miss Eleanor Hart a most decorative woman who should marry, and marry well, as soon as possible. But sitting next to this sublime woman on this summit, on this clear day, she seemed more real and deep than he had previously imagined.

"You know Julia's mad at me," Ellie said, staring in front of her.

"She's not."

"Well I've annoyed her, and I've annoyed myself. She's mad about the whole P. G. Gryce thing."

"What Gryce thing?"

"She thinks I ought to have married him."

"Gryce?!" Trenor was now a picture of outrage, though he would have agreed with his wife just a few hours ago. "I can't see you with someone like him. So uptight and . . . and plain. Gryce? I mean, what was she thinking? I could have told Julia that you and Gryce weren't a match. But then she doesn't consult me about stuff like that," he said sulkily.

"She made a decent point. I don't have a lot to fall back on."

Trenor stiffened; any talk of money made him anxious. People constantly hit him up for loans, charitable donations, seed money for start-ups going nowhere. "What about your mother, your settlement?"

"Mother has enough trouble keeping herself afloat, and I'm afraid I signed a fairly severe prenup."

"Lawyers can deal with that kind of thing."

"My lawyers say it's ironclad."

"Here's an example of a time when a Randall Leforte would come in handy," Gus said, trying for levity, poking her side just under her ribs.

"Great," Ellie said flatly. Even this small touch from him felt hugely intrusive.

"But you did get something . . . I mean, some money."

Ellie nodded.

"Are you having someone invest it for you?"

"I have to live."

"You live at your mother's for free and then there's clothes and such, but you must have some left over."

"Some."

"Who's investing it?" he asked again, looking at the view, not her.

"Some firm in New York that my lawyers recommended."

Trenor seemed to mull this over.

"Don't worry," Ellie said. "They're very conservative. I won't lose anything. But I'd like to buy a little place for myself. Maybe in Cleveland. And all the money's tied up right now. The market's a mess. It's a terrible time to liquidate anything."

Eventually Gus said, "I could invest some of it for you."

"But the money's all tied up," Ellie said again.

"I can get them to hand over the management of some of it to me. You're so young." How Ellie loved to hear that, even in this context. "You don't need to be super-conservative. You can afford to take some risks that'll pay off bigger for you in the long run."

Yes, Ellie thought, risk-taking right now was exactly what she needed. She was still young, still able to gamble, as she had the other night. Gus seemed to do well with his own money. He and Julia were comfortable, to use Viola's word. Why not entrust a portion to Gus? He might actually make her some money.

"What kind of fees would you charge?"

"Friendship fees," he said, smiling.

"I wouldn't feel comfortable unless you charged me the same thing you charge—" And here she hesitated just a fraction of a minute. "Everyone else," she finished.

"If that's how you feel about it, then fine." He stuck out his hand. "Strictly business."

As Ellie shook his hand she felt a lightening of her load. Here was a friend who might take care of her. And she would be helping him as well—giving him a chance to prove himself with someone else's money.

She got up and said, "I think I'm ready now."

Gus showed her how to hook into the harness and explained in detail how to rappel down. As he attached the harness, Gus's hands seemed to linger on her waist and once she was sure he unnecessarily brushed her bare stomach under her shirt when fastening a rope. He hooked her up with many safety cables and a helmet. Though she'd never done it before, she felt an odd confidence that she could handle this, that with Gus guiding her, she'd be safe.

· *8* ·

The Stepney-Mingott Wedding

Now, you might be wondering why Ellie even came back to Cleveland. It took me a while to convince Jim he wanted to move back here with me. And Ellie, I mean, she was used to New York, so why not try Boston or Chicago? Hell, even Los Angeles if she was feeling like really starting over. The thing is, there is something about being raised in Cleveland that draws you back.

Everyone I know in Cleveland went away to college, found a spouse, maybe lived in a larger city for a while, but eventually they moved home. They chose to come back. When you do, it's because you've lived anonymously long enough. You want to come back to the place where people know you and your mother and your grandmother, and probably even your great-grandmother. Where people are still house-proud and throw dinner parties. Where the gray lake shocks in the winter with its cover of ice, and shocks again in the summer with its tropical blue. Where you can get your child into one of the swanky preschools without college-level stress. Where you can find the best of anything you need—a doctor, certainly; hairdresser; psychotherapist; acupuncturist; artisanal baker. It's just that Cleveland has one or two of each, not a full page in the phone book like New York has. But really, how many do you need?

It's an ideal place for nesting.

You return because a hundred years ago Cleveland's iron and steel barons built the neoclassical art museum, and John Severance built his wedding tribute of a concert hall. The Terminal Tower, formerly the tallest building outside New York, still looks proud. You return because the brownfields are slowly being turned into urban gardens, and Tremont hasn't lost its bohemian blue-collar vibe despite being overrun with luxury SUVs on the weekends as suburbanites jockey to eat at the trendy restaurants. You love the Ritz's sushi happy hour. I mean, I wouldn't eat the walleye. That's just me; let's not get crazy. You love the huge white windmill that churns next to Browns Stadium right on the edge of Lake Erie, not far from the closed steel mills. It's Cleveland's beacon to those who want to move forward, to change, and why wouldn't Ellie, in her present state, want to come back and absorb a little of that energy?

In the weeks that followed my trip to Ellicottville I didn't see Ellie as I was distracted by prenatal testing, which pronounced the baby fine, a little boy. Jim was ecstatic. With this news, I started decorating the nursery and stocking the pantries and cleaning out closets and performing all the other nesting clichés of the pregnant woman.

But Ellie lingered in the back of my mind. I fretted over her, whether she was still sober, whether she'd started her job. I kept telling myself to call her, but somehow with the baby and the preparations, I couldn't psych myself up to do it. Funny that with a friend that old I'd need to gin myself up to call her. But the truth was that after seeing her at the Trenors' I wanted to store up a little energy, don a small bit of karmic armor, before I talked to her. Sounds awful, I know; she's my oldest friend after all.

In any event, I didn't see her again until the Stepney-Mingott wedding.

Vivian Mingott was the rather plain daughter of a family that had been the original partners of John D. Rockefeller when he started out in Cleveland. The hangover from that type of wealth had lasted to the current generation. Jack Stepney was a distant cousin of Ellie's. He worked downtown in a bank and hadn't a dime to his name. Vivian would take his name, but no one in Cleveland would ever refer to her as anything other than Vivian Mingott. Such was the power of her family name compared to his.

The wedding was a country affair, meaning that the ceremony was held in a tiny white country church east of the city, next to the Chagrin River. An invitation to the actual ceremony was extended only to close family and important friends—and was considered quite a get. Invitations to the reception, held at the bride's family's home in Hunting Valley, were not limited by space, and most everyone I knew was invited. I thought I might see Ellie there.

Waiters strolled through the living room and dining room with silver trays of champagne. French doors opened to a slate terrace tented for dancing. Heaters kept the whole thing cozy in the late autumn chill. Fourteen Meissen urns from Vivian's family held masses of fall flowers intertwined with bright autumn foliage by Cleveland's florist of choice.

After the bland dinner of salmon and the appropriate toasts and well wishes, couples headed out on the dance floor. There'd be no first dance, no father-daughter dance, no spotlights—just the huge orchestra, sixteen deep with a substantial string section, playing all night for the bride.

Out of the corner of my eye I saw Percy Gryce in his dark gray suit looking less like a caricature of a mountain man and more like an engraving of a monocle-wearing gentleman that hangs in some barber shops. The Trenors were there, of course, Julia chatting to a clutch of fashionable ladies, Gus barking orders at the bartenders. Of course the Dorsets were there, and the Mathers, young and old. The Lincolns and the Morleys and those glamorously bohemian, yet genuinely old-school, Moore-Frontinis were huddled in groups chatting and laughing. Both U.S. senators, one from each party, were there.

The Chesterbrowns, or should I say Mr. Chesterbrown, as his wife had recently left him for another woman, was there. In a corner the surviving heads of the great Cleveland triumvirate passed judgment on all: the Hays of the steel money, who had given it all away; the Rushworths of the coal money, who had pissed it all away; and the Dagonets of the shipping money, who had managed to hang on to it all. The whole Van Alstyne clan seemed spread over all the rooms. To my utter surprise I saw Randall Leforte looking as shiny as a just-waxed car and clinging to the bar as if to a life raft.

"The groom's taking Leforte under his wing," Jim said sotto voce in my ear. "Trying to get me to play squash with him."

When he saw Jim, Leforte made a straight line for him and dragged him off on the pretext of introducing him to one of the senators. Vivian's father kissed my cheek and asked about my parents, who were traveling in Europe and had missed the wedding. I was chatting with the proud father of the bride, practically bursting out of his tuxedo, when Cinco Van Alstyne interrupted us.

While I'd known Cinco all my life, his family had known mine for longer. He kissed my cheek and heartily shook the hand of Mr. Mingott, who then quickly begged off, spotting a group of guests to greet.

"How are you?" Cinco asked. He was as tall and lanky as I remembered. "I've been meaning to call and get you out to the house soon. Did you have a good time at the Trenors'?" I hoped the smile on my face wasn't too goofy as I remembered the conversation about him and his wife adjourning upstairs during their dinner party. I'd been having recurring dreams about him since then.

He was in his element here, cloaked in an air of respectability signaled by the way he kissed your cheek, the cut of his shirt, and the way he chatted with old ladies. Seeing him here made the tacky story seem as unlikely as a tabloid story in the supermarket. But from certain angles the boy I'd known, who was a vicious mimic and often full of mischief, peeked out at me. Perhaps the dinner party story was real after all.

"I had a great time," I said, blushing. "How'd you know I was up there?"

"Diana and Dan were over the night before they left. They said they'd see you."

"I hear there's a lot to be done out at the farm," I said. Anyone who knew the Van Alstynes called their country estate a farm. Of course nothing had ever been farmed out there but generations of Van Alstynes.

He nodded, shifting around so we were standing next to each other, leaning our backs against the stone wall of the house, shoulder to shoulder in the way of old comrades, which I suppose we were. I felt comforted and oddly intimate. He propped a foot up on the wall behind him. "But we've got the funds now," he said.

I leaned my shoulder into him. He was surveying the crowd, smiling at people he knew. No one talked money at a Cleveland wedding.

"You didn't hear?" He shoved my shoulder after I'd remained quiet. "A Saudi sheik's representative knocked on the door last spring. Some member of the royal family had a heart thing done at the Clinic this summer. He wanted somewhere secluded to recover and with a couple wives and a passel of kids, he needed a place big enough for his whole family."

A waiter offered a tray of hot shrimp. He swiped one off the silver tray. I waved no. He must have realized then that he didn't want to stuff the shrimp in his mouth mid-story and so it became a kind of baton.

"So a real estate agent is driving the sheik's right-hand man from place to place." Cinco smiled and nodded at someone across the way while continuing his story. "And he doesn't like any of them." Whisk of shrimp from side to side. "I guess they were driving past the farm on their way to another house to rent when he told the driver to stop. Next day this representative guy knocks on my door." Shrimp pounding at imaginary door. "As they say, he made me an offer I couldn't refuse." He finally popped the shrimp in his mouth.

"You sold it!" I turned toward him, genuinely pleased. The house was one of the worst white elephants in Cleveland. That Cinco would cut himself free of it excited me more than was probably appropriate. This was not the judgment-ridden boy I'd known when I was younger.

He was changed and free—selling the house, the story of his wife and him at the dinner party.

He held a hand up and chewed.

I continued, gushing. "I think that's really great. I always thought it'd be such a drain on you. I mean, I know it must be hard to find a buyer, but a house like that has got to be an albatross—"

"God no," he said as he swallowed the shrimp. "Calm down. I rented it to them for the summer. It's already paid for a new roof, shoring up the foundations . . ."

My mind scrambled for a way to remove my foot from my mouth.

But he seemed unfazed by my glee at the idea of the house being sold; perhaps he was used to skepticism about his family seat.

Cinco prattled on. "Amazing, right? We had to get every stitch of furniture out of there in a week. I mean every effing dish towel, for crying in the night, everything in the basement, every everything. But for that price, I did it."

"Is that rope swing out in the bower still there?" I thought a bit of nostalgia might erase my faux pas.

"Still there." He smiled at me then, and I had the strongest memory of what it had been like to kiss him. As I mentioned, the first time was in a sandbox; I couldn't have been more than five. And then there were dances at the country club in middle school where we'd sneak off to the golf course. The summers I'd come home from college we'd get a group of friends and a bunch of beer and skinny-dip in the pond at his family's farm—now *his* farm.

"I'd love to see it," I said again. At the end of summers we'd each go back to school with no strings attached. Neither of us had returned to Cleveland. He'd visited me a few times in New York, staying at the University Club, where he hosted huge cocktail parties for his New York friends—mostly Clevelanders doing their big-city thing and searching for their imports.

Speaking of which, his wife came over then—dressed in neat black with her chic haircut and massive pearl-and-diamond-encrusted earrings, something out of the Van Alstyne vault no doubt.

He reintroduced us, and she whispered something in his ear. He blushed, heaved himself off the wall next to me, and took her hand. "I think we're leaving," he said. At first I thought he was embarrassed by her rudeness. I was starting to think he'd really chosen a social hindrance, as everyone said. But I noticed how quickly he seemed to fold her under his arm with that unmistakable air of anticipatory pleasure, and it dawned on me, from the look on his face, that she'd whispered something suggestive. We were at a wedding, so there's always romance in the air, but this seemed pretty tawdry. She'd not talked to me.

I raised an eyebrow. "They haven't cut the cake."

But they'd already turned their backs and didn't hear me. I was stunned as I watched them walk toward the door—and disappointed, as if the party was over. I'd enjoyed standing there next to him, feeling a buzz I hadn't felt in ages. Neither Jim nor I would ever leave a wedding or a dinner party so blatantly to go home and get in bed. Cinco just didn't seem to care what Cleveland thought anymore.

He and his wife greeted Ellie quickly on their way out.

Ellie wore what looked like an ancient flapper's dress of ombré moiré silk—no spangles and no bugle beads, just a long close-cut column of silk starting at pale blush near her face and ending in deepest mauve, like a bruise, at the hem. A long sash tied loosely around her hips almost trailed on the floor. She waved and came over, kissing me on the cheek.

"You look amazing," she said to me.

"Amazingly large," I said.

"Hardly," she said. "I can't even tell. Are you scared?"

Now this is a question an expectant mother is almost never asked. Are you excited? Are you feeling well? Are you tired? Yes. Are you scared? No.

"Yes," I said. "I guess I am."

"If it was me, I'd be terrified," she said.

We watched as the couple cut the tremendous marzipan wedding cake and then fed it to each other, sealing each bite with a kiss. This particular wedding tradition had always embarrassed me—the mess of it, the innuendo.

"Look at that," Ellie said, watching her cousin with detachment.

"They're very sweet together," Jim said, arriving at my side and putting an arm around my waist.

"I guess everyone should have that sort of lovey-dovey, puppy-dog love once in their lives. Look at her," Ellie said.

They say love is the most effective makeup on a woman, though I'd never really understood it until looking at plain Vivian Mingott radiant with triumph and adoration in her grandmother's Brussels-lace wedding gown. I could just barely remember feeling that way at my own wedding.

I turned toward Ellie. "Haven't you ever felt like that?"

Ellie shook her head. "Not like that."

"Not yet," Jim said.

"You're hopeful for me?" she said, swatting his elbow. "How sweet. Don't you know I'm too old?" She turned toward him. "What about you two?"

Jim smiled and kissed my cheek, but I noticed that Ellie kept his eye.

The Engagement

Ellie watched William Selden dodge through the wedding guests, who were busily eating cake and chatting. Though he stopped to say hello to a few people, he was intent on his destination. Her. She looked around, seeking a way to avoid him, when he caught her eye and smiled.

A waiter offered her a slice of cake. She declined. Selden had been a participant in her debacle at the Trenors', and he had a knowing smirk on his face as he closed in on her. He swiped a glass of champagne off a passing tray and offered it to her.

"Not drinking," she said when he arrived. "That's what got me in trouble last time."

A look of annoyance crossed his face but was replaced almost instantly with his usual jovial smile. "I'm trouble?" He took a short swig from the rejected glass.

"You left without saying good-bye."

"I figured I'd see you. I didn't figure you'd not return my phone calls."

He leaned against a doorjamb, languidly looking at her body. It'd taken an almost superhuman amount of self-control only to kiss him that night in Ellicottville. Selden was an expert kisser. One who'd gained his skills from much diverse practice. It hinted that he was an accomplished lover. Thinking about it now, seeing the new confident look on his face, she blushed.

"Oh, you don't have to worry about me," he said with a wave of his hand. "I know I'm not your type." He seemed changed since their night together in Ellicottville—older, cocky even. It wasn't appealing.

"How do you know I have a type?"

"Gryce is your type," he said, moving closer. "Or maybe Randy Leforte, yeah?"

"I don't know Randy Leforte, but I can't think of two more different people," she said primly. "Clearly I have no type. What are you implying?"

"Not implying anything." He leaned toward her. "I'm a realist, and I see who you are."

"Really? Who's that?" Her face was hot now.

"I'm saying you're a pragmatist. Aren't you?"

Perhaps she'd upset him more than she realized by not returning his calls. "That sounds vulgar," she said.

"You think you're the only one?" He looked around the room. "How many of these marriages are based on less than that?"

She considered the Wetheralls in front of her, a union based on his business connections and her social ambitions. Just looking at them made Ellie depressed.

"How many still have passion?" he asked, waving a hand.

"I don't think anyone really knows what goes on inside anyone else's marriage."

"Right." He shrugged.

"Passion is fine," she said, grasping his glass and taking a sip. "What I really want is freedom."

He raised an eyebrow. "Freedom in marriage?"

"Freedom from everything—from money, from poverty, from ease and anxiety, from all the material accidents. That's the only thing money can buy."

"Money doesn't buy that," he said.

"The hell it doesn't," she said with a snort.

"What you are talking about is a republic of the spirit, a context of the soul." He deposited his now-empty glass on a silver tray and took the full flute offered by a waiter. "It can't be bought." He ran a hand through his unruly hair. "What you are talking about has nothing to do with money and everything to do with your state of mind. You've had money."

"That's where the passion comes in. Need that too."

He grasped her wrist. "Ribbon's gone."

"Fell off." Ellie shrugged.

"You need another," he said. He looked at the couple next to them, saying good-byes now that the cake was cut. "The Hindus say the rich man and the poor man have the same troubles, except the rich man has money," Selden said to her.

"Eastern wisdom from a corn-fed midwestern boy—you know that's annoying as hell, right?"

"Want me to read your aura?" he asked, smiling.

"You can do that?"

"No, but I actually read things besides *Vogue* magazine."

"Didn't realize you read *Vogue* magazine," she said with a smirk.

He snorted. "You know what I mean."

"You mean I'm an idiot." Ellie took a plate from a passing waiter and turned toward Selden. "Lemon," she said, offering him a forkful of cake as a little peace offering.

"You're not an idiot." He ate the bite from Ellie's fork. After he swallowed he said, "It means we all have to deal with the same shit. Some can throw money at it, but they still have to struggle with the same major questions of life. Always have."

Just then Jack Stepney came over with Randall Leforte. Ellie kissed her cousin and congratulated him on his bride, his happiness, his beautiful day. Selden leaned back against the doorjamb again, watching her. Randall Leforte bent low over her hand and kissed it with a loud smack.

"Yes, we've met," Leforte said when introduced by Jack. "At the orchestra. I'm a big patron. I love music." He said this with a flourish that embarrassed Ellie. The man may have been rich and not bad looking, but he was impossible socially. Now was the time to glide over any awkwardness and introduce him to Selden, to be her usual charming self, but she couldn't. She didn't want Selden to think she was hunting Leforte. Selden had that effect on her. He invited her into his own world to abide by his views. They were brave views and romantic. Her concerns were trivial and small when she was with him. It was when they were apart that his heroic stance was hard for her to maintain on her own. She was smiling distractedly and silently at Leforte, who was gradually reddening.

"I hear you're a good friend of Gus Trenor's," Leforte said. "I was playing squash with him the other day." She thought she saw Selden smile at this thudding name-drop.

"Gus and Julia are some of my best friends."

"I love your dress," Leforte said, grasping at conversational straws and sinking. "Where'd you get it?"

Ellie winced. It was one thing for a woman to quietly inquire about a dress's provenance, but a man? It was strange and aggressive. It put her on the spot if the dress was from Target, even worse if it was from Prada. "From my parents' attic, actually. It was my grandmother's."

Leforte laughed heartily, trying to cover his discomfort. "Digging in the attic, huh? The fancier the family, the more you're allowed your eccentricities, I guess. Or maybe you just can't afford a new one?"

Ellie smiled a tight, close-lipped smile. He'd never understand the gradations of old Cleveland, she thought. Never be able to parse that the Hays were the tippity top, though they had no money, because they had given it all away. The Dagonets remained at the top because they retained their money, though one rung under the Hays. The Harts were just a nice old family that had produced some pretty women. Ellie's dress was so old she kept hoping the seams wouldn't disintegrate and cause the whole thing to fall off her. Her cousin Jack gave Ellie an apologetic smile. Selden shrugged off from the doorjamb and raised his empty glass at her, leaving to find another drink.

Looking at Leforte's bright lapis cufflinks compared to her cousin's dull onyx shirt studs, Ellie was conscious then of an overwhelming need to find P. G. Gryce. She'd seen his broad shoulders moving through the crowds earlier.

"Mr. Leforte," Ellie said.

"It's Randy, please."

"Have you had any cake yet?"

She took Leforte's arm and started walking toward the terrace in search of Gryce. Leforte kept up a litany of questions and comments that she volleyed back with charm and wit. She was conscious of eyes following them questioningly and with amusement. And she was conscious of her companion's satisfaction in being seen with her.

The terrace was empty, and the whole place had the air of dispersal when she saw Viola Trenor slicing through the thinning crowds and heading right for them.

"Come get a drink with me after this," Leforte said low in Ellie's ear.

Before Ellie could answer, Viola swept her up in a breathless hug.

"I just had to find you and tell you. P. G. and I, we're engaged! He just asked me. It's all so fast, but when it's right, it's right. I think cousin Vivian's wedding just carried him away. I wanted you to be one of the first to know since you and P. G. are such friends. Look . . ." She flourished a massive emerald-cut diamond offset by two dark blue sapphires. "He even paid extra to make sure it wasn't a blood diamond. The gold is recycled."

Ellie smiled her most brilliant smile. Viola's face floated in front of her, red with joy and victory. P. G. hung in the background accepting congratulations from the people who would no doubt approve of joining two of Cleveland's richest families. Ellie hugged her friend in congratulation. She widened her smile until her face hurt, telling herself that not all options were yet closed to her. There was still door number two. She turned to Leforte. "Yes," she said. "I'd love to have a drink with you."

· 10 ·

The Downtown

I drove downtown on an overcast fall day, nearly winter, to meet Ellie at her new job. She'd been sending me e-mails asking me to come see her and her new boss, the fashion designer, for lunch in a renovated building across the street from the Cleveland *Plain Dealer*. The building had been a textile mill but now was filled with artists' spaces, a theatrical company, a Pilates studio, and an Internet café. The building next door was a decaying warehouse, the windows smashed out and boarded up from the inside, the mortar crumbling.

I'd rummaged together a pregnancy outfit. I'd only just outgrown my normal clothes, and now my choice was either to highlight the bump or wear a fashionable tent. I'd recently been rocking my mother's djellaba from the seventies with the hood out over a tiny jean jacket and flat boots. It somehow looked just crazy enough to seem a choice and not a default. I'd actually gone shopping for something to wear to this lunch, such were my nerves at meeting Ellie's fashion designer boss. But I'd been unable to find anything that didn't feel contrived, and so I'd decided Mother's vintage was best.

I was still feeling nervous when the freight elevator deposited me on the top floor. I could hear her boss before I even walked down the hall.

"I wanted to say to that damn idiot on the radio that, first of all, it would never, never be Adam and Steve."

I couldn't hear a reply, but as I opened the door I heard her laugh and him speak again: "It's Adam and Steven, for God's sake."

"Hey," Ellie said, laughing, as I walked in the room. She was sitting on the windowsill, smoking a cigarette, wearing a gleaming astrakhan wrap around her shoulders, a thick cashmere sweater, and a tiny gray skirt that showed off her perfect legs swathed in black jersey tights and ending in precariously high-heeled black suede booties.

The space was white with floor-to-ceiling windows on one side, but dingy and many times painted over.

Clear late fall light flooded across Ellie's face and for just an instant I saw her as she must have seen herself in the mirror sometimes—perhaps in the morning or late at night. There were crosshatched crinkles under her eyes and the beginnings of apple-doll lines above her mouth as she took a last drag of her smoke. Her skin looked sallow and rough next to her black clothes. Then she flicked the butt out the window and smiled at me, and again she was radiant and returned. The moment passed.

A tall, fair man, well scrubbed and youthful, came over and hugged me. He wore a ripped black cashmere sweater that showed wide swatches of neon yellow T-shirt, sharply cut pin-striped flannel trousers, and dark expensive-looking shoes. Two steel hoops glinted when he smiled—piercings right next to each other on the left side of his lower lip. Viper bites, Ellie would later tell me they were called.

"Steven, this is the friend I was telling you about."

He kissed the back of my knuckles, and I thought I felt the graze of warm steel for just an instant. "I'm dying to do a maternity line," he said, pulling me in close. "She told me your little secret," he whispered. "But you don't look pregnant at all. Look at you." He held me at arm's length. "Now spin."

I looked at Ellie, mortified, but also relieved that I seemed to pass muster. "Please, Steven, don't scare her," Ellie said. "She's not going to spin."

We went down to the Internet café for sandwiches and salads. The place was done in midcentury modern—steel chairs and white tables. The walls displayed art for sale by artists working in the building. I ordered a grilled cheese, Steven some superior salad, but Ellie ordered only green tea with honey.

"Not feeling well," she said unconvincingly.

"Nice piece," I said, slipping into a chair next to Ellie. I petted the black Persian lamb wrap she was wearing. "Have you always had it?"

"New," she said.

I raised eyebrows.

"She has a sugar daddy," Steven said.

"I do not."

"That luscious Randall Leforte. You know he probably oils himself up before he goes out. Smells like Gucci heaven when he comes to pick her up for lunch." He flicked his tongue over the piercings in his lip.

"You've been seeing Randall Leforte?" I was surprised.

"Saw. A few times. Just curious," she said.

"Haven't you seen the picture of them?" Steven asked, forking around in his spinach salad.

"How did you know about that?" Ellie asked him a little sharply.

"It was in the newspaper, hello—the picture of you guys at the benefit for the playhouse. But Mr. Leforte is also my Facebook friend," Steven said smugly. "And he posted the picture on his wall."

"He has a Facebook page? Why is he your friend?" Ellie asked.

"Probably trying to get in good with you," Steven said. "The man can wear a tuxedo."

"Well?" I said, turning to Ellie.

"Well, I'm having fun. He's so not my type. No, this," she said, stroking her fur, "is the result of wise investing. Gus Trenor is taking care of my money for me."

"Does Gus Trenor actually manage people's money?" I asked, taking a bite of my gooey cheese sandwich. "I mean, besides his own."

"That weekend in Ellicottville he offered to invest some of my settlement for me, and he's done well so far. So I bought myself a little treat."

"As long as you're okay with it," I said after I'd swallowed.

"He actually has quite a few clients. You'd be surprised."

"He's one of those what-do-you-call-'ems, Ells," Steven broke in, snapping his fingers.

"Dead-end WASP," Ellie said, bored, elbows on the table.

"I love that," Steven said. "All of the expectations and none of the abilities." He forked a bite into his mouth.

"So not hot," Ellie said.

"No," Steven said, shaking his head when he was done chewing. "And you, my dear, definitely need someone hot," he said, poking his fork at her. "What is wrong with Leforte? The man's hot as blazes. His first name's Randy, for God's sake. I'll bet he's a tiger in the sack." He nibbled his viper bites, pondering this.

Ellie rolled her eyes and took a sip of tea. "From the person who told me he went to the clubs Saturday night to get his man on."

"Well, why the fuck not?" Steven asked.

Ellie shrugged, lapsed into silence. A line was forming of dark-suited businessmen picking up their gourmet sandwiches. Every one of them did a double take when he saw Ellie. She sipped her tea, used to the attention her beauty attracted.

"Because I want more."

"He has money," Steven said.

"Maybe I don't give a shit about money."

I smirked; I couldn't help it.

But Steven was nodding. "Good girl. Maybe you don't. Maybe you don't give a shit about marriage or kids either. Maybe you're just some super-fabulous post-millennial babe who's going to blaze a new trail for women worldwide."

I smiled. I was really starting to like Steven.

He waved a hand toward my belly. "Frankly, I don't see you with all that." He leaned over and whispered in my ear, "Sorry, darling." Then he turned back to Ellie. "But the suburbs-and-security thing . . . doesn't really suit you, Ells, not in my opinion. And seriously, not to get all bra-burning on you, but shouldn't you be thinking about more than that?"

I was hoping to make space for something more too. Once the children were in school, maybe. I was about to stick up for myself, to try to explain that I wasn't some patsy of male hegemony, when Ellie spoke up.

"What else is there?" she asked quietly.

Steven moaned and leaned back in his chair. "Jesus, woman, this is the two thou. You can do any damn thing you want. Be secretary of state or a Supreme Court justice or some other brand of complete ass kicker . . ."

Ellie snorted. "Come on, be real."

"Why don't you believe in yourself?" Steven asked, leaning over the table, suddenly intensely serious. "Why don't you want something dreamed up by just you and no one else?" He poked her fur, high on the left side of her chest. "What the fuck is in there?"

I remembered that they'd been in rehab together. That he probably knew things about her that I never would. I was touched by his concern for her, his ability to see clearly.

"Is this the part when you sing 'Climb Every Mountain'?" she asked.

He rolled his eyes and gave her the finger.

A young boy in a tight black T-shirt and a barbell through the cartilage of his ear, maybe a student at nearby Cleveland State, came to refill our water. He knocked Ellie's glass right into my lap.

"I'm so sorry," he said to her, not me. He flicked a rag out of his back pocket and wiped up the spill with a shaking hand.

"It's okay," I said, swiping my lap with paper napkins.

His eyes didn't leave Ellie. "Can I get you another water?" he asked.

"Sure, thanks," she said.

"More tea?" he asked her.

She looked up at him then and smiled. "Yes, please."

He smiled a wide grin at her, a little dazed, I thought. He walked away but came right back.

"I'm sorry, did you say you wanted water *and* tea?"

Steven rolled his eyes. I watched the two of them, amused, as always.

Ellie had a little smile on her face. "Yes, please."

He gave a sheepish grin and left. He never did come back with her drinks.

When the boy was out of earshot Steven turned to me.

"Everyone wants her to get married," he said. "Look at the effect she has." He gestured toward the counter, where the boy was helping another customer. "They want her tied down, not corrupting the young."

"You want a piece of that?" I asked Ellie in disbelief, hooking my thumb toward the counter. "He's young enough—"

"Don't you dare say it," she interrupted with a smile.

"Marriage," Steven said, turning to me. "Your marriage is hot?"

"Don't pick on her," Ellie said to him while sweeping a hand toward me. "You should see her adorable husband—straight out of a J.Crew catalog and not with a flat Waspy ass either."

We all laughed, though I felt vaguely uncomfortable that Ellie had been appraising Jim's ass.

Steven leaned back. "I mean, don't get me wrong, I'm no man hater. A woman without a man is not like a fish without a bicycle. A woman without a man can get lonely." He gestured toward Ellie. "She's going to need lovers."

I snorted at the word.

He laughed. "You breeders—so stuffy. You must know someone eligible for her," he said to me seriously. "If she doesn't like randy Randy Leforte."

"Ellie knows everyone I know," I said.

"Everyone knows everyone in Cleveland," he said, sighing. "It's like Sweden." He rose, straightening his impeccable trousers. "I'll leave you ladies to your estrogen talk."

Ellie stuck her tongue out at him. He kissed each of us on the cheek, faint click of steel, and then left.

"Do you want to go shopping?" Ellie asked suddenly.

"In Cleveland?" I said, surprised.

"Don't be provincial. You just have to know where to go."

"Don't you have to go back to work?"

"Steven won't mind."

She scrabbled up her phone, her car keys, her wallet, and a lipstick.

"Why don't you carry a handbag?" I asked.

"It's such a luxury not to. Don't you know? To have your hands and shoulders free. Freedom is the true luxury. The new black." She smiled at her corny phrase. "Besides, it ruins the line of clothes." She tucked the lipstick and her phone up the sleeve of her fur and grabbed the rest of her things.

I nodded but wondered if she couldn't afford a nice bag right now.

We walked out to her car. Noontime groups of women from the surrounding office buildings were headed out to lunch wrapped in their practical woolen coats with their sensible low-heeled shoes and huge black shoulder bags. Ellie towered above them with her great mass of caramel hair flying out over the glossy sleekness of her fur.

"So Steven doesn't mind if you just take off for the afternoon? Nice work if you can get it."

"I don't know how the whole Steven thing is working out."

"Why not?"

"He's hired me to be his muse. Have you ever heard of anything more bizarre?" The wind off the lake was rapidly turning her face red. "I go and sit around the studio and try things on and brainstorm with him. But I don't know how much longer something like this can last. I mean, when I stop amusing him, or he stops thinking I'm fabulous, or I stop laughing at his jokes—what then?"

"I thought he needed PR help."

"It's not exactly advancing my career or my skills. I can't put on a résumé 'muse for an ex-junkie nobody designer,' can I?" We turned the corner, walking past a police precinct straight out of a thirties noir movie—stone pillars, globe streetlights. Next to it, a vacant lot was covered in trash.

I was surprised by her vitriol. "You don't know where it will lead. You could meet someone in the industry—"

"You know, you always say that. 'You don't know where this will lead.' But I think I do know where it will lead. If not to a husband, then to a boss. Look at these girls," she said, gesturing to four twentysomething women walking toward us. "You think they don't live in fear of some boss and his tirades or don't sit by the phone waiting for some man to call? They live by men's whims. God, I'm so sick of it. I just want to opt out of the whole thing."

She had unnerved me, and I was worried about her. Ellie never seemed to worry, or perhaps she didn't worry with me. "But that's life," I said. "We are all of us, always, accommodating others, unless you want to be a hermit."

She put an arm around me as we walked. "I know. And you're about to do the biggest accommodation act of all. I'm just saying in the balance we accommodate men, much more than the other way around. And I'm a little bit sick of it. I want to know what it would feel like to have someone accommodate me for a change. Or everyone—how delicious would that be?" We kept walking and when I didn't say anything she said, "Okay, maybe just one fabulous man to do my bidding." When I didn't laugh she added, "Just for a while."

"So opt out. Buy a house. Live alone." Her attitude annoyed me today.

"I'm thinking of buying a condo. Gus's investments are going so well I might have a down payment soon."

I was constantly amazed at Ellie's concern about money. She had a prenup with her first husband, yes. But surely he'd settled something on her? Then again there'd been those whispers of an affair, a few even. Maybe such things canceled out any payments.

We both climbed in her car, an ancient red BMW with a dent in the hood.

She drove fast and parked in front of Potter and Mellen, the city's oldest jeweler.

"This is where you shop now? Niiiice," I teased.

"Baubles," she said, and smiled.

All her life money flowed out of Ellie's pockets as quickly as it came in. When she was married in New York, her husband had kept her on a short leash with his cash. "We could have walked," I said.

"Not in your condition."

We stepped under the royal blue awnings and then into the warm room as hushed as a vault. Immediately two saleswomen welcomed Ellie with hugs and kisses.

"Have you come to visit it?" they asked in the well-modulated tones of nurses on the maternity ward.

"To show it to my friend," Ellie answered.

The impeccable women smiled and went behind the counter. One carefully spread a blue velvet swatch on the case as if unfurling a baby blanket. The other settled an enormous brooch on the cloth.

"Isn't it wonderful?" Ellie whispered. She wasn't used to having her own money, to commanding a decent sum from her own work and deciding exactly how it would be spent. I could see that she was enjoying mulling over this purchase.

It was an immense gold brooch, in the Art Nouveau style, depicting a tree with a twisted trunk and spreading branches. Nestled inside the branches were old mine-cut diamonds and smooth cabochon emeralds.

"Oooh, pretty," I said. "Old, yes?" I asked the lady behind the counter.

"Turn of the century. We don't get pieces like this very often."

I could see why; jewels like this weren't often sold out of families. It brought to mind my mother once describing a new family in town as "the type of people who buy their jewelry." Ellie had picked the piece up and was holding it to her shoulder.

"It's something very special," the woman now said to Ellie and me.

"But it's too beautiful to be kept in a safe. I'd wear it all the time. Every day," Ellie said.

The lady behind the counter smiled wider. "It'd be wonderful with jeans," she said in a whisper.

"Or a green velvet gown," the other murmured.

Just then Viola Trenor, wearing a sack dress that looked like it was made out of hemp and golden suede boots, emerged from the other side of the shop, where the china and crystal and silver were kept. She held a stack of manila folders with notes and paper clips hanging out. We all hugged and kissed.

"Are you registering for the wedding?" I asked.

"I'm trying," Viola said with a wan smile. "I'm having a hard time getting into the spirit of it. P. G. and I are such practical people. I don't know when we'd ever use half this stuff."

Thinking of all the brides who'd be thrilled to be in Viola's place—immense wedding and the lavish present fallout from it—I said, "This is your chance. People want to give you things. Think of family Thanksgivings and Christmases, stuff to pass down to a daughter."

"Yes," she said distractedly. An avalanche of family china and silver probably overflowed Jefferson Gryce's house; as a widower he'd give P. G. and Viola everything they'd need to entertain twenty-four generously. But to my surprise Viola said, "I think today was a particularly bad day for me to do this. I've just come from a Dress for Success board meeting, and they're having a hard time meeting this year's fund-raising goals. They might have to actually close it down. Can you believe it? They do such good work. The stories you hear from the women they help . . ."

"I have some suits from my accounting days," I said. "I can bring them by."

She smiled sweetly. "That would be nice, and they'd appreciate it, but what they really need is money. There's so much more to it than outfitting—there's training and résumé writing and interviewing skills, general operating costs, and the economy's so bad right now . . ."

To my utter shock, Ellie said, "I'll help." She took a slim lizard wallet out of her skirt pocket and started writing a check right there. I didn't see the amount but noticed a generous number of zeros.

Viola turned to me while Ellie was writing.

"And Cinco Van Alstyne's wife is helping too." She smiled. "Corrine. Do you know her?" I felt a pang then. Perhaps Cinco's wife wasn't a complete social idiot. Cleveland smiled on anyone who helped Viola.

"Not well," I said. Corrine was her name; I'd forgotten.

Viola had been there in Ellicottville when we'd all heard the story about the Van Alstyne dinner party. It didn't surprise me she had roped in Cinco's wife. The story had probably jogged her memory. Viola could round up help from anyone, and she wasn't squeamish about pressure. I wondered how long it'd be before P. G. and the entire Gryce family were opening their wallets. It made me smile to think of it. In this one area, as far as changing a man, Viola might have had even Ellie beat.

Ellie gave Viola the check, and after Viola quickly glanced at the amount, she tried to keep the surprise out of her voice. "Ellie, this is so nice of you! You must come to the next board meeting and let us thank you. Or, I know, you should come . . . Well, you should come meet some of the women." Viola continued to gush. "Not to push my luck because you've just been so generous, but I know they would love to meet you. A lot of them aspire to the fashion world. And of course you're so glamorous. It'd be a thrill for them, an inspiration."

Ellie blushed. I couldn't help but think that Viola's response was all the most ardent moralist would have wanted. Ellie promised to come meet some of the women, and we left the store.

"That was nice of you," I said as we drove back to my car.

"I'm a sucker for a cause like that. Helping people get back on their feet." She looked at me quickly sideways. "And doing it all through clothes—what could be closer to my heart?"

I smiled and she continued.

"But for the grace of God that might be me," she said. "Putting on someone's old suit and trying to type a million words a minute. I know how it feels to be in that spot. Everyone needs someone to take care of them."

I nodded, but such retro musings out of Ellie surprised me. We pulled up next to my car.

"Not buying that jewel and giving Viola some money—it actually made me feel for a moment that things were going to be okay, you know." She leaned over and kissed me on the cheek. "Tell your lovely husband I said hi."

I got out of the car and watched her drive off toward the Terminal Tower, which proudly rose at the end of the street like a Gotham lighthouse. It was then I realized she was driving in the opposite direction from her job.

· 11 ·

The Ritz

Ellie was driving downtown to meet Randall Leforte for a drink. He'd asked her to meet him at three o'clock. An absurd time, but she figured it ensured she'd see no one she knew. She walked into the empty bar at the Ritz, sat on the leather stool, and ordered a glass of champagne. If she were going to have a rendezvous with Randy Leforte, she might as well go all the way and order the champagne. They'd had a few dinners, attended that benefit where he'd been obsessed with getting their picture taken. She was initially repulsed by his slick appearance: she was pretty sure he went to one of those spray-on tan places, he'd had his teeth whitened, his watch flashed with diamonds, and he wore too much gel in his dark curly hair. Despite this, after a few lunches she'd decided he was sexy. He was tall, and under his sharply cut suits she detected evidence of daily workouts. By now she saw his grooming as a desire to please that might translate nicely in bed, or a healthy dose of vanity, which hinted he'd be concerned with his performance. Really he was quite handsome, and a fling with a tall, dark, handsome lawyer with a Maserati might be just what she needed. Perhaps Steven was right.

Perhaps *this* was the woman she would be now, taking pleasure where she found it, yet independent and on her own. Men did this sort of thing all the time—slept with unsuitable women.

He walked in wearing a ridiculous suit—navy blue with a heavy chalk stripe, and tight, in a Cleveland tailor's parody of a Savile Row. But it made his broad shoulders look larger and his waist narrower. His white teeth almost glowed in the dim bar, and he kissed her on the cheek, sat down, and ordered a Macallan rocks.

"No clothes from the attic this time, or was this Granny's?" he asked, nodding at her fur.

"New, actually. I've come into a bit of money."

He smiled.

"You're in a good mood," she said.

"I'm always in a good mood when I see you." His BlackBerry vibrated, and he glanced at it, then set it aside. "I have a little question to ask you."

Leforte slid a hundred-dollar bill on the bar without acknowledging the bartender. "Look, I'm not good at this. But I like you." And here he swung on the bar stool to face her. "A lot." He drank his scotch down. "I didn't think I'd be nervous, but you make me nervous, you know? You're about the only one who ever has." His BlackBerry vibrated again, and he checked it with a shaking hand, then set it back on the bar.

Ellie didn't mind the interruptions. Leforte's career intrigued her; it was true. She remembered as a girl telling her mother that one day she'd make her own money.

"That's right, dear," her mother said distractedly, putting her tennis racket away in the front closet and heading toward the kitchen to make lunch.

"Maybe I'll be a lawyer."

Her mother washed her hands at the kitchen sink and then leveled her gaze at Ellie. "With your face, I think it'd be easier to get one man to take care of you than to get a courtroom full of men to think you're smart."

She'd felt slapped and embarrassed.

When Ellie didn't say anything, her mother continued. "Maybe you'll marry a lawyer."

But her mother's comments made Ellie feel oddly powerful too. Her face was pretty enough to get someone to take care of her? And looking back, she supposed that was where it all started.

"I've been bored as hell in Cleveland for a while," Leforte was saying. "It's a hick town when you get right down to it. Everyone here is so provincial. Old Cleveland is a stuffy, prehistoric group of geriatrics."

Ellie thought this herself sometimes, but it jarred hearing it from him.

"Anyway, I was bored until I saw you at the orchestra that night. I thought, There is a woman with real class."

Ellie winced at the word, though Leforte didn't notice.

"And these past few weeks, I just know that you're the type of woman I could be with, that I want to be with."

Alarm bells started sounding in Ellie's ears. This was not the sort of talk she expected from her afternoon tryst.

"And because I've never done this and never thought I would do this, I'm going to be really bad at it. I have to just get what I'm thinking out on the table."

He leaned forward then, took her face in his hands, and kissed her. It was a fine kiss; technically it was quite accomplished. There was nothing wrong with it. The scotch after-burn covered a faint taste of stale coffee in his mouth. But Ellie felt nothing in her stomach; it didn't flip. When he was finished he said, "I want to marry you."

"What?!" Ellie gasped.

"Look, just listen to me. I suspected this might take a little convincing. You are the type of woman I want, and I'm sick of being a big fish in a small pond. I'm ready to go to New York."

Ellie furrowed her brow.

"Don't you miss it? You can't tell me you don't miss it. I have more money than I know what to do with. Something tells me you'd know what to do with it in New York." He leaned in and kissed her again. "Don't you want to go back and show them all?"

Ellie was stunned. She sipped her champagne. She'd been expecting a proposition and ended up with a proposal.

Leforte smiled at her and leaned in close. "I reserved a room upstairs. I'm all checked in. Come up with me. Let me convince you how right we are for one another."

She remembered someone telling her that his nickname was the Persuader. It was, quite literally, his job. Some lawyers advised, some mediated, some resolved, but Leforte's specialty was big-time litigation when the case was certain for trial. It was then you called the Persuader. She'd thought it implied a slippery finesse, but now she realized it referenced the surprise of a blunt instrument, a sledgehammer of directness, and a complete lack of pretense. No wonder he did so well.

Her head was reeling. "You've kind of caught me off guard here," she said. "You're going to have to give me a minute."

Leforte leaned back and glanced quickly at his BlackBerry. Ellie got up and straightened her skirt. "Be right back."

In the bathroom she dabbed water on her temples, swilled a little Ritz mouthwash and spat it out. A handsome, rich lawyer was offering to marry her, take her back to New York, and let her spend his money situating them in society. If possible it was an even less romantic proposal than that from her first husband, who'd been drunk and panic-sweating.

Yet there was something about Leforte. He was ambitious and hungry for the limelight, and when she thought about it, those things actually appealed to her. He knew what he wanted out of life; he had passion, and he wasn't afraid to go balls-out to get what he wanted.

But she didn't love him, and she'd been down that aisle with her first husband. She'd learned that she wanted love, the at-first-sight, toe-curling, can't-live-without-him—or something closely approximating it—love if she was going to marry again. She wanted that and the money, because Ellie didn't think she could live in a hovel on toe curls alone.

She actually did want to go upstairs with Leforte. She hadn't gotten laid in months, and she was curious about what he'd be like in bed. She'd been looking forward to a blissful afternoon, but it came with strings. How did men do this? How did they sleep with someone who had expectations and then blow them off? Could she do it too?

She sat down next to him again at the bar. He'd had her drink topped off.

"Take your glass," he said into her ear. "And come upstairs with me."

She kissed him this time—a long kiss, a searching kiss. She was glad they were the only ones in the bar. And as they parted she smelled his overpowering cologne and detected just a whiff of a stale corn chip smell—the smell of self-tanning lotion.

As she resettled on her seat, out of the corner of her eye she saw two gray-haired women enter the end of the lobby used for afternoon tea. Sparkles flashed in Ellie's eye as she recognized Betsy Dorset and her diamonds from across the room. Betsy smiled a minute in recognition and sat down with her back to Ellie. Betsy Dorset was no gossip. Ellie could be pretty sure she hadn't seen the kiss and wouldn't run around town telling people she'd seen Ellie Hart and Randy Leforte having drinks. I mean, frankly, no one would care. But if Ellie took her champagne and got in an elevator going upstairs with Randy Leforte? Well, even Betsy Dorset would talk about that.

"I can't today," Ellie said to Leforte.

"Come on," he said, leaning in close and running his hand down her arm. "I'm dying for it."

"I can't."

"You knew why I asked you down here in the middle of the day. What did you expect?" he said, testy.

"I didn't expect a marriage proposal."

"Don't be so serious. We'd be great together. And if we're not . . ." He shrugged.

"Let me think," Ellie said.

"You can't think properly unless I take you upstairs. You won't have all the information." He had a wicked gleam in his eye that would have appealed to her a minute ago, but now the lasciviousness looked more like acquisitiveness, and he suddenly became less attractive.

"I can imagine," she said, getting up. "Let me mull." She kissed his cheek and went to leave.

"Okay," he said, grabbing her hand and pulling her toward him. "But don't make me wait too long."

The Dinner Party

A few weeks after my lunch with Ellie, I was invited to a dinner party at Julia Trenor's massive 1920s faux-Tudor pile in town.

It was the same night as Jim's and my wedding anniversary. We'd agreed to go to Julia's dinner and tell no one. Since moving back, I'd thought it best to accept all invitations as we established ourselves—especially Julia's invitations. I didn't want to miss out on anything.

We'd celebrate together the next night at home with a cozy dinner and going to bed together early, I hoped.

I was upstairs, trying yet again to find something to wear that fit me, when I heard Jim come through the back door.

"Lovely wife," he called from the kitchen. "Come down here. I've got a surprise for you, darlin'."

Now, I love surprises; I always have. But Jim was an awful gift giver. He knew it too, I think, which is why he'd taken me shopping for an engagement ring and let me pick out exactly what I wanted after he proposed.

We'd agreed no gifts for our anniversary this year as the baby and the ensuing expenses were coming. But I'd figured it'd be okay if I made him a silly little box that I'd filled with folded notes, each one describing something I loved about him—from the valleys on either side of his hips, to the way he held doors for me, to the way he calmed me, to his agreeing to come live in Cleveland. I planned to give it to him tomorrow night—preferably while naked in bed.

Despite Jim's gifting track record, I cinched a robe around my ballooning waist and skipped down the stairs as gracefully as I could, hoping for a lovely present.

In the kitchen Jim stood with a shiny red mountain bike with a huge green bow on it.

I raised my eyebrows, shocked and unable to think of anything to say.

"Happy four-year anniversary, shug," he said.

I felt myself flush, shock and disbelief clouding my thoughts.

He smiled, wary and watching me. "For getting back in shape after the baby. You've been talking about that a lot recently."

I took a deep breath. Jim loved mountain biking. I'd never tried it. Not when we were dating or newlyweds, and not now when I was pregnant. It'd be a while, with a new baby, until I'd have time for anything like that. I'd never even expressed an interest in it.

And the bike looked expensive—glinting and tricked out with shocks and gears—clearly violating the purpose of our no-gift rule.

And I hated that he seemed a little too eager for me to return to my previous size.

I felt like he didn't know me at all.

And then he asked the question I was dreading, though I suspected he already knew the answer.

"Do you like it?"

I took a deep breath, went to him, and kissed his cheek. "Thank you, sweetheart," I said.

"I knew it," he said. "You hate it." It was more an accusation than a question.

I felt a tremor of annoyance. If he'd known I would hate it, why did he buy it?

"It can go back," he said. "I made sure at the store."

"No," I said. "Don't take it back."

And so it started, as it had many times in the past—me begging for a gift I didn't want so as not to hurt his feelings, him resentful that I didn't like his offering. I'd long ago told myself that the gift may not be perfect, but since the gift giver was, I would be gracious. However, I was having a hard time holding on to my resolution now.

"We said no gifts, remember?" I said.

"Yes, but I wanted you to have this."

"Right, you wanted me to have it," I said, picking at the hem of my sleeve, looking anywhere but at the red bike in the middle of the room.

"What's that mean?"

"Nothing."

"It means you don't want it. I want it," he said flatly.

"You want it for me." I tried to sound kind.

"Whatever."

"Oh, don't be mad." I sighed, exasperated, turning from him to the sink with the dirty lunch dishes in it.

"I can't help it if it hurts my feelings."

"Well, you're basically telling me to get my fat ass in shape, so I'm not sure whose feelings should be hurt," I said, turning on the water, picking up a dish.

"Christ you're sensitive. You've been talking about getting in shape afterward—"

"For the love of Mike, when have you ever seen me ride a bike?"

"Never," he said quietly. "I thought you'd like a total surprise, something out of our usual routine."

I didn't think we were in a usual routine. Everything seemed full of potential as we waited for the baby. "It's the thought that counts," I said with a tight smile as I put the dishes in the dishwasher and turned to him.

"It's going back," he said, heading toward the stairs, dismissing the bike and me.

I sighed. "We're due at Julia's in twenty minutes," I called after him.

He came back down. "Right. Wouldn't want to miss spending our anniversary at Julia Trenor's." He snarled the last words.

"You said you wanted to." He'd agreed to go to the party, and now he was going to act like I was dragging him there?

"Only because you suggested it. If you didn't want to spend our anniversary alone with me—"

"We will, tomorrow night," I said, growing exasperated.

"It actually matters," he said, coming close. "The actual day. It matters to me."

"So now you're the romantic?" I gestured to the bike and instantly regretted it. He shook his head, turned, and walked up the stairs.

I said nothing, and when I heard the shower turn on I went back up to our bedroom. In the top drawer of my dressing table was the small box I'd made for Jim wrapped in plain butcher paper with a heavy brown satin bow. I couldn't give it to him now. It'd look like an accusation and would certainly not be taken in the spirit in which I'd made it. I didn't want to save it; it was now associated for me with another gift exchange gone wrong. I took it downstairs and threw it in the kitchen trash.

Something silly would have been fine, I thought. Or a piece of paper where he'd written "I love you more than anything or anyone." That would have been ideal. Or even saying that, just now. Not a bike. Not a fight. And I started to wonder, when was the last time he'd told me he loved me?

After a silent drive, a caterer opened the door to Julia Trenor's paneled Gothic entryway, took our coats, and offered champagne. In Julia's dark living room, the walls covered in watered green silk, were a few couples I knew and many I did not. Silver bibelots sat tarnishing away on Julia's early-American tables. The room was trademark Julia style— cultivated to give the impression that these tasteful knickknacks had been Grandmama's. They'd certainly been someone's grandmother's, just not Julia's. She'd bought them at antique shows. I'd recently heard her decorating business was picking up. She'd signed some clients who weren't related to her.

Ellie was seated on a threadbare needlepoint French settee in between a woman I didn't recognize and Julia's acupuncturist. Ellie lit up her corner of the room in a shimmering little sequin dress—a perfect sort of dress with a hint of sex at the leg but not revealing too much skin at the neck. In my larger state I wore a velvet Zandra Rhodes dress that I'd once again unearthed from Mother's closet, more loot from her Gypsy phase in the seventies. Jim absolutely detested it and all the women adored it.

When she saw me, Ellie excused herself, stood up, and came over to kiss me as Jim left to fetch drinks.

"Your mother always was glamorous. You look like a Rossetti." I blushed at her effusiveness. "This," she said, gesturing to her leg, "is Steven's doing. It's a little hoochie, but I promised I'd wear it tonight."

"You're very scrupulous. How would he ever know if you wore something else?"

"He's here. He's my date," she said, pointing.

Steven looked polished in a black tuxedo with a gray shirt open at the neck, no tie or cummerbund. The hoops in his lip glinted as he grinned and leaned slightly forward, listening to our hostess.

I saw Cinco and Corrine Van Alstyne then, holding hands as they chatted with a woman I didn't know. Their holding hands was almost as suggestive as excusing themselves during their own dinner party. No one did that at Julia's soirees, where spouses were separated for dinner and not expected to talk to one another until the car ride home, where they could compare notes and share hearsay. I assumed Corrine was terrified of having to make conversation and so clung to his hand. When he saw me, he waved his drink with a little wink.

Jim confidently maneuvered across the room to me, stopping and chatting with just the right people, saying hello to others and moving on quickly, his calculations in this spot-on. His hands were full with drinks for Ellie and me; his manners were impeccable even when he was pissed off. He'd adapted so well to Cleveland, had been so quickly accepted into the right circles, the right clubs. I'd never wondered if it'd been a strain for him at all. Watching Cinco and Corrine I knew I should feel lucky. My husband always had been a social animal.

Jim came over with sparkling water for both Ellie and me and a beer still in the bottle. I wondered how he'd managed that given the caterers and all.

"He's considerate, this one," Ellie said, taking her glass from him and cocking her head in his direction.

"I heard Gus Trenor is handling your money," Jim said after kissing her cheek.

I elbowed him in the side. I'd told him that in confidence.

"He is." Ellie shrugged.

"I don't think he's been doing too well recently. I've heard about some setbacks." Jim had told me this, and I'd promised to pass it on. Jim's mentioning it to Ellie first thing made me think that Gus's situation must be worse than I imagined. Either that or he was trying to get me in trouble with Ellie. Was there something he wasn't telling me? "Wouldn't want you involved in a bad situation." Jim took a swig of his beer.

"It's been good so far," Ellie said.

"He's over his head right now." Business gossip in Cleveland flew faster and farther than any other kind, save that concerning adultery.

"Actually, he's helping me find a place to live. I've been looking at some condos, and he thinks he knows one that's an excellent investment. That's pretty solid, right? Real estate?"

"They're saying we're probably at the bottom of the market. Great time to buy." Jim nodded, but I could see he'd gone a bit pale. "Anyway, I just wanted you to have the information."

"So sweet," she said, suddenly turning to me. "So protective. You really did nab one of the last decent men out there." She took a canapé off a passing tray.

I was going to ask Ellie where she'd been headed after our lunch the other day when we were besieged by Gus.

"Ellie-belle," he said with a strange proprietary air. "Come let me introduce you to some people." He guided her off with a hand low on the small of her back, almost on her ass. Jim was swept away by a group of men wanting to discuss the latest squash brackets at his club.

William Selden came over to me then, dressed in a dark blue suit with a rumpled white shirt open at the neck, no tie. He looked both rakishly handsome, as if he'd just fallen out of bed, and plainly austere—a pleasing combination.

"Half of the happiest couple I know," he said, kissing my cheek. "How do you feel?"

The perpetual pregnant-lady question. For just a moment I thought of answering with the truth: "Every day I feel like I'm slightly hungover—either tired or nauseated or a little of both." But I thought this unbecoming in a mother-to-be. And so I said, "Fine, thank you." His calling me happy echoed around in my head—a compliment that lingered like a question in my mind.

"How's your new class?" I asked. "Ellie told me."

"Hard to teach the first term of a new course, but it's going well."

"You know, I've been thinking about auditing a class. I thought it might give me something to do while gestating."

He smiled. "You'd be more than welcome to sit in on a few of my classes. I didn't know you liked poetry."

I cocked my head to the side, considering for a moment whether or not William Selden would ever give his wife a bicycle for an anniversary gift, and decided probably not. Some poetry maybe; certainly Selden plied women with poetry, not workout gear.

"I'd love that. Maybe I'll bring El," I said.

"Oh, don't do that," he said quickly, and then to cover: "It's just hard for me when someone I know sits in, yeah?"

I left aside the obvious fact that he knew me. But it was then that I noticed that his gaze never seemed to leave Ellie as she chatted her way around Julia's foxhunting-inspired living room.

For dinner, I was pleased to be seated next to Cinco. He'd probably scoped out the place cards and had thoughtfully avoided me during cocktails so we wouldn't talk ourselves out, his dancing school manners impeccable.

On my other side was Gus Trenor's cousin Jeff, who was visiting with his wife from Manhattan and had three boys. He came home to Cleveland often and was sought out by my mother and her friends at intergenerational Christmas parties and benefits because he was chatty and wore a bow tie, which they adored.

Cinco held out my chair for me, part of Julia's massive Chippendale set that seated twenty-four with ease. Her mother's Venetian green glass filled with orchids and foliage sparkled in the center.

Even though our hostess was young, Julia's dinner parties maintained a formal schedule where guests were expected to talk to the person on the left for the first course and the person on the right for the next, and dessert was served in the living room, where people could then jockey for their preferred gossip partner.

I knew how painstakingly Julia arranged her table. A reason lurked behind each seating choice, if only that you were the old friend whom she could inflict her dull cousin-in-law from New York on, as was the case with me seated next to Jeff. I knew that in consolation she'd put Cinco on my other side.

"So now we run into each other all the time," Cinco said, placing his napkin in his lap and nodding to the waiter when offered wine.

The table around us started buzzing with conversation and laughter aided by the cocktail hour. I shook my head no when offered wine and stilled myself. The smiles, the overwhelming scent of the flowers—the room suddenly felt hot, and I felt huge. I tried to catch Jim's eye, but he was listening closely to what Julia was saying to him. That she seated him next to her was a sure sign of her fondness for the both of us.

"I've been thinking about what you said at the wedding," Cinco said, interrupting my thoughts. He'd been talking for a while, and I hadn't heard a word he'd said.

"What'd I say?" I asked, but I knew exactly what he was referring to.

Endive salads on tiny plates appeared over our shoulders and were set down in front of us.

"You were so happy at the idea that I'd sold the farm . . . ," he said, trailing off, forking up a bite.

"It's a lot, especially for someone as young as you. Especially since your wife's not from here."

"What do you mean?" he asked. "You're saying a Clevelander wouldn't be overwhelmed with the farm?"

"No, no," I said, backtracking. The edge in his voice startled me. "But it might have been easier if she had her own family here. Or she might have known what she was getting into, maybe."

"I think it would have been way more difficult with anyone but Corrine."

"Way," I agreed, mocking his slang, but it came out bitter.

We ate in silence, listening to the conversations buzzing around us for a few minutes. The sharp salad dressing made me feel a little sick. I'd only taken a few bites. Cinco was almost done with his. I took a deep breath.

"I should apologize," I said. "It's not really any of my business what you guys"—I nodded toward Corrine—"do out there."

"No, I think I should apologize," he said.

"No, no," I said, interrupting him. He stopped, smiling, and I went on. "I really didn't mean anything other than I would be daunted by a project like that myself."

"Yes, you've made that clear."

"Good, then I hope you know I didn't mean anything by it."

He chewed a bite of salad. "No, really I should apologize to you. The way we left you at Vivian's wedding was a little . . ."

I shrugged. "You're married."

"And trying for a baby." He winked at me.

I never know how to address this information. I mean, what does one say to a person like Cinco Van Alstyne? "Have fun"? "How's that going?"? And of course it immediately brought to mind the idea of them having sex. I looked at Corrine across the room as she nodded at what Dan Dorset was mumbling in her ear. Very calm, very comme il faut. I couldn't picture them in bed, and not only because she looked like his sister. I'd never slept with Cinco. As I mentioned there were kisses and things. I'd always suspected he was tightly wound. But given his recent attentions to his wife, perhaps I'd judged too quickly.

I nodded.

"We're going to have to go down that whole . . ." Here he waved a hand in front of his face. "Doctor thing soon, I think."

Was he mentioning this because of my pregnancy? I was wearing a velvet shroud; surely he knew. Did he want to compare notes? I wasn't sure, but this subject demands a careful tread, and so I thought I'd wait for him to speak.

But before he could, the waiters cleared the salad plates and like a weather vane, Julia turned to her right, as did everyone at the table.

"So you don't know what you're having?" Jeff Trenor asked me as the unobtrusive help placed a plate of shepherd's pie in front of me. I hoped it was the Oprah chef in the kitchen.

I tried to swallow my bite so I could tell him. Unfortunately the potatoes were gluey.

"But you want a girl."

I smiled. "I want healthy." I didn't want to correct him after he'd just answered his own question. He was on a tear anyway.

"Well, let me ask you something. Let's say you have a boy." I smiled. "When he comes of age—I don't know what that age is nowadays," he said with a world-weary sigh, as if bemoaning the state of the world. "But I've been thinking about this with my own boys." His oldest was eight. "What will you tell him about marriage? What advice will you give? About how to do it well. What would you say?"

"I don't think I'm the expert on doing it well," I said.

"You have a happy marriage, no?" he said, twirling the stem of Julia's etched crystal wineglass. There it was again, this calling out my marriage as a happy one. It wasn't something I thought about very often—whether I was happy or not—which is likely a sure sign that one *is* happy. But twice in one night and with the fight this afternoon, I was beginning to feel like an example—and a fraudulent one at that. It made me nervous.

I nodded. "Yes, I do."

"Well then, what advice will you give?"

"My advice," said Cinco on my other side, "is don't have a baby in the first year."

There were murmurings of assent.

"I had a close friend who had a honeymoon baby, and it looked like an awful time," he continued.

Jeff nodded. "You're getting used to being married to this person and then you've got a newborn on top of it to deal with as well."

"Plus"—Cinco was not done—"I think you should have some time to enjoy being a young married couple, newlyweds." He nudged me. "Don't you agree?"

"Oh, absolutely," I said.

"Well, my advice, and Jim"—here Jeff raised a glass toward my husband—"listen up." The table fell silent at this. "My advice is to take the kids every once in a while. Don't ask, don't plan, just take them off your wife's hands for a chunk of time each weekend, or one weekday night. Let your wife have some alone time that she doesn't have to beg for."

The table started twittering in approval. Jeff's wife, seated on Julia's other side, nodded. "It's true, he does it almost every weekend," she said. Everyone was talking at once about fathers pitching in.

Jim winked at me quickly across the table.

Jeff turned back to me then. "You'll see."

This bit of advice alarmed me. I was not naïve enough to think that Jim and I would be sharing all child duties equally. He worked, and I was at home. But I wasn't anticipating needing to beg for anything. Jeff's advice filled me with dread.

"My advice on marriage," said Ellie, and here the room fell silent, "would be, don't try to change someone."

"That old saw," someone said.

Jeff sliced his dinner with a clack on the china. I noticed Selden was listening attentively.

Ellie continued. "People can't really change. It is true some men can be changed a little, but they wind up hating you for it. Look at Anne Boleyn." She dragged a finger across her neck. "Why do you think she got the ax?"

"She couldn't produce a male heir," Cinco said.

"Trivial in the face of true love," Ellie replied. "I think she just required that he change too much. Change the church for instance. Change what he believed about the purview of God and the role of man."

The entire table was quiet for one full beat. Ellie's wrestling with questions of divinity had distracted everyone.

"It works both ways though," she continued. "Women end up not respecting men they change. Look at Camilla Parker Bowles or the Duchess of Windsor—do you think either could even stand their loves after the men changed so completely?"

"All royal examples," someone said. "Why is that?"

"They have everything, and they can't get it right," Julia said at the head of the table. "Making these huge messes. I mean, why did he have to abdicate for her? She wasn't even that pretty."

"But so stylish." This from Steven. "The way she wore clothes—"

"Men don't care about that," Selden popped in. "Contrary to what people think, men actually care about what's on the inside. I mean, beauty is the attractor. But connection at the soul level, that's what everyone's looking for, right? I mean, that had to be the attraction to Camilla Parker Bowles. No matter what might be ruined, that had to be true love, yeah?" Here Selden looked directly at Ellie.

"I forget there's a poet in the room," Gus Trenor said, giving Selden a withering look.

"Yes," Ellie said, taking a little sip of water. "He changed so much, put so much in jeopardy. Everything he loved, really. Don't you think he must hate her a little bit for it?"

Talk overtook the table now. I heard agreement with Selden,

agreement with Ellie, and then a loud "Those royals are all emotion-ally retarded inbreds anyway," from I don't know whom.

I saw that Jeff had a little smile on his face. His job as ringmaster raconteur had been fulfilled. "So," he said, turning back to me. "Why do you think we're fascinated by royals in another country? I mean, who cares about them anyway?"

"We're like the Greek chorus," I said. "We need something to comment on."

"Yes . . . ," he said, taking a bite of the shepherd's pie. When he finished chewing he said, "So, Ellie," and gestured with his emptied fork to the other end of the table where she sat. "She's a good friend of yours?"

"I've known her since we were girls."

"I knew her in New York a little. I'd run into her at parties."

I nodded. "Oh."

"You know, contrary to what she said, people can change even if you've known them all your life," he said, considering me out of the side of his vision. "Don't you find her changed?"

"We all grow up, but a person's core doesn't really change—does it? She's essentially the same person I knew."

"You don't think our moral compasses change after childhood?"

I was taken aback by his dropping his bantering tone and tried to cajole him back into it. "Isn't that what we were just talking about? How things really don't change?"

"I'd watch out," he said sourly.

"Watch out for Ellie?"

"I used to hear things about her. She used to go after people's hus-bands. Not just random people's actually, her close friends'. I know someone who got involved—"

"Ellie's like family to me," I said, cutting him off here. I really didn't want to hear this kind of thing about her. It made me nervous, and it seemed like he was ramping up for a confession—sounding very sour grapes.

He looked at me for a beat and then down at his plate. "Of course

I hear she's likely to end up with Randy Leforte, of all people. Do you know him?"

"Only a little. Do you?"

"Not at all. But my mother tells me she was introduced to him at a cocktail party for some congressman, and Leforte advised her to hang on to the cameo she was wearing and never sell it as it'd appreciate a hundred percent by the time her granddaughter got it."

"Come on. He didn't say that."

"Hand to God."

"Ewww."

Jeff raised an eyebrow. "Old Ellie could probably straighten him out." He looked up at her then, taking her measure. "A project like that would be good for her. Give her something to do. She could tone down the bling, bring in a little sophistication, like Carla Bruni did with Sarkozy."

I regained my breath. Here was my opening to steer things past this treacherous territory. "Have you heard the last album?" I asked.

"She calls him her drug in one of the songs," he replied with a glinting smile. "Can you imagine?"

Julia served dessert in her living room. A group of men started a game of pool in the library next door, preferring cigars to dessert. We sat on her Fortuny covered chairs as she passed around dishes of berry cobbler with homemade honey ice cream. The walls were hung with paintings from the 1920s of industrial scenes downtown—men in steel factories, steamships under the bridges, the flats in full production. The great-grandchildren of that industry now sat cosseted and comfortable far away from the actual mechanics of Cleveland.

I enjoyed my dessert, wishing I could have more without being conspicuous when Cinco came and sat at my feet, with legs crossed and his back to me. His wife was chatting across the room with the acupuncturist.

He twirled his fork over his dessert. "This ice cream is like all the mortal sins of the world in a bowl."

I laughed.

"Speaking of which," he said, tilting toward me, "have you been offered drugs yet?"

"Hardly." I laughed. "You?"

He whispered out of the side of his mouth. "You can tell if you're in with the in crowd if they do. Only to special friends, you know." He lolled his head back on the seat next to me and smiled. "Too bad you're not cool enough."

I made a face at him. "I don't think it has anything to do with being cool."

"Right." He rolled his head to look at me. "You might think it doesn't, but that's exactly what it means." He grinned at me, teasing.

I looked at him and laughed. "Or it could be because I'm pregnant."

I'm not sure if I imagined it or not, but it seemed his face fell. He regained his composure quickly. He looked neither shocked nor delighted. "You're pregnant?"

"Look at me." I gestured to my waist. "What did you think?"

He shrugged. "I thought you'd gained a little weight."

I was dumbstruck. "A little? I'm a whale."

"You're not a whale." After a pause he said, "Still beautiful." He said it softly to the room, not looking at me.

A stunned thrill of excitement and revulsion ran through me. Cinco still thought I was beautiful? It made my head spin in both alarm and pleasure. He wouldn't have given me a bicycle or been worrying about my getting back into shape after being pregnant.

He got up then, unfolding his long legs and rising to join the men in the library shooting pool.

Jim took me home early, about midnight, but the party was in full swing. Gus was in the corner revving up his complicated music system to blast hip-hop songs currently popular at frat parties. As far as I could tell, Ellie hadn't drunk a drop. Jim and I left when small groups were making their ways into different rooms of the Trenors' house—den and library and bar—for a little illicit activity, be that cigarettes or drugs or couples meeting in secret to hook-up or have fights. At

Julia's parties a contingent of guests left soon after dinner and another group wouldn't leave until after breakfast was served in silver chafing dishes in the dining room.

I saw Ellie seated on a low banquette in a dimly lit corner of the Trenors' library talking to a man whose back was to me with his arm propped against the wall, as if shielding Ellie from something. She blew me a kiss over his shoulder and mouthed "I'll call you." The man didn't turn around.

· 13 ·

The Texts

Ellie leaned back against the Trenors' green velvet library banquette and enjoyed the feeling of Selden's company. Though he made her doubt herself sometimes, tonight his presence soothed. Here was a man who would never propose a business deal instead of true love. Here was a man who would never primp. Here was someone who saw her, even if his gaze sometimes made her squirm. It calmed her, the feeling of being known.

He'd brought her a small glass of tequila rocks, *his* favorite, she noted. He also held a glass for himself, and he'd managed to tuck a half-full bottle under his arm. He set a third glass on the table in front of them with limes, and out of his pocket came a crystal salt shaker in the shape of a hunting dog. She sipped at her drink, discreetly enjoying it out of the view of prying eyes. She couldn't remember the last time she drank tequila. She smiled at Selden, who, in the low light, looked young and rough with his rumpled hair but bright with his burnished skin, his polished glasses.

"I should call you Selden the corrupter."

"I like that." He leaned in closer, picking up her wrist. "Makes me sound dangerous, yeah?"

"Yes, I believe you know how to corrupt in more ways than one."

He took a lime and rubbed it across the inside of her wrist where the ribbon used to be. Then he sprinkled salt on it.

"You're not going to—"

"Hush," he said with a grin.

She stiffened for a second. If he expected her to hold a lime in her mouth for him, well, she had to draw the line somewhere. He leaned down, arching an eyebrow with irony, and she smiled at his boyishness—a body shot, so retro, so deliciously crude.

He licked the salt and warmth shot up her arm and landed as sparks in her stomach. Then he drank down his tequila quickly, without drama, and put a lime in his mouth with a wink.

"Your turn," he said, after he'd sucked on the fruit.

She felt the age difference between them then. This hadn't been popular when she'd been in college. She'd never done it. "You've got to be kidding."

"It's part of my corruption—seduction," he said, and pointed to a spot under his left ear.

She rolled her eyes, hefting the crystal salt shaker in her palm, considering his neck. How would she get salt on there? She wasn't going to be caught licking the side of his neck at one of Julia's parties.

She picked up a lime, and he raised his eyebrows, excited. But she squeezed the wedge in her glass. He frowned at that, licking juice off his fingers.

"Be right back," he said. "Sticky."

She'd annoyed him, she knew, not playing along. She did a shot of tequila by herself while he was gone. Selden actually made tequila look pretty good. She felt it burn down her throat and winced a little, remembering that tequila didn't agree with her. But Selden's outlook, the way he walked through the world, his body, those fingers, even his drink—all looked appealing to Ellie right then. His fingers, she thought again, shivering a bit.

On the small table in front of her, next to the bottle of tequila, Selden's phone lit up and started vibrating. The ringtone sounded familiar, but she couldn't place it with the background noise of the party.

Prince? Ellie thought. It was too tempting; she had to see who Selden would assign to an old Prince song.

She picked up the phone. Diana Dorset's name was on the display: text message waiting.

So maybe things weren't as over as Ellie had thought. Men were so unknowable sometimes, she thought. Diana Dorset was a class-A bitch. Didn't Selden see that? Though Ellie supposed there were men who liked that sort of thing, Selden thought Diana was his sexy motherfucker?

Her thumb hovered over "OK." It was outrageous that she'd read it. But she really wanted to know where things stood between them. Was this a booty text? For a brief moment she wondered how she'd explain it if he caught her. But she was less likely to get caught if she just went ahead and read it without stalling, and so she pressed "OK."

S—MISS U TERRIBLY 2NITE. COME SEE ME. CUM FOR ME? D OUT OF TOWN.—DI

Ellie hit "Close" and practically threw the phone back on the table and wiped her hand.

Ick. If only brain bleach were real, she'd scour that out of her brain.

She supposed it wasn't *that* surprising. Selden liked them stylish. Selden's mother had been chic. A charming woman, Ellie remembered her mother saying of Marianne Selden, with a light touch in every area of her life. Some found her enchanting, others thought her flighty, spacey. And that, Ellie supposed, was where the fondness for a self-sufficient woman came in. The son of a flake would choose a self-reliant lover, and being married would make Diana autonomous. But judging from that text, Diana's independence had fallen away.

The phone vibrated again, the funky groove line starting up.

She had to look. If he caught her, she'd laugh, flirtily ask him what he had to hide. If it came down to that, she hoped he was drunker than he looked.

MISS ME?

Before she'd even closed the message, another came through.

It was a picture of Diana, looking a little drunk Ellie thought, undressed except for a lacy red bra mashing her breasts together. Underneath it said:

WHAT ABOUT NOW?

Ellie smirked. Diana had aired Ellie's dirty laundry in Ellicottville, successfully ruining things with Gryce. She'd tried to sink Ellie with Selden. Who knew what further damage Diana would try to do to Ellie? Who knew what advantages having the goods on Diana Dorset could bring her? With one eye out for Selden, she quickly forwarded the messages and the picture to her phone.

She saw the messy top of Selden's hair from across the room as he made his way down a tightly packed hallway. She deleted the original messages—if Diana mentioned them to Selden, they'd likely chalk it up to a technological glitch. She tossed the phone back on the table and leaned back, taking a deep breath. It didn't actually confirm that he was still sleeping with Diana—the ringtone, the text, the pictures. But it certainly looked that way. Ellie was both repulsed and sparked; she'd always been competitive.

Selden settled down next to her again with a smile. He leaned in, taking her hand, and was about to say something when Prince's voice warbled through the air.

Selden stilled, and his eyes got wide. Then he frantically scrabbled at the table for the phone, almost knocking over the tequila. The song kept playing, winding up to its crescendo.

Ellie sniggered. Diana was certainly tenacious. Selden found the phone next to him and silenced the ringer.

"Who was that?" She was all-out laughing now, thinking of Diana's desperation, thinking of the picture she now had custody of.

"Your mom," Selden said peevishly, which only made Ellie laugh harder. He rumpled a hand through his hair. "God, I don't know how to switch that thing. I don't know what she did to it," he mumbled.

"Who?"

Selden sighed and leaned back. "Diana," he admitted.

"She's your sexy motherfucker?" Ellie teased.

"No," Selden said quickly. "No, but she put this ringtone on here when—" And here he stopped himself, realizing he'd gone down a road he didn't want to. "It's annoying."

"When you were together?" Ellie asked.

"I'd hardly call it together."

"What would you call it?"

He looked away. "I don't know."

"And now?"

"Diana is . . ." His eyes searched the ceiling.

"Awful." Ellie couldn't help it.

"Troubled," Selden corrected, and Ellie detected a kindness in his tone that confirmed there'd been something between him and Diana sexually.

"And married," Ellie said.

"Plus that," Selden snorted, and it made Ellie think that he'd definitely been the one who'd ended things.

"Is it over?" It was shocking and even a little exciting to her that Selden had participated in an affair. Maybe, like Ellie, he'd been counting on regular sex with no strings and gotten in over his head. Maybe that's why he called it off.

He furrowed his brow at her. "Definitely."

"A mistake?" she asked, wanting to hear him say it.

"I don't go in for regret."

"Doesn't mean you can't make a mistake."

"Right," he said, and that was good enough for Ellie.

She was pleased, satisfied that things with Diana were over for now. And if anyone could erase the memory of another woman, it was Ellie.

"It makes sense though, you have the reputation," she teased.

"As a bookish professor who can't change his ringtone?"

"As a Lothario."

"Makes me sound like I should be wearing a pinkie ring." He leaned in closer to her, relaxing now. "I much prefer 'corrupter.'"

"Speaking of which, I shouldn't be having this," she said, tipping her glass toward him.

"Really? A few drinks are going to kill you?" He leaned to the side, still shielding her from the party but resting his head on the wall.

"You know I've had issues in this area."

"Drinking?" He furrowed his eyebrows.

"Rehab."

"For alcohol?"

"No."

"Well, there you go. Moderation in all things," Selden said, nodding to himself. "Moderation's what's needed."

"Obviously I've found it pretty hard to be moderate. About most things, really. You?"

He shrugged. "I'm moderate. At least I like to think I am. I go a little overboard—with running, with drinking sometimes, with literary minutiae. Maybe I'm moderate in some things and not in others, and that in itself is moderation."

"The Selden moderation. You should write a book."

"You have to make space for passion," he said, rolling his head to face her. "For a little craziness in life. Balance it out with some non-crazy aspects, yeah?" Here was an almost perfect answer, read right from Ellie's own thinking.

"You always have everything so figured out. It's very comforting to be around. I wish I did."

"Don't you?"

"No."

Selden picked up her hand then and kissed it. She shivered from the simple feel of his lips on the back of her hand. "Let's figure it out together," he said.

"William . . ."

He stopped her. "I love you, you know. I've loved you since we were kids." He leaned forward and kissed her then, and her mind stopped. Her world shrank until there was only the taste of him—salt and citrus—and the smell of him, like burning leaves. The feel of his lips was the only thing in the world. She couldn't breathe. She wanted to take his clothes off. She wanted to feel the weight of him on top of her immediately.

She pulled away. He quickly backpedaled, thinking he'd crossed some line. "Ellie, I—"

"Randy Leforte asked me to marry him," she blurted out.

Selden leaned back. "What?"

"Yesterday."

"How do you even know him?"

"We've been dating."

"You've been dating Randy Leforte," he said in a bewildered voice.

"Yes."

"Are you marrying him?"

"I don't know."

"Why not?"

"I might be in love with someone else."

"Who?"

She grabbed his lapel and pulled him toward her. Selden made her forget about so many things when she was near him.

· 14 ·

The Estate Sale

Every Thursday morning if you're driving through the better parts of the Heights, or maybe at the end of a long driveway in Hunting Valley, you'll see them—people lining up at six o'clock in the morning for estate sales.

Jim teases me about my Yankee love of a bargain, but furnishing a house requires a lot of money. So I'd become a member of this dawn patrol, picking up a number at six A.M., leaving to get coffee, and then returning to take my place in line for the frantic door opening.

I tried to avoid the moving sales. The economy being so bad, sometimes families in foreclosure had to pack in a hurry and sell the rest. These sales depressed me, with the children's playhouse, too big to move, and the newly upholstered furniture, perhaps too big for the next, smaller house.

No, the best sales were the true estate sales after a death. After the family had been through and taken what they wanted, they'd hire the one firm in town that would round up everything that was left—from the embroidered place mats to the Tabriz rug to the Knabe piano—place a price tag on it, and let in the thunderous herd of bargain hunters.

I watched for these sales in the paper, and since I knew each address, I could picture the house. So I was excited one morning when I opened the paper to see that one of the big estates in Bratenahl—one of the mansions right on Lake Erie—was the location of the sale for that week. I actually knew the family. My mother had attended the patriarch's funeral a few months back. Though I was exhausted daily, a sale like this came around only once every few years.

I arrived at the scrolling green copper gates of the neoclassical mansion at six the next morning. It was cold, winter now, and I blew steam out of my mouth into the freezing morning. Next to the stucco garden walls, I saw the usual cast of characters.

The son of one of the main antiques dealers in town was stamping his feet, dramatically I thought, for there was no snow on the ground yet. He rarely bought anything given that he only wanted the finest pieces, which he bought without bargaining. I secretly suspected that he was simply nosy, enjoying seeing the insides of the houses. There were the society decorators of choice, a gay couple whom I'd occasionally run into at cocktail parties. They'd done houses for a few friends of mine, and they pretended not to see me, which was silly, given that everyone knew where they sourced their Sheffield silver and Regency dining chairs. There was the picker who was only looking for Federal period furniture made by Duncan Phyfe or the Seymours, which he'd buy, add a few zeros, and sell to a fancy dealer in New York. God only knows what the dealer in New York then charged for it. There was that strange man who collected records and went straight for the old vinyl without saying anything to anyone. There was the main antiquarian book dealer in town in his camel cashmere coat with his takeout latte. His Internet site was prospering. I saw a woman I always saw at these things with coral lipstick on her teeth who only bought costume jewelry. I was no competition for any of them as I was looking at practical things, pieces they couldn't resell. They smiled indulgently at me, the young pregnant wife trying to furnish her home.

Off to the side, huddling against the chill wind from the lake was a group I hadn't seen at sales before. Some were acquaintances of my mother's, some I recognized but had forgotten the names, and some just looked out of place. They were all older ladies who usually spent their mornings in group exercise classes or walking their sporting dogs or clipping foliage in their gardens for ikebana arrangements in their front halls.

The antiques dealer's son came over to talk with me.

"When are you due?" he asked, looking warily at my belly, as if I might momentarily explode.

"Three months," I said. He sipped coffee. "A new group," I said, nodding toward the ladies.

"You must know them," he said. "Don't you all go to the same benefits and things? I've seen some of them in the paper."

"I know some of them," I admitted. "But I didn't expect them to be—"

"Picking the carcass?" he interrupted.

"Exactly. I wonder if some of them have been eyeing things for years, you know? Looking at the old silver hot-water urn and waiting to get their hands on it."

"Is there one?" he asked, interest peaked. "An urn?"

"It was just an example."

"I thought you might have been in there."

I saw a sparkle in the corner of my eye.

"That's Betsy Dorset, right?" he asked, following my glance.

I nodded.

"Oh my God, is she wearing the—"

"She almost never takes it off," I said.

"Well, no, but diamonds at a house sale?"

"I saw her once at a Christmas party," I said. "Black tie, pheasant under glass, a very fancy host. And she wasn't wearing it. The one time you thought she really would. She was wearing this immense hunk of glass around her neck. When I told her I liked it, she said it was a Lalique ornament from her son and he'd given it to her the day before to celebrate his daughter being born. So she said, 'I'm wearing it in honor of my first granddaughter, my little Christmas angel. It really belongs on the tree.'"

"Huh," he said. "Sweet."

"It made me like her."

He took my elbow and steered me toward the front of the line. People parted the way for me, the pregnant lady, the schooner at full sail.

The manager of the sale walked down the driveway, which was lined on either side with bare, pruned Japanese lilacs. She crunched on the frosty gravel and opened the green creaking gates. She started taking numbers in her gloved hands, letting in the first twenty-five people. I rushed as fast as I was able toward the grand pilasters that flanked the entrance to the house.

Stepping into the house was always the part that felt strange at these sales, a violation for sure, though the house had been opened for this. It's what they wanted, but it made me a little sad, divvying up the scraps.

Inside, the group quickly dispersed to their areas of interest—the book dealer went to the dark library, the lipstick lady dashed up the stairs. The house overwhelmed me, and I ambled into the first room on my left. The music room was filled with japanned English furniture and a matching gilt harp with pianoforte. The crystal chandelier twinkled at me. I heard the group of ladies come in behind me, shrugging off their sensible fleece-lined balmacaans and folding them over their arms.

"Look at this room," one of them breathed. "When Nancy was alive they would have music in here during parties. Are they actually selling that harp?"

I tried to keep a room's length between me and them but was interested in what they said. There were updates and talk of their children and grandchildren, and I was distracted by a nice little pen-and-ink drawing on the wall when I heard a familiar name.

"You know, like that Randy Leforte," one of them said.

"Isn't he your new friend, Betsy?" another asked, chuckling.

I could hear the smile in Betsy's voice. "He's interested in the new wing of the museum, if you can believe it. He's already become involved in raising the funds for it."

"What's he want in return?" one of them asked.

"I can't figure that out. The orchestra wooed him, but he never gave them anything but a few thousand. He doesn't seem to want to be on the museum board. Seems content to let us pick his pocket." She said the last three words low. "In exchange for just knowing he's done the right thing." She said the last louder.

"Unique."

"In this day and age, yes, I'm afraid." Betsy picked up a crystal paperweight and turned it upside down, looking for a price tag.

"He thinks it gives him some air of legitimacy, some social status?"

Betsy slowed her speech like she was speaking to a dim-witted child. "As if such things matter anymore, Helen. This is the new millennium. Young men don't care about society. There isn't any society to care about."

"Don't say that."

"It's true," Betsy said, moving on from the desk.

"Well, society's not the same, but it still exists," one of them said as if consoling herself.

"No." Betsy shook her head, diamonds twinkling. "We're all that's left."

"Perhaps he's interested in you," one of them said. I almost laughed out loud imagining Randy Leforte as Betsy Dorset's arm candy. I was also a little offended for Betsy; the question was catty.

"Hardly. At our age you're either a nurse or a purse, and Mr. Leforte needs neither."

I smiled. That put the questioner in her place. I was surprised at Betsy's savvy, though I shouldn't have been.

"And I hear he's dating Ellie Hart," Betsy said.

This confirmed that though Betsy Dorset was no gossip, she knew everything that went down in Cleveland. Come to think of it, perhaps her discretion was why she was so well informed.

There was a collective gasp.

Betsy continued. "They were in the bar at the Ritz drinking champagne at three o'clock in the afternoon." Maybe that's where she'd been headed the other afternoon, I thought.

"Can you imagine such a thing in our mother's day?" one asked.

They shook their heads in unison.

"A nice girl having a drink with a man at a hotel in the middle of the afternoon," someone said.

"It's not like we were in purdah," Betsy said.

"But you didn't do that."

"Such a pretty girl." Someone clucked her tongue.

"Always was," another said wistfully.

"She made a mess of that marriage in New York." This was whispered.

"She's out to make a mess out of marriages right here in town," Betsy said.

"No." There was a delighted gasp.

"Diana told me that she flirts horribly with all the husbands. I wouldn't be surprised if she made passes at them . . ."

They were walking my way, and I was quickly making for the door into the dining room when one of them spotted me and descended.

"What on earth are you doing here? When are you due?" asked a recent acquaintance of my mother's whose name I always forgot.

"You should sit down." This said by a woman I didn't recognize.

"Go home and put your feet up," said another one.

"Are you nauseated?" someone inquired.

"How's your mother?" asked Betsy.

It took me a half hour to answer their questions and deflect their advice. It was comforting, being fretted over as only those women of my mother's generation could, making me feel as special and rare as if this were some sort of immaculate pregnancy. We walked into the butler's pantry, which broke my heart with the entire contents of the cupboards on the counters, and I heard a low voice at my elbow.

"Find anything you need?"

"Cinco Van Alstyne." Betsy Dorset beamed at him.

Cinco had always been a great favorite of this crowd. Why hadn't *their* daughters married someone like him—someone who would take on family obligations? They professed to want their children to marry spouses with minds of their own, not pushovers but wholly formed people. But when these spouses in question then actually *had* minds of their own? Here was one member of the next generation, they thought, who understood the importance of roots and family—or at least appeared to.

I watched him hug them and chat, donning his cloak of respectability, playing the good son. He answered questions about the new roof being repaired on the family farm.

"Come look at this little pen-and-ink drawing I'm interested in," Cinco said, taking my elbow and steering me toward the little picture I'd been admiring earlier. "Shouldn't you be home in bed or sitting on a tuffet or something?" he asked once we were alone.

"Couldn't miss this one."

"I know what you mean," he said.

We both faced the little artwork, a rendering of the harvest coming in.

"Isn't your house furnished?" I asked.

"Hardly. It all got divided up and so now we're slowly furnishing it with things from these sales. She," he said, meaning his wife, "can't stand to come. So I do it."

"I don't mind it. I won't go to the foreclosure sales though."

He paused and then said, "So you look good."

I blushed, thinking back to what he'd said to me at the dinner party. "Thanks. I feel huge."

The ladies came over to us, curious to see what Cinco was interested in buying.

"I think I should take you to get something to eat," he said, turning to me then.

"You two go off now and discuss things," they clucked in approval. Cinco, doer of duties and keeper of familial flames, *would* be protective of pregnant ladies, likely old women and small dogs too.

"What? Are neither of you buying a thing? Cinco, go buy that pair of huge candelabras in the front hall," one of them said to him with a friendly push on the arm. "Your farm is about the only place besides this house where they'll fit."

He and I smiled and said good-bye and went out past the card table where a large cash box was already overflowing with money and a lady wrapped newly acquired treasures in tissue paper.

"You can thank me for my chivalry now," he said, wrapping a tartan scarf around his neck.

"You saved me?" I asked, barely able to button my grandmother's car-coat-length mink. It was well preserved, having spent summers in cold storage. I'd never have bought myself a fur and was slightly mortified to be wearing it. But as Gran had said many times, it was the warmest coat in the world.

"They're more vicious than they look," he said, his respectability cloak slipping off him now.

I scowled. "Please."

"Don't cross them when they're in a pack," he said mock-seriously.

I laughed as we kept walking down the long drive.

"Nothing for you?" he asked with a raised eyebrow.

"Some days I can't think straight enough to buy anything."

We walked in silence for a minute as I pulled my gloves out of my pocket and slipped them on. The sun was melting the frost, but I could still see my breath. "Life on the farm?" I asked.

"Is good."

"Does Corrine like it?"

"The farm?"

"Yes."

"I think so. It was a very big adjustment for her. She grew up in Manhattan, you know."

"Surprising she'd want to leave it."

"She didn't really want to."

"So you forced her?"

He screwed up one eye like I'd hit him on the head. "No, I just . . . she knew what she was getting into when she married me. She knew the farm was part of the deal."

"You guys had a deal?"

"You know what I mean."

Thing was, I knew exactly what he'd meant. I think I'd known it even when we were children. I saw it reflected with approval in the eyes of Betsy Dorset and her friends. They knew that the driving passion in his life, the thing he was going to love more than himself, wasn't going to be a wife. It was going to be a house. This stability unconsciously attracted them.

I couldn't think if Jim and I had ever had a deal between us and decided we probably hadn't. But I nodded at Cinco now to be polite.

"I don't mean it was explicit," he said, backpedaling when I'd stayed silent too long. "But she knew the farm existed. Knew I'd want to live there one day if we got the chance."

"What if she didn't want to?"

"Then we wouldn't have." He turned his face to me. "Luckily my wife's crazy about me."

I laughed. "Oh really?"

"Does everything I say. I know you feel the same way about Jim. The obey part of the vows you took." He was joking.

"I took that vow out." I laughed. "As did everyone else I know. But it's true I give him everything he wants." I said it in a silly, flirty tone.

This stopped him up short. "Yes, well . . ." His eyes flicked down to my belly and then he started walking again. "Do you remember," he asked, "when I came to see you in New York?"

"Which time?" I asked.

"The time when you were hanging out with Ellie a lot."

"In the beginning, when I first moved there?"

"Yes." We crunched down the gravel path to the road. "Do you remember that night I took you out to that dive bar around the corner from where she lived?" he said.

"The one with the excellent jukebox? Why doesn't Cleveland have a place like that? You'd think it would do really well. Maybe we should open one." I linked an arm under his. "With crappy beer, a dartboard, and a tremendously awful open-mike night . . ."

"Cleveland has plenty of places like that," he scoffed.

"I've never been to one."

"Then they must not exist," he said in mock-seriousness. "It doesn't surprise me that you don't get out. Look at the crowd you run with."

"Ummm, that would be the *same* crowd you run with," I said. "Besides, mother-to-be getting tanked at the pool hall is just a little too . . ."

"Ghetto?"

"That word again, it kills me—especially coming from someone like you."

"Like me what?"

"Like living on his manor-estate-thing and calling things ghetto."

"Point taken." He squeezed my arm closer to him, and I had a flashback of this same move with his wife at the Mingott wedding. "But I was talking about New York. You remember that night?" he said.

I did, but I didn't know what he was driving at. "Sure, my squandered youth."

He smiled. "Do you remember what you said to me?"

"About?"

"Home."

I looked at him blankly.

"You said you'd never come back here." He stopped us and turned to face me. I couldn't read if I saw regret in his eyes, concern, or mere curiosity.

"Changed my mind." I shrugged, trying to shut down this line of questioning. Cinco made me nervous, especially now, bringing up our past.

"You sounded so final. I remember wondering what the deal was with your certainty. Now here you are. Was Jim the one who wanted to come?"

This grated, as if he assumed Jim must have been the one making the decisions in my marriage. After a moment I realized that perhaps it gave me insight into his marriage—perhaps he made all the calls. "No, it took some serious convincing on my part."

"So why the change?"

"That's me. I'm a puzzle," I said, shrugging, again trying to close this subject. I didn't want to discuss this with Cinco. Not because I was embarrassed by my change of mind, but maybe because I didn't want to hear from him that he'd been right all along. He knew me well. He'd often told me I couldn't escape coming back to Cleveland. No matter how much I objected, he would insist he was right. I guessed he was ramping up for a gigantic I-told-you-so.

He paused, not content with my evasions. When the silence got uncomfortable I said, "Because we all come back. You of all people know that. Even Ellie came back."

He considered this for a moment, started walking, and squeezed my arm a little. "Even me."

"What do you mean even you? You were always coming back."

"Is that what you thought then?"

"I mean there was never any question for you—was there?"

He looked me in the eye and then quickly looked out over the lake. "There could have been."

My arm burned, tucked snugly as it was under his. I wondered what my husband would think of me walking so cozily with Cinco.

"I don't think you could be happy anywhere besides here," I said.

"You wouldn't be happy anywhere but here either."

"Yes, I remember you saying that," I said. "I thought it'd be claustrophobic."

"Oh, it's definitely that," he said.

"So why come back?"

He shrugged and took my arm out from under his. We'd arrived at my car.

"Why indeed?" he asked, opening my door and helping me into the car.

· *15* ·

The Benefit

The holidays came and went in the usual blur that is Cleveland Christmas. With my pregnancy, Jim and I made a new rule—only one party a night, no doubling up lest I feel exhausted. The week leading up to Christmas was packed with multigenerational parties each night. I dragged myself to all of them, again not wanting to miss a thing. I saw Ellie at only two parties—both given by old families, not the sort of invitations you could turn down, even if you were Ellie. I felt sure she'd been invited to lots more, but she'd declined these invitations.

Jim redeemed himself from the mountain bike incident by giving me earrings for Christmas, and his family sent an ancient silver porringer that had been his grandfather's, as an early gift for the baby.

At the end of all this celebrating, Cleveland collectively goes into hibernation. No one entertains in January; people barely go out. It's as if people can't stand to see one another after so much cheer.

And so I was actually looking forward to the art museum's annual black-tie benefit in February, though I still didn't have anything to wear in my current size. Jim assured me daily that I looked beautiful, that my body was amazing. But his constant attention overshot the mark, and I wound up feeling even more self-conscious. Though I agreed with the amazement part, my body felt out of control, like it was running amok, which it was—albeit for a good cause.

The theme of the benefit was 1916, the year the museum was opened. Diana Dorset's development job put her in charge of the party, and she had decided that a series of *tableaux vivants* would be the attraction for the evening. Each of a dozen young Clevelanders would be paired with a local designer or artist and play a part in depicting a painting currently hanging in the museum. The participants' names were listed on the back of the invitation, and among them was Eleanor Hart, who would be posing in a tableau created by Steven, the designer she worked for.

The museum had never done anything like it before, and the idea was so retro it was chic. Diana and the benefit committee of young up-and-comers and old-school movers and shakers went to great lengths to ensure that the tableaux would be tasteful and fast as quicksilver, nothing staid and fixed but a morphing and changing vision.

The night of the party, the glassed-in courtyard was set with chairs, and the doors leading into the 1916 galleries were transformed into a stage with old damask curtains, gold cording, and potted palms. High heels clicked on the marble floors as glasses clinked at the bar, and the room hummed with the slightly intoxicated breath of the guests.

I watched Diana move through the room. Her position in development meant she knew almost everyone. She knew their net worth, their interest in the museum, whether they'd donated in the past. I watched her calculate who needed a big showy hug—marking them as an insider with the museum—and who preferred the less showy, but equally impressive, tête-à-tête before solemnly being turned over to one of her staff to be shown to their seats. Diana knew who liked to be acknowledged in the program and who preferred to have their name on a discreet "Reserved" card on a chair in the front row. She excelled at these small calculations, making people feel comfortable and superficially special. Tonight she was shining, at the height of her power.

I was walking down the rows, looking for a seat, when I saw William Selden. He looked more groomed than usual, and I sat next to him waiting for Jim to catch up with us.

"I'm so excited about this," I said.

"Have you seen Ellie?" he asked.

"No," I said. "Do you know which painting she's going to be?"

"I don't. She was so secretive about it. I barely saw her all week."

So Ellie and Selden were seeing each other.

"I hope she chooses something gorgeous. One of the Muses or something," I said. "I've always thought someone should paint Ellie."

Jim settled in next to us, and then the lights went down.

The first scene was the museum's famous Degas painting of a dancer in four poses. They'd chosen four close friends, all brunettes, to pose in white tulle skirts on chairs. The crowd applauded enthusiastically, a good start.

The next was a Modigliani, *Portrait of a Woman,* perfectly cast to feature Lulu Melson's long neck. They'd gotten her clothes just right too; the long pendant between her breasts was an exact replica of the one in the painting. Her gaze was wistful, the blush on her cheek intense.

"Lulu Melson always looks good in black," a voice behind my shoulder whispered, and I turned to see Steven, the designer, sitting in the row behind me.

"But not as good as Ellie," I whispered back, and he winked at me and nodded toward the stage.

The next was Dan Dorset and a man I didn't know bare-chested in loincloths as George Bellows's *Stag at Sharkey's.* Dan Dorset had clearly been working out for this, and though his stomach looked well muscled, his depiction somehow lacked the fearsomeness of the raw and violent original.

They'd chosen the pale and frail Elizabeth Corby for the Van Dyck portrait of a woman and child. Mrs. Corby looked the part with her high blue-veined forehead and watery eyes and lashes, so it was easy to forgive the fact that her blond-haired daughter in blue embroidered velvet did not quite match the original painting. The child blushed adorably but held the pose next to her mother.

Kate van den Akker portrayed the muse of history in a bright yellow silk gown with gargantuan feathered wings on her shoulders. She was wrapped in a purple silk banner and held a stone tablet. The classical dimension of her features made this the most exact representation so far.

Finally it was Ellie's turn, and when the curtain was drawn to reveal her the audience gasped. She'd chosen a Rubens, though her voluptuous curves weren't as decadent as the Diana in *Diana and Her Nymphs Departing for the Hunt*. Ellie was clad in a diaphanous white toga that hinted at her excellent form beneath. Around one shoulder hung a leopard skin, draped to expose one pale perfect breast.

There were immediate whisperings in the room. Some of the older women looked away. The older men stared agape. Diana Dorset stood off to the side in her supervisory capacity with a delighted smirk on her face.

Ellie held a greyhound at the end of a short leash and the dog, sensing the excitement, was trembling, needing to be calmed. Ellie's hair flowed down her back in loose waves.

She'd never looked more beautiful to me.

I looked to my left to see my husband staring at her in wonder.

When I looked back at Ellie, I saw her beam a wide loving smile out to my right. I, along with everyone else in the room, realized she was smiling directly at Selden. Her smile broke the pose; in the painting, Diana didn't smile. Then, to my utter shock, she winked—at Selden.

Selden started and then blushed deep magenta. People turned in their seats to stare at him. He kept his eyes fixed straight ahead, not smiling.

I realized then that Ellie had made a serious miscalculation. For all his bohemian, world-weary, pot-smoking ways, at heart Selden was still a conventional boy from the Midwest. However much he might not mind, might applaud even, a wild display like Ellie's tonight, the woman he loved should never do such a thing, never be seen as aggressive, especially sexually aggressive. Such conservatism, such modesty, had been bred into him. And when something like that was bred into you, you couldn't get it all the way out.

The dog jumped on the end of its leash. Ellie reached down to settle it and then rose, striking the pose with an intent look on her face, and I knew that she'd realized her error.

I hardly remembered any of the other tableaux. No one did. There was great applause at the end.

During the cocktail hour I found Ellie and Steven surrounded by admirers. Her chest was covered now, and she wore the leopard skin around both shoulders as a wrap. A newspaper reporter was asking questions. Steven was expounding on the human form in art, Diana the huntress, and Jeff Koons's porn star ex-wife showing a breast during Italian political rallies. Ellie slipped away and took my arm.

"Incredible," I said. "You're the talk of the evening."

"I didn't think it would be that big a deal."

I smirked. "Seriously?" I asked. "Ummm, Janet Jackson at the Super Bowl? You had to know all of Cleveland would talk."

"About a boob?" She shook her head. "They're not scandalized by the painting, and it's been hanging there for years."

"Yes, but you showed your actual breast."

"Much more exciting than a painting of one, I guess." I noted with concern that she took a glass of champagne off a passing tray and gestured with it toward a group of Gus Trenor's friends in close conversation. "All of them probably watch porn on the Internet. Really, I thought it might cause a little talk, but what *is* the big deal? Steven wanted me to do it. He told me it'd create a ton of publicity for him."

She had to know it would cause a scandal, much more than a titter. I suspected she wanted to be the talk of the evening. I wondered why. "Well, Steven was right," I said as we both turned toward the group swarming the designer. "Good for him. Do you think he'll be able to do anything with it?"

"I hope so," she said.

Steven looked sharp in jeans, a white T-shirt, and combat boots with a halo of blond stubble highlighting his jaw and his lip piercings—very much the artist in residence tonight. His outfit was calculated, I'm sure, to stand out among the other men in their black tuxedos.

"The Amazons fought with one breast exposed," I heard him say. "It's said the sight of just one female nipple stopped male warriors in their tracks." All the reporters laughed.

Diana Dorset came up to introduce Ellie to an important board member, the head of a large tire company in town—a florid, fat man with a cane who stared at Ellie's now-covered chest.

I'd lost Jim, and in looking for him I wandered over to one of my favorite pieces in the museum, the *Cocktails and Cigarettes Jazz Bowl*. The large black ceramic bowl had been glazed in turquoise with Deco scenes of the city, people dancing, cocktails rising up toward the skyline, smoke curling up from their cigarette holders. It'd won the museum's May Show back in 1931.

"I've always loved that," a deep voice said, and I turned to see Cinco Van Alstyne standing next to me.

I smiled at him and gestured toward the small plaque next to the piece stating that it had been a gift from his family. "Apparently your great-grandmother did too."

"My uncle found it a couple years before my grandmother died when they were trying to sort out the farm. It was in a bottom cupboard in the pantry. Someone had filled it with Tupperware and old keys that didn't fit any locks anymore—amazing it didn't get chipped. Still beautiful, isn't it?"

"Nice of them to donate it," I said, feeling oddly uncomfortable as I remembered when we'd talked, at Julia's. He'd said the same thing about me.

"The easy way out when everyone wants it," he said. "Eleanor Roosevelt had one too."

"Did they ever use them?" I asked, hoping to keep the conversation light.

He shook his head. "Completely nonfunctional." He smiled at me with an arched eyebrow. "Insert joke about my family here."

I laughed.

"Crazy to see it here, though," he said, looking at it, and then more quietly, "Crazy to see you here."

"I've always loved this place." I gestured around at the galleries. "Love to support it."

He nodded. "I meant in Cleveland."

My heart skipped a beat, and I felt my face grow hot.

"I just can't figure out why after everything, you came back here," he said, moving closer to me.

I said nothing, looking at the bowl in front of me.

I couldn't believe he was picking up our conversation from the estate sale again. Our parting years ago had been mutual. What was he trying to start? I thought it best to brush him off.

"I told you why." I smiled. "I'm nesting, same as you."

"But like you said, I was always coming back."

I shrugged.

"You coming back here changed everything, and you know it," he said quietly in my ear, standing right next to me.

"No," I said.

"Yes," he said. "And you know it."

An elderly lady in a sequined jacket admiring the bowl on the other side of the case gave us a quick glance before she politely moved off.

"You're happy," I said, thinking of his wife, of the wedding, of the dinner party. "Don't pretend you're not."

He ignored this. "I want to know why."

"Why not? It's a good place to wind up. To raise a family."

"No," he said, clear gray-blue eyes staring me down. "I want to know why it wasn't me."

Did he really want to know, or was he trying to stir up some drama, some excitement in musty old Cleveland? "The condition to being with you was coming back here," I said. "I didn't want someone with conditions."

"But you came anyway."

"Like that matters. We were never like that. You had conditions. You'd never be with someone who wouldn't come back here and that, to me, isn't true love. You have to be willing to give up everything."

"Everything?" he asked. "What complete bullshit."

"Everything, no conditions, no strings."

He narrowed his eyes at me. "So if Jim cheated on you, you'd still love him."

"What does that have to do with anything?"

"I mean you have conditions of your own—fidelity, responsibility. Don't tell me you love him with no strings. Love is not some unconditional thing."

"I do love him with no strings," I said. "Love should be completely unconditional."

He snorted, drained the last of his drink, and muttered, "Bullshit," under his breath.

Jim interrupted us then. Sensing the tension between us, he immediately drew me under his arm. He stuck his other hand out at Cinco, who shook it with maybe more vigor than was needed. Cinco's cloak of respectability descended as he leaned over to accept a kiss from a stout older woman in heavy gold jewelry who hustled up to him. Then he begged off, claiming to see someone he needed to talk to.

Jim studied me. "You okay?"

I nodded. "What do you think of this piece?" I asked, turning toward the Van Alstynes' bowl.

He watched Cinco across the room. "So you and Cinco?" he said. "You grew up together?"

I shrugged. "I knew him growing up."

"Were you ever together?" he asked. I should have known Jim's intuition would be as strong as ever.

"We dated a little," I said.

He was staring at me, and so I turned back to the bowl. "Love the idea of that era," I said. "The flapper, the cropped hair, the women getting the vote and their smokes."

"The idea is probably better than the reality. Look at the first thing they did with their vote."

"What?" I said.

"Prohibition." He smirked. "Sick of getting the snot beaten out of them by drunk husbands, you know. Decided to try and get the law on their side."

Here was a bit of conditional love. I'll love you as long as you don't hit me. I'd never thought of it that way.

I was glad for Jim's arm around me. My past with Cinco wasn't something I had brooded over, until now. He hadn't loved me like that. He'd been looking for someone to come back and deal with the farm—a partner—even if he wouldn't admit it to himself. I hadn't wanted someone so convention bound, so decided.

I suppose we would have looked perfect on paper—two good Cleveland backgrounds. A part of me did wonder what it would have been like with him. Could I have gotten him to leave the farm and his preconceived life? Not that it mattered. My head looped around these questions, circling back and forth—all over someone I hadn't thought of seriously in years.

Yet, I was convinced that Jim and I belonged to one another. I suppose I was naïve, yes. But I really didn't think there was anything Jim would ever do to make me love him less.

"Everything okay?" Jim asked low in my ear.

"Of course," I said, my voice sounding forced and unnatural, even to my ears. "What do you mean?"

We made our way to the food, where, to my surprise, I saw William Selden and Randy Leforte having what looked like an intense conversation while each stared into a platter of vegetables. Jim shook hands with a tall balding man in a tie printed with tiny dachshunds, a business acquaintance I was sure.

I hated playing the adoring pregnant wife with Jim's business contacts of the older generation. They rarely attempted conversation with me in my pregnant state. It was as if I was an untouchable or wearing a sign around my neck stating that, yes, I had sex with my husband.

And so I edged my way over to Selden and Leforte. They stopped talking the minute I was close enough to hear, and though I realized I was interrupting, I grasped on to them.

"Do you know Randy Leforte?" Selden asked, turning to me.

I was about to say that I did when Leforte stuck out his hand.

"Randall Leforte," he said formally. "Nice to meet you."

I'd met Leforte a half dozen times before, and he always forgot and greeted me as if we'd never met before. I should have said "Yes, we've met," but I already felt bad crashing his conversation, and so I smiled and shook his hand.

Leforte turned to Selden then. "We should get a drink sometime. You should call me."

Selden gave a little jerk of his head up once—an agreement and a dismissal. "Sure."

"Just thought you should have all the information," Leforte said, as if in apology, and then edged into the crowd.

"Asshole," Selden breathed. He turned then, as if he realized I was there. "Sorry."

I was taken aback by his uncharacteristic acerbity. "I've met him a few times," I said. "Jim knows him better than I do."

"He just told me the goddamnedest thing," Selden said, and then took my elbow and steered me toward the bar. "I need a drink."

He ordered straight tequila, which gave the bartender a start. Selden rolled his eyes at that, downed the drink, and then asked for another. When he'd finished that too, he turned to me.

"I know you're her good friend," he said, nodding. "Leforte just told me that Ellie is being kept by Gus Trenor."

"Kept?" I scoffed. "Like this is the nineteenth century or something?"

"Like they're having an affair."

"I know Gus has made some investments for Ellie. I think he's managing her money." I started twisting my cocktail napkin.

William shook his head. "He implied they were lovers and he was supporting her, had bought her an apartment."

William was usually so easygoing that it unsettled me to see him upset. "People can be mean about Ellie, you know, because she's so beautiful. Ellie's still living in her mother's house, I'm pretty sure," I said, the napkin fraying in my hands. I was actually used to setting the record straight about Ellie. Rumors always flew around her. But Selden's intensity made me nervous.

"He told me he'd been seeing Ellie for a while, but she broke it off. I don't understand you people sometimes," he said, gesturing toward me.

"What people?" I asked, confused now.

"You guys. Women. Is that what you like? Leforte?" He was angry. Things must have been serious with Ellie.

"Umm . . . no . . . ," I said, the napkin coming apart in my hands, bits of it fluttering to the floor.

"The man's as slimy as they come. And Gus Trenor? I suppose he's powerful. That's what you guys like—right? Being dominated?"

I almost choked on my sparkling water. "Dominated by an old gym sock like Gus Trenor? Yes, most women are dying for that."

This brought a weak smile from Selden.

"Plus he's married," I said as I set my drink and my shredded napkin on a passing waiter's tray.

Selden rolled his eyes. "Naïveté doesn't suit you," he said acidly.

"Harsh," I said, wincing.

"Oh right," he said, looking at me. "Of course you're married to a solid guy, yeah?"

"Ellie's not interested in Gus Trenor beyond his keeping track of her money. She has enough options without resorting to married men."

Selden gave me a funny look then.

"It's probably just gossip. Leforte's not the most subtle man in the world."

Just then Ellie walked up and kissed Selden on the cheek. Seeing this register no effect on him she said, "Please don't tell me you're scandalized. I am catching so much grief for showing a little tit. You're an intellectual." She kissed his other cheek. "Aren't you supposed to be above the middlebrow flock?"

"Drink?" Selden asked, taking her champagne glass and walking away before she could answer.

I didn't like Selden's tone or that he was getting her another drink. She gave me a puzzled look, and I shrugged as if to say I had no idea either.

But I did understand, and I thought Ellie probably did too. Selden idealized love. His specialty was the Romantic poets, for God's sake. So though he might have affairs, he was looking for a true love to settle down with, someone to have children with and grow old with. He was a romantic, an innocent, at heart a hypocrite. Even though he might be involved in an extramarital affair, the woman he loved and eventually married should never be involved in such a thing. Now that I saw this clearly, I realized this was probably why he was still a bachelor. Add the wink and the boob, and things didn't look good for Ellie.

As Selden was heading off to the bar, Randy Leforte circled back around to us. He greeted Ellie with a stiff little bow and a curt nod for me. He complimented Ellie on her "performance" and quickly moved off.

"So, I take it you're not seeing him anymore."

"Oh, he's mad as hell at me."

"Why?" I asked.

"I turned him down. He wanted to marry me."

I watched Leforte's retreating back with alarm. Underneath his stiffness I'd detected a sense of injustice, like a child punished for something he hadn't done. And I wondered then if Leforte had told Selden other things besides the rumors about Gus.

But I was a little bewildered at Ellie's rejection of his proposal too. For the older I get, the more I realize that I too, like Selden, am a product of the pragmatic Midwest. With Leforte's money and Ellie's chic, they'd rule Cleveland. Ellie had to know that, and it surprised me that it didn't matter to her. She could tone down his clothes and redirect the interests away from exotic cars and over-priced liquor to land in the country and philanthropy. Marriage to

Leforte was not something she would have passed up so easily just a few months ago.

"Who needs him?" she asked, as if reading my thoughts.

"You know, he's not bad looking."

"I think so too," she said, tilting her head, as if admiring one of the paintings that surrounded us on the walls. "But there's nothing there. I tried. I swear."

"What do you mean?"

"I mean, I slept with him, and it just wasn't . . ."

"Good?"

"He knows what he's doing. But there was just no . . ."

"Heat?"

"Very unsentimental."

I made a little grimace. "Paint-by-numbers sex?"

"I guess I'm old-fashioned, but I need a few sweet nothings in the ear."

"Such a girl," I teased, but I agreed. Sweet nothings or not, if she didn't love him, or think she loved him, if for only one night, it just turned into "insert tab A in slot B," didn't it?

"Besides, I'm going to be able to support myself. Gus is working out all these fabulous investments for me. Between that and William's salary, we'll be fine."

"What do you mean William's salary?"

"I mean two people could make a life on that, plus what I have if I manage it well."

I was stunned. "You and Selden for real?"

"For real," she said with a smile and a nauseating giggle.

I paused for a second.

"What?" she demanded.

"Nothing." I shook my head, but I was alarmed. Hadn't she seen the look on Selden's face just now? He struck me as a man who'd had his vision permanently readjusted, and she was planning their life together.

Ellie waved me off, annoyed, I knew, and walked across the room, where she inserted herself into a conversation with a museum curator and a local restaurant critic.

I watched her charm them—their smiles widening, the writer leaning in as if he smelled something delicious, the curator twinkling at her comments. Ellie could charm anyone, it was true. But I didn't think mere charm would help her now with Selden. It seemed his feelings had undergone a tectonic shift this evening, and you didn't shift a man back easily, especially one like Selden.

16

The After-Party

Ellie stood in the middle of the swirling party talking to what had to be the two most boring men in town and wondered, as she had in similar circumstances, what the hell she was doing there. She'd liked the idea of the tableaux when the museum approached her. Here was something a little artsy, a little creative. She'd thought her pose might cause a *petite scandale*—just a small delicious amount. But now that she was the spectacle for the evening, frankly, she was finding it tiresome—men talking to her chest, blushing, stammering, or flirting ham-handedly. She'd wanted to entice one man—Selden—the one who'd seemed disgusted. She decided another glass of champagne was in order.

She watched William Selden out of the corner of her eye. He was the last person she'd thought would be provincial about her pose, but there was no ignoring his dismissal of her just now. She'd miscalculated. Based on Diana's tawdry text, Ellie thought that maybe Selden went in for exhibitionism, a little voyeurism. And if that was the case, Ellie could do sexting one better. She should have known better, should have known that Diana wasn't smooth enough to calculate what Selden liked and then give him a little more to lure him back. Ellie should have seen Diana's message for what it was—a desperate and probably drunken attempt to find something, anything, to get his attention. Straight-up amateur. Ellie sighed.

Ellie had been hanging out with Selden for over two weeks. There'd been kissing, and she'd spent a chaste and deliciously restful night asleep in his bed. Neither of them wanted to rush this. Selden was hesitant around her. Was he unsure of himself, or intimidated, or did he have her up on a pedestal? She'd decided that tonight she'd jump down off that pedestal and give him a little encouragement. And so she'd kept her pose a secret, thinking he'd be surprised, turned on. She'd have a whole room of men at her feet, literally, and then she'd make it known she only wanted him. Okay, so maybe the wink was taking it a little far, but she'd wanted to get the message across. She'd thought it would get him hot, that tonight would end in his bed, both of them excited by her display, their attraction acknowledged and consummated. But his reaction? As tightly wound and convention bound as any of them, despite his licking booze off her like an oversexed frat boy, his binding her wrist, his insistence that pleasure was what mattered. She watched him leave—without her—out a side door and knew he wasn't coming back.

"Bastard," she breathed, so that the director leaned in closer over her chest.

"Sorry?" he said, blushing.

Gus Trenor, in a thick pink silk tie, broke into her conversation then, winking at the curator and shaking hands with the writer.

"Star of the evening," he said to Ellie as the other two men drifted away.

Ellie sighed, and Gus exchanged Ellie's empty glass with a full glass of champagne off a passing tray.

"Better?" he said, nodding at her. "You caused quite the sensation." He smiled down on her as if looking at a favorite child.

"It's not hard in Cleveland, is it?"

Gus laughed. "No, I suppose not."

They surveyed the room, which was slowly emptying.

"Are you going to the after-party?" Gus asked Ellie.

"I don't have a ride."

"Don't you?"

"He left."

"Selden?"

"How did you know?"

Gus laughed again and downed the rest of his champagne. "You must think I'm an idiot. His mouth was practically hanging open—like he wanted to hang you on his wall."

It mollified Ellie somewhat to hear that she'd had some effect on Selden. She scanned the room, looking for what, she didn't know. Diana Dorset was busy at the back of the room, talking to the head caterer.

"Come with me," Gus said, leaning in close. "I'll take you to the party. It's bound to be more interesting than this."

He bundled her into her grandmother's fur, and they headed for the car.

"Where's Julia?" Ellie asked, looking around the parking lot.

"She'll meet us there."

Gus started up his German sedan, and they glided out of the museum parking lot into the night. The streets were freshly plowed from a recent snow. The gray mounds on either side of the streets were covered with a new white dusting. They passed Wade Oval and then the fine arts garden hung in the silver and white of snow and ice under a dotting of streetlights, and then Gus made a sharp right, cutting through the Case Western university campus.

She leaned back in the heated seat, the windows fogging from their breath and the cold. So what if someone saw her leaving the party with Gus Trenor alone? It felt good to have him driving her in his luxurious, heavy car, not knowing where she was going. To relinquish responsibility for the moment was leather-scented bliss.

They pulled up in front of a new row of condominiums in Little Italy. Gus parked in front and got out.

"Julia's meeting us?" she asked.

Gus bounced up the unshoveled stairs, jingling keys in his hand.

"The party is here?" she asked again, following his footsteps through the snow, the hem of her costume peeking out from her coat and trailing behind her.

Gus opened the door and ushered her inside. "I wanted to show you this first."

He flicked on the light and she was standing in a modern two-story space with pale bare floors, hushed and chill. "Why?" she asked, hugging her coat tightly around her.

"A good investment for you," Gus said. "I told you I'd been checking out real estate. This neighborhood is only going to go up. But you'll have to act fast on this little place. It's not even on the market yet."

It was straight out of her imagination, a little place on Murray Hill, close to the university and to Little Italy. She could see the mix of Noguchi and Gustavian in these spare rooms, though she didn't think Selden's Arts and Crafts pieces would mix well. Selden. She'd managed to forget him for a moment.

She walked into the living room—a full wall of windows with a view of downtown Cleveland. Gus turned on the lights. "No, no, turn them off," she said. "Look at that view."

"A view like that will hold its value."

She walked over to the window and stood, touching the freezing glass. There was the whole city laid out before her in blinking lights—the Terminal Tower, the steelyards, the lake. Below in the street was a car she thought she recognized as it slipped past in the night on the tire tracks in the snow left by previous cars. And then she felt Gus Trenor behind her, and she froze. He seemed to wait just a moment, and then his arms were around her waist and his mouth was next to her neck, then kissing her ear with a loud wet smack that echoed in her head. She jumped, squirmed, and tried to remove his hands.

"Now, wait," he said into her ear. "I thought you liked me."

She twisted so that she was facing him. "Gus—"

"I like you." He lunged forward, again trying to kiss her. "You seem to like me."

"But Julia . . . ," she said, brandishing the first thing she thought would bring him to his senses. In her panic she instantly realized that the situation was dangerous on multiple levels—her good friend's husband, her money manager, her old family friend—on every level, really. And would she tell Julia that Gus made a pass at her and suffer ostracism when Julia turned a blind eye? Or not tell and look guilty by omission and have Julia imagining the worst when she eventually found out? You could never keep anything a secret in Cleveland.

"Julia's frigid. You're her friend, I thought you knew."

Ellie continued squirming until she was out of his grasp and on the other side of the room. "I think you have the wrong idea about things."

"I don't think I *do* have the wrong idea about things. I think you know how I feel about you. And you were willing to let me finance you because you knew I liked you. And I was okay with it. I thought it might lead somewhere eventually. But after seeing you up there onstage tonight, I thought, I've got to get me some of that." Here he made a step toward her, but she backed up. "I've always had a thing for you."

Ellie started edging her way around the room toward the front door. "Of course I'm flattered, and you've been a really good friend to me—"

"I could be an even better one. And unlike Leforte, I don't kiss and tell."

This stopped Ellie.

"Yes, he's been talking," Gus said, moving closer to her. "Locker-room chitchat now that he's been waived into the club to play squash. The man's a jackass. You should be more discreet, El. Choose more carefully. Frankly I was a little disappointed. Now, I . . . I can be really discreet." He reached out for her arm.

This time she went straight for the door. She fumbled only a minute with the lock and then fell on the doorstep with a gulping of cold night air. She ran down the steps, snow spilling in her shoes, her thin costume slipping off her shoulders inside her coat as she looked up and down the wintry street for a cab. The air felt delicious—safe and unbound. Seeing no cars and no people, she guessed at the lateness of the hour and saw a man—there was something familiar in the outline of his overcoat—turn from the opposite corner and disappear down a snowy side street.

17

The E-mails

To: William Selden (wselden@cwru.edu)
From: Eleanor Hart (ehart@gmail.com)
Subject: Your ribbon

You left without saying good-bye. I hope this old e-mail address gets to you as I have no other way of getting through.
Your cell says the voice mail is full. I was wearing your ribbon
in the tableau. Steven freaked out, said it ruined the authentic-
ity. But I insisted. Did you see it? I'd send the ribbon back to
you, but I don't have your address. If you want it, let me know
where you are . . .
E

· · · · ·

To: Eleanor Hart (ehart@gmail.com)
From: William Selden (wselden@cwru.edu)
Re: Leaving

I'm sorry I had to leave so quickly. The offer demanded it, and
I was packing for a day and then on the plane the next. The

dean was a nightmare about covering my classes, but when he heard it was the Sorbonne and I'd be back, he made it easier for me. You don't need to send me a ribbon, or anything else. I have no claims on you and never did. I get that now.

Best—

WS

. . . . .

To: William Selden (wselden@cwru.edu)
From: Eleanor Hart (ehart@gmail.com)
Re: Claims

If this is all going to go to shit over e-mail and you won't even call me or tell me where you are then you should at least know some things. It wasn't about claims on people. Didn't you tell me that? A meeting of souls? A kinship of spirit? How could I misread everything so completely?

I think I love you. I don't think I've ever loved anyone else. I'd come and find you now, if only I felt you wanted me to. Do you want me to?

Did it ever occur to you that I maybe needed something from you?

Love (I can't believe I'm reduced to doing this all over e-mail),

E

. . . . .

To: Eleanor Hart (ehart@gmail.com)
From: William Selden (wselden@cwru.edu)
Re: Misreading

I had no idea you were seeing/sleeping with Randy Leforte. Are you still?

. . . . .

To: William Selden (wselden@cwru.edu)
From: Eleanor Hart (ehart@gmail.com)
Re: You're pissed at me?!?!

I had no idea you were seeing/sleeping with Diana Dorset. Are you still?

. . . . .

To: Eleanor Hart (ehart@gmail.com)
From: William Selden (wselden@cwru.edu)
Re: Confusion

I'm not. It was over a long time ago. And you know that. Is that why you were seeing Randy, and Gus Trenor for that matter? To get back at me? That sounds like I'm mad and I'm not. It's just that I realized that we come at the world in two different ways, El. I should have seen that more clearly earlier on. The night of the museum thing just made me see that we're very, very different people. I see that now. You've always been wild, Ellie. And I'm kind of, well, I'm kind of not.
But I do wish you the best, truly—
William

Selden's e-mails left her fuming. His suggestion that she'd sneak around with married Gus Trenor offended her. He should have known her better than that. And it was the height of hypocrisy to call her out on it when he'd been seeing Diana Dorset, who was married. That he was upset about Randy was ridiculous too—the double standard, alive and well in a modern man. She wasn't raised in a convent and neither was he for that matter—raised in a monastery, that is. She'd heard rumors that Selden had been seeing one of his students.

Seriously, this was the twenty-first century, not a hundred years ago. She'd been married, for crying in a bucket. He'd had innumerable girlfriends, so who the hell did he think he was judging her? Sending her those crap e-mails.

She'd thought twice about firing off angry e-mails to him. Her mother's admonishments came back to her, as they often did at the strangest times.

"Anger isn't pretty," her mother would tell her, rinsing dishes in the sink. "Avoid it when you can, and when you can't, fake it. Nothing is uglier than a wrathful woman."

But Ellie couldn't just let him leave and say nothing. She thought briefly about flying to Paris to find him and make him listen to her but decided she couldn't. It was just too clingy, too desperate. And Ellie had been taught to never appear desperate.

"Always remain self-sufficient," her mother had told her one hot summer afternoon as they drove in her mother's stifling red Saab to make a deposit at the bank. Ellie's ears had perked up. Most of her mother's advice regarded insulating her looks from decay and complex techniques for keeping a man guessing. "Always keep a bank account, a credit card, and a car in your own name."

Ellie had looked at her questioningly.

"You never know when they might come in handy," she said as they parked, and her mother snapped her purse shut with a tidy click of the ball-snap closure.

Now Ellie leaned back in the old slatted chair at her mother's breakfast table rereading Selden's e-mails and getting progressively more angry. No, she wouldn't go begging after him. She took a swig of Grey Goose out of the glass next to her. Selden just proved himself to be the same as any of them, judging her against his suburban morals. She'd honestly thought he was different, thought he adhered to a different set of principles guiding his life. But when it came right down to it, he'd shown his inherited conventional view of women and sex. It didn't escape her notice that he likely thought no less of Gus or Randy for that matter, though he'd never liked them to start. Being involved with Ellie didn't lower them in his eyes.

Selden's conventionality probably applied to his views of marriage as well. He probably expected dinner every night at six o'clock, wouldn't want to smell cleaning fumes when he got home, would refuse to eat leftovers. She'd heard friends complaining about their husbands doing these exact things. When Ellie had been married to Alex, he'd had enough money to hire someone to take care of all of that, rendering moot any conflict between them over housekeeping. But at the time she'd wondered why her friends didn't just tell their husbands where they could go. But now she kind of got it. Some men were that conventional, and you didn't change a man once you'd married him. If Alex had taught her anything, he'd taught her that.

Her computer dinged.

. . . . .

To: Eleanor Hart (ehart@gmail.com)
From: Randall Leforte, Esq.(rleforte@lefortelaw.com)
Subject: Get together?

Was wondering if you're free on Friday for a quick drink after work? Have a business proposal for you.
Sent from my BlackBerry wireless device

She was surprised he'd written. He'd not taken her refusing him well. And he was so stiff and weird at the benefit, she didn't think he'd want to be friends. But apparently the Persuader didn't give up that easily. She hit "Reply," knowing that somewhere out there his Black-Berry would vibrate and he'd read her message instantly. He wasn't able to resist that toy. It was another thing that oddly appealed to her. He was kind of powerless against his petty addictions.

. . . . .

To: Randall Leforte (rleforte@lefortelaw.com)
From: Ellie (ehart@gmail.com)
Re: Get together?

Am intrigued. Three o'clock at the Ritz tomorrow?
E

Why not three o'clock? she thought. It was his favorite time, wasn't it?

· 18 ·

The Aftermath

The first week of March I gave birth to a healthy nine-pound baby boy we named Henry. Jim and I brought him home, and I immersed myself in those initial weeks of baby care. Stalled labor had ended in a Cesarean section, and so I hobbled through those first few days in a haze of pain pills and exhaustion. It amazed me that the doctor advised against eating blue cheese while I was pregnant for fear of some bacteria harming Henry but sent me home with a generous supply of OxyContin. I managed nursing after a few tearful nights when neither the baby nor I knew what we were doing. Jim ran the most effective blockade of visitors save my mother and the few people who dropped off casserole dinners, which allowed me to exist in a cozy cocoon with the new baby. I put the pain pills away in the medicine cabinet as I healed. A huge spray of pale lavender roses, their color almost silver, was delivered from Cinco Van Alstyne. Cards came in the mail by the handful.

The smell of my baby's head and the sleeping smiles and the tiny fingernails so enraptured and fascinated me, and the sleepless nights and the nursing and the constant rocking so exhausted me, that I existed almost solely in the baby cocoon for a good six weeks, sending only thank-you notes out into the world.

Jim tried to coax me out. He wanted me to go watch his club's annual squash tournament—a black-tie event where the members watched professional players competing for a sizable purse. But the thought of entrusting Henry to some new sitter so I could attend in a too-tight cocktail dress—I had lost weight but there was still a lot of work to do—and watch grown men chase a little ball? I passed. But in appreciation of my husband's constant tending of Henry and me, I encouraged him to go and suggested he take Ellie. Despite, or because of, the tableau, having Ellie on his arm would make Jim seem cool and make me seem magnanimous.

For three days after the tournament Ellie called and left messages with increasing frequency. When I called her back, she asked to see the baby right away, and so we decided she'd come the next day.

I felt self-conscious about seeing her with my belly still looking like it had a batch of risen bread dough sitting on it and dark circles shading my eyes. I showered and attempted makeup in an effort to feel a little less frumpy when Ellie showed up.

She arrived wearing enormous sunglasses. She took them off and revealed under-eye circles darker than mine. She'd lost weight, and her dry hair was raked back in a sloppy ponytail that revealed an inch of undyed roots dotted with gray hairs. I tried not to stare. As much as Ellie displayed a just-rolled-out-of-bed sexiness in her style of dress, she was always perfectly groomed.

Henry was napping, and we peeked in the nursery. Ellie cooed distractedly and pronounced him beautiful. It wasn't until we were sitting downstairs with peppermint tea and the baby monitor light blinking that the real purpose of her visit became clear.

"I suppose you've heard what happened."

I shook my head. "I haven't heard anything. I've been in the land of baby."

"So? You can still hear stuff," she said, sharp.

"I'm exhausted. I don't return phone calls," I said, appeasing her. I'd been feeling guilty about my inability to do anything but take care of the baby. Silly of me, but I know women, maybe you know them too, who jump in and swim a week after giving birth—whipping up dinner with the baby in a sling, jogging with the baby rolling in a stroller while they exercise the pounds off. I was over-whelmed, triumphant if I made it out of pajamas into real clothes by the time Jim got home. "I only called you back because you left eighty messages."

"I left four."

I smiled. "I'm saying I'm out of it."

She sat cross-legged on my couch with her shoes off and constantly jiggled one foot, distracting me. She was studying my face, worrying a chapped spot on her bottom lip, and I thought that whatever gossip was going around must have been bad.

"Julia's pissed at me," she finally said.

I made a face. "I'm sure she's not." I fumbled with the tea bag in the pot and retied it to the handle.

"I'm getting bits and pieces back from people, but the night of the museum . . ."

My discussion with Selden at the benefit flooded up in my mind.

"She thinks something happened with Gus that night," Ellie was saying.

I poured more tea in my cup and sat back, waiting. But Ellie had stopped.

"Why would she think that?" I asked.

"I left with him, which in retrospect was stupid. I thought he was giving me a ride to the after-party. He took me to this condo. I thought he wanted me to buy it. He made a pass at me."

"Come on," I said.

"Now Julia thinks something happened, that we're having an af-fair." She paused, fiddling with her cup and saucer. "Gus has tried talking sense into her, but she doesn't believe him. Frankly I don't blame her after all the shit he's pulled."

"Doesn't she know about you and Selden?"

Here Ellie looked down, and I thought I heard her voice waver as she said, "He left to teach at the Sorbonne for a semester. Very short notice. He was gone in less than a week." She looked out the window. "It was like one day he was here and the next . . ."

I don't know why I said what I did next. I guess I was trying to make the best out of the situation. "Well at least you'll get to visit him in Paris—so romantic."

"I haven't talked to him. I've been reduced to e-mailing him. I don't even have his phone number. His cell doesn't work over there." She uncrossed her legs and leaned back in the couch, closing her eyes. "Him leaving, plus what Julia's saying—it looks bad."

"Who cares how it looks?" I thought about the night of the benefit. "You know, at the museum benefit Selden said something to me."

"What?" She opened her eyes and looked at me, panicked.

"He seemed a little pissy, and he said he'd been talking to Randy Leforte."

Ellie groaned and leaned back again, looking at the ceiling. "Randy's been talking about me all over town too. Or in all the locker rooms in town, I guess. Selden knows about that too. Cleveland is so damn high school."

She seemed oddly calm given the inferno of gossip raging around her. If it were me, I'd have been panicked. But she voiced perspective, almost as if it were happening to another person, yet she sounded defeated. I sat there in silent solidarity with her, felt bad for her. Cleveland *was* a good bit like high school.

"And the old double standard is alive and well. Is anyone talking about Gus, or Randy for that matter? No. Just about a potential catfight between Julia and me. Nice how nothing ever changes." Her bitterness did strange things to her mouth, her lips wobbling like it was all a bite too big to swallow.

I realized she was right, of course. "So leave," I said. "It gets provincial here, you knew that."

"It's the same in New York. Alex's substance abuse gave him a disease, the poor thing. I was just the bitch who cheated on him when the chips were down. At some point you have to say 'Fuck it, I don't care what anyone thinks.' Tried that too. Although I do care when they're whispering behind my back at parties, not inviting me places, and in general treating me like I'm diseased and disgraced."

"Fuck them," I said.

She snorted. "They wish."

We both laughed.

I didn't know how to ask, but I had to know for sure. "El," I said quietly. "You didn't, did you?" I had no illusions about Ellie's lack of scruple. She could convince herself that almost any action she took was justified, and the stories I'd heard about her making passes at other people's husbands lingered.

She raised her eyebrows.

"With Gus," I clarified.

She looked at me with utter contempt. "After all I just said, you think I'd sleep with Gus Trenor?"

"No, no," I said, realizing instantly that I'd offended her.

She sighed. "I can't believe you'd ask me something like that, though I guess I shouldn't be surprised. William believed it. I did not sleep with Gus. But I might as well have in this town. And Randy Leforte was a huge mistake."

"But he liked you so much. The proposal—"

She shook her head. "I told you at the benefit. I'm not doing that again. We went for drinks though. He had a business deal for me. He wants to start a foundation of all things—with his name on it, of course. Wants me to help him with it."

"Ells, that'd be great for you." I was enthused.

She shook her head no. "Can't even think about it. Of course he won't actually pay me anything decent—there's that. But he really just wants to keep me close. Is trying to convince me we're right for one another. No one tells him no. It's so pushy."

I thought her too cynical. With her contacts she might actually be pretty good at the job, and she'd feel altruistic even if it was with someone else's money. Perhaps Leforte wasn't after her. When I suggested it, she snorted. "Wake up," she said. "He's not going to pay me anything, and I have no training or idea what I'm doing."

"You could learn."

She waved a hand. "Disaster."

Not knowing what to say, I got up to refresh our teapot, and Ellie headed for the bathroom.

When we got back and settled, I leveled my gaze at her. "So go get Selden."

She scoffed. "What? Go get him like a caveman or something?"

"Go to France. Talk to him. Show him how you feel." I doubted that any man, especially Selden, would be able to resist Ellie making a grand gesture.

"He was pretty dismissive in his e-mails."

"This is love we're talking about."

She smirked. "Love? Please."

"You told me that night at the benefit—you two together for real."

"I was wrong."

"What else is there really?" I asked. "When you get down to it, what else matters besides love? If you think you've found it, then go show him he's being an idiot. I know I would."

Ellie had a strange look on her face. "You've always been a good girl."

I was startled. It was such a strange thing to say. I'd done my share of "bad" things—sneaking cigarettes as a girl, sleeping with messy boys in college, trying drugs when I lived in the city. "The hell are you talking about?"

She stood up. "Never done anything really bad, anything you're ashamed of." I saw tears welling up in her eyes, and I didn't want her to cry. We'd both be uncomfortable if I witnessed her losing control.

I heard the baby stirring through the monitor—soft grunting, perhaps just waking.

"Ellie, come on." She was scaring me. I was thinking fast, and not very clearly. I was trying to avert her tears. Just the thought of seeing her cry had me panicked. She was my oldest friend, and in that moment, looking at her in a ratty T-shirt with the gold chain her mother gave her around her neck, I felt protective of her and oddly responsible for her. I don't know why. Ellie had seen more of the world than I probably ever would.

"Well, I know something that will take your mind off all this. I was going to ask you today," I said. "Maybe it will cheer you up. Jim and I . . ." Here I paused, and she looked at me, gulping back her tears as I rattled on. "We want you to be Henry's godmother."

She just looked at me blankly. I don't know what I'd expected. Ellie never showed any interest in babies, but I grasped at something that would have been meaningful to me.

Henry's cry came louder now; he was definitely awake.

"I should go," Ellie said, drying her eyes.

"No, no, stay. See your godson," I said with enthusiasm, trying to make her smile, trying to make this okay for her.

"No, I'll see him later." She sniffled into a napkin. I was nervous she was going to start crying in earnest.

"You haven't actually said you'll do it," I said.

"Of course I will," Ellie said listlessly, gathering her things. "I've known you my whole life. Can you imagine what our mothers will say when we tell them?"

I smiled but felt irrationally disappointed by her lack of enthusiasm. Foolishly I'd thought the reality of Henry would change her into a baby person.

Henry's squawking was becoming more urgent now. "I should go up there and feed him. You can come if you won't get freaked out by the size of my boobs."

I wasn't going to mention the tableau, but Ellie said, "You saw one of mine, so I shouldn't be uncomfortable with yours."

We laughed.

"I should leave you in peace," she said.

The baby was crying in earnest now.

"I should get him," I said, heading up the stairs.

Ellie quickly kissed my cheek. She fumbled in her bag for her sunglasses.

"El, I'm sorry for asking . . ." I started to apologize for mentioning Gus, not wanting her to leave so sad.

She leaned over and kissed my cheek again, put her glasses on her red-rimmed eyes, smiled a weak smile, and then she was gone.

In taking care of Henry that afternoon, I completely forgot about Ellie's visit. Jim and I had not discussed godparents at all. We hadn't even planned the baptism yet. So I was little jolted when he came home from work and asked about Ellie's visit while rummaging in the back of the fridge for a beer. I told him that I'd asked her to be a godmother.

"Ellie Hart is the person you're choosing to guide our son spiritually through his life?"

"Yes, what's wrong with that?"

"She's a party girl."

"She's not."

"Does she even go to church?"

"Doesn't matter. You only need one Catholic godparent, the rest can be—whatever. You can choose the godfather."

"Then I'm choosing Dustin Cunningham."

Dustin Cunningham was his roommate from college who'd graduated from NYU film school and headed to Los Angeles, where he was running an adult Internet site while trying to come up with money for a documentary on composting.

"You haven't spoken to him in years."

"Makes as much sense as 'Ellie Hart, Godmother.'"

"You're in a bad mood."

"I'm not, but this is a serious thing."

"It's not. There's no limit on the number of godparents. We can pick four more if you want. Ellie was upset. I thought it might cheer her up, and I've known her all my life. You think she wouldn't take this sort of thing seriously? I'm worried about her."

"Why?" He eyed me, nervously, I thought.

"She looked tired. I think she's going through a hard time."

"She wasn't on something?" Jim took a long pull on his beer, but he kept my eye.

"Drugs?"

"She has a history."

"No, I think that's all behind her." As I said this, it did occur to me that Ellie had looked haggard.

Jim looked down at Henry, who was happily kicking in his bouncy seat on the kitchen floor. "I just want everything to be perfect for him."

"It will be. Was there someone you wanted for the godparents?"

"I was thinking of P. G. and Viola."

"P. G. and Viola would make perfect godparents," I said, nodding my head and smiling. As I've said, Jim surprised me sometimes with his clear reading of other people. "They'd take the role very seriously."

That night as I was washing my face for bed, I noticed one of my hand towels in a damp pile on the sink. Strange that Ellie would come up here and not use the powder room. When I opened my medicine cabinet all the OxyContin were gone, and she'd left the empty bottle.

19

The Laundry Room

A few weeks after Ellie's visit, Diana Dorset had us over for dinner. I'd found a regular babysitter I liked, and she came an hour early so I could enjoy getting ready for my first night out.

If Julia Trenor's parties had the best champagne, dinner served by caterers, and copious illicit substances, Diana's parties usually had some over-the-top theme, featured the latest potent cocktail, and ended with new illicit couplings. This night she'd moved all her furniture out of her living room and replaced it with huge Moroccan cushions and tribal rugs so we could all sit on the floor. Red paper lanterns hung from the ceiling and a low Japanese table ran the length of the living room. Down the center were tea roses in every conceivable hue in short mercury-glass vases that reflected tiny white candles and her grandmother's silver service for twenty-four, a set so complete it included oyster forks and fruit knives. The whole thing was like a million-dollar opium den and very Diana.

The guests included those fabulous conversationalists the Ahujas, those well-read Downings, and other young Clevelanders I knew. I'd not been out socializing since the birth and people were welcoming and asked about baby Henry and were kind. Diana had invited a few artists, and I was surprised to see Ellie's boss, Steven, but no Ellie, which worried me.

I'd also expected to see the Van Alstynes. I was looking forward to it, actually, after Cinco had sent those beautiful flowers. But as I scanned the crowd clustered on the floor of Diana's living room inhaling at hookah water pipes, I didn't see them. Given that this was the beginning of the party, I suspected there was no pot in those pipes yet.

Dan Dorset was accosting his guests with an origami cootie-catcher, the type we made in grade school.

"Come on," he said to me. "Pick a color."

Jim gave me a helpless shrug as if to say I was trapped and he couldn't help me.

When Dan was done shifting his fingers around he said, "Choose a number." And after he shifted his fingers again, I chose another number, and he lifted a flap to read my fortune.

"You'll end up on your knees tonight, much to someone's delight." The room erupted in laughter.

I quirked an eyebrow at Jim as if to say, "Really, that's funny?" But apparently the room thought my look challenging or suggestive and people just laughed harder.

"Jesus, you're a pervert, Dan." Diana got up off the floor, blowing a mouthful of apricot tobacco smoke away from me and fanning the air. "All the fortunes are nasty. Sorry. You actually got one of the tame ones."

She hugged me, and her eyes, which everyone described as glittering, I now noticed had an edge of fear or restrained panic in them that kept them moving, as if double-checking the exits.

"How's the little man?" she asked.

"Exhausting. Growing all the time."

"Sleeping and such?"

"He's up at three for a quick snack and then back down. It's pretty reasonable."

She took my arm and led me back to the bar. "A real drink. I must have a real drink." She got us tequila shots, Selden's drink, I noted with chagrin. She clinked her shot glass with mine. "Come on," she said. "You've been pristine too long."

I threw the shot down my throat, slightly gagging at the peppery taste that brought memories of early mornings filled with regret.

"Another," she said to the bartender, but I waved it off.

She drank the liquor, and as always, I was amazed at her tolerance given her petite stature. She wasn't affected at all.

She took a glass of wine. I took a glass of water. And she steered me back into the living room, away from the smokers.

I scanned the rooms—no Ellie, no Selden, no Van Alstynes.

"He's not here," she said.

I was embarrassed, thinking I'd been caught canvassing her party, looking for Cinco.

"He went to Paris, you know."

When I didn't say anything she nodded distractedly. "You're friends with Selden, yes? I thought you two were close." I was trying to ignore the topic, hoping she'd get the hint.

"I know William," I said.

"Then you know he's in Paris."

I was disappointed she wasn't going to move on. "Yes."

"And you know he claims he saw Ellie and Gus coming out of the condo Gus keeps on the other side of town for, well, you know . . ." She all but waggled her eyebrows at me. Ellie and Selden were her new chew toy.

I was about to feign disbelief, wanting to protect Ellie, when Diana interrupted.

"Oh God, everyone knows about that place. I think he actually had one of his girls living there like a mistress for a while. Now he just keeps it for his 'meetings.' Everyone knows about it," she said with her foxy little grin. "Even Julia."

"I can't believe that."

"Julia's not jealous of Gus, but she doesn't want to be left. That's why she had such a fit about Ellie."

"She wasn't having an affair with Gus. That is total fiction."

Diana raised an eyebrow. "William called me one night this winter," she said with a triumphant gleam in her eye. "Right after he saw her coming out of Gus's condo. He was blown apart by it. It was that night after Ellie's Janet Jackson moment at the museum. Really, I think she must have been on drugs. She's out of control."

It was becoming clear to me now. After hearing Selden so upset on the phone, Diana realized that he was in love with Ellie. Diana had known he'd been seeing Ellie a little, and she'd been prepared to let this fascination run its course, thinking he'd come back to her. Ellie would lose interest soon and dump him anyway, Diana guessed. But Selden had fallen in love, which meant Diana would lose him forever. So after a moment's calculation, and for Diana's brain it would take only a moment, she decided to destroy Ellie.

I knew that the moment after Diana hung up with Selden, she'd called Julia, in the guise of a concerned friend, and relayed that Selden had seen Gus and Ellie together.

Diana knew, as I did too, that Gus's indiscretions with girls ten years his junior meant nothing to Julia. Young girls with neither the chic nor the education of his wife might provide a distraction for a few months, but Gus would tire of them. He'd been raised by an understated mother who set the bar for how a wife behaved—she threw dinner parties and sat on charitable boards, was a member of the garden club, bought her clothes in New York twice a year, and made sure her husband's money was tastefully spent. When children came along, she'd make sure they were properly educated and socially prepared. Gus wasn't leaving his wife for some hard-bodied receptionist, no matter how explosive the sex. He was a conventional midwestern boy.

But Ellie was a different matter. Here was a true threat. A woman of taste and the same background who held every advantage Julia did, but with the body of a Venus. Gus could easily fall in love with Ellie Hart. Julia would have seen that. Julia would imagine she'd done the only self-preserving thing she could do. She took Ellie out by quietly getting the word around that Ellie was a home-wrecker and a slut.

Diana and Julia's alliance would be formidable as so much was at stake for both of them. Diana was vanquishing her rival for Selden's attention once and for all. Julia was saving her marriage.

"I don't know how she does it," Diana said. "I barely have enough energy to fuck my own husband, let alone anybody else's."

I smirked at this. "Where's Julia tonight?" I asked.

"She and Gus went to Buenos Aires for the week. To reconnect, she told me. It's very French, don't you think, trying to woo back your husband after he's had an affair?"

I was about to object that there was no affair when Steven came over and air-kissed Diana on the cheek. "You're stunning tonight," he said to her.

"Of course," she said. "I'm wearing your clothes." She turned back to me. "We were just talking about Ellie."

"I'm worried about her," Steven said. "She looks awful." His tongue darted out over the viper bites in his lip. "She stopped coming to work. I had to fire her. Didn't want to; goddamned accountant made me."

Diana smiled. "She's having a rough patch."

I realized then how far Ellie had fallen if both Steven and Diana were comfortable talking about her like this to me, one of Ellie's oldest friends.

"We're concerned," Diana said, assuming a cozy solidarity with Steven.

"And you're close to her," Steven said.

"You should talk to her," Diana said.

"I just worry about her health," he said. He turned to Diana then and said, "Darling, would you get me a glass of water? I'm parched."

Diana was taken aback. No one broke up a hostess's conversation at her own party. He could have easily flagged down a waiter.

"You're sure just water?"

"Yes, I don't drink alcohol," he said flatly.

She registered what he meant, that he was in recovery. And I knew then they couldn't be that close if she hadn't known about his past.

"Thank you, beautiful," he said, all but patting her head and sending her off. When she was gone, he steered me into Diana's kitchen. It was hot, food spread everywhere and the caterers bumping into each other and us—giving us dirty looks for crowding their working space.

Steven led me into Diana's laundry room, clicking on the light.

"Have you talked to Ellie?" he asked, real worry in his voice.

I shook my head.

"She won't take my calls. I think she's mad as shit that I fired her. But I can barely make the business work right now, and I had to. I just need a couple more of these bitches"—he twirled his finger in the air—"to start wearing my shit, and I'll get my head above water. I mean, I love Ellie, and she's the world's best walking advertisement. But I can only give away free clothes for so long." He hopped up on top of the dryer next to a basket of folded white towels. "So what have you heard?" He nibbled at his piercings nervously.

"Nothing."

"After that boy left, that Selden? She fell apart."

"I'm getting that," I said.

"With a history like hers there's a real possibility of relapse at times like these. I mean, I should know," Steven said. I'd not thought about Ellie's recovery. She seemed to be doing well enough. But Steven's well-informed comment filled me with dread.

"She was at my house the other day," I offered.

"She looked like shit, right?"

I nodded because she did, but I felt a little disloyal, though I shouldn't have. Steven seemed genuinely worried about her, even if he had used her at the museum to shock and drum up publicity. "She seemed worried about rumors going around about her."

Steven groaned and said, "Why? I mean, why would a girl like that care what people say about her? Everyone wants her to get married. They're obsessed with it. Like this is the eighteen hundreds or something. It's so not modern. A girl like Ellie? All she's ever been told is that she's beautiful." He frowned into the open washing machine next to him, as if pondering this. "She's spent so much time getting people to want her, to like her. She doesn't even know what she wants." He pulled a pack of organic cigarettes out of his jacket. "Smoke?" he asked.

I shook my head no, and he lit up right next to the basket of clean towels.

"These people work at time-filling, bullshit jobs, if they work at all. No children, except for you. None of them have a goddamned original thought in their heads. Stupid fuckers." He rested an arm on the basket. "She should have said yes to Leforte. At least the man made his own money."

"I agree she should have married him," I said.

He gave a little sneer. "You think she's getting old? Past her shelf life? A woman better catch her man before she's forty or she'll be alone her whole life?"

I'd thought I was agreeing with him, and he'd turned on me with acid. I moved to go, but he grabbed my wrist.

"Not you," he said. "I'm sorry. Sometimes it all gets to me, watching it." He exhaled. "I agree she'd have been comfortable with Leforte. I just don't know if safety should be Ellie's thing, you know? You're the only one who was ever a real friend to her. That's what she said. And I could see it at lunch. You'd help her, I know."

He stuck the cigarette in the side of his mouth opposite the little hoops.

"What's there to do?" I asked.

He shrugged. "Fuck if I know. But I'll be damned if I'll let that witch Diana take her down." He put the cigarette, only half smoked, out on the bottom of his shoe and rinsed it down the laundry sink. "Diana came down to the studio sniffing around, asking where Ellie was. It's the greatest pity I had to tell her I fired Ellie. Luckily I managed to get her to buy some clothes, so it wasn't all for naught. God knows what her malfunction is. I think she needs Lexapro, or a vibrator, probably both."

At seeing the look on my face he laughed. "Don't be shocked that some people need a little assistance. Not everyone has a hot DILF at home, you know."

"Like MILF?" I asked, laughing. "'Dad I'd Like to Fuck'? Why have I never heard that before?"

"Brad Pitt would be on the poster, with child, of course—though I prefer Gavin Rossdale. Now, come," he said, taking my hand. "We'll see if we can possibly get Diana to shut up. Plus, we've been gone too long and I don't want her forming a search party."

We emerged from the kitchen and attempted to mingle, but our absence was as conspicuous as if we'd been playing seven minutes in heaven. Luckily Steven's preferences were well known.

Diana all but attacked us with Steven's glass of water. "You disappeared." She sniffed and then smiled in understanding.

"Quick chat outside," Steven said with a wink.

"So I was saying about Ellie . . . ," Diana started in again, and I was shocked at her doggedness. She was intent on grinding Ellie to dust.

Suddenly the idea of staying and eating her food, of spending the rest of the evening with her, of being beholden to her in any way, was awful. I was angry with her and disgusted with the whole scene.

Steven had gotten Diana off the Ellie topic and onto some actress and the dress she recently wore at an awards show.

"You know," I said, putting my glass of untouched water down on an inlaid table, "I should find Jim."

"You okay?" they both asked in unison.

"Fine, I just feel a little woozy all of a sudden."

This had the effect I intended as Jim was summoned instantly. Diana bundled us into our coats and whipped us out the door with zealous concern for my health.

When we got in the car Jim asked, "What was that about?"

"I miss the baby," I said, which was true. "I think it was just a little too soon for me to be out."

"We could have called the sitter."

"I didn't want to call. I want to hold him," I snapped. A tear slipped down my cheek.

"Are you crying?" Jim said, looking at me, horrified, and almost missing a stop sign.

"No. Hormones."

"Seriously, what happened back there?" he said, pulling over.

I explained about Diana. "She was so mean tonight," I said, drying my eyes, getting ahold of myself.

"Well, that's Diana. You don't get too close," he said, taking my hand.

"She's just destroying El, and why? Because she's jealous? Diana's married, for God's sake." In saying the words out loud to Jim, I realized that the panicky feeling I had was born of the suspicion that should I ever step even the slightest degree out of line, Diana Dorset would hesitate not one instant to grind me into gossip hamburger as well.

Jim was silent. The sodium streetlights cast a golden glow on him. "Okay, I hesitate to tell you this because I do think you are a little fragile right now, but I think I have to."

"Tell me what?"

"You remember that squash tournament at the club two weeks ago?"

My heart beat in my ears. My breath got short.

Jim continued. "I think she really is out of control."

"Oh God," I whispered, images of Jim and Ellie together filling my mind. "You're scaring me."

"Ellie drank a lot. Although now that you mention it, sweetheart, she could have been on something too." I thought of the pills she'd filched from my bathroom. I hadn't mentioned it to Jim. "She was wearing this corsetlike dress thing. The chest was on display. Every-one wanted to meet her. I think because of the museum thing. Even the old codgers—especially the codgers. Anyway, I was introducing her around and the top-ranked traveling player—young guy, just out of Brown—comes up. The attraction between the two of them was pretty clear."

Relief started to seep into my brain as I tried to focus on what he was saying. Was he saying nothing had happened between him and Ellie?

"I didn't want to tell you because I thought you'd be mad at me for not stepping in and trying to get her out of there, but the rumor is she slept with him."

Relief took over my brain, followed by love for my husband.

"So she slept with some guy, so what?"

"She slept with him in the club."

This may not sound so bad, but it was bad in Cleveland. Jim's club was an all-male holdover from the 1920s, housed down-town in an immense Tudor brick mansion, the halls lined with taxidermy. It had been like a fraternity for industrialists—a place where they could play squash, play cards, shoot pool, smoke cigars, tell dirty jokes, and drink. They'd once held hunting dog trials—complete with live birds and ammunition—inside the club. Now nice young men, many the great-grandsons of the founders, still went there for the same distractions. Every once in a while wives were invited for an evening, but it was rare. There were bedrooms upstairs where, in the 1920s, members housed visiting friends for a society wedding or debutante season. Now when professional squash players came for a tournament, or professional boxers, as the club hosted a smoker every year, the contestants stayed in the bedrooms.

"What do you mean she slept with him in the club?"

"She's the first woman to actually stay overnight in the club. I've caught hell from the governing board since she was my guest. I think they've decided not to do anything formally to me. She almost got the squash player thrown off the professional tour. I was going to tell you, but I thought you'd worry. After what those guys were saying tonight, I thought you should know."

I was repulsed, I admit it—repulsed that Ellie'd be so stupidly pro-miscuous. She had to know everyone would find out. But I was also a little disgusted with myself for showing my provincial stripes, because

I didn't care that she had a one-night stand. I cared that she'd done it in a men's club. I was scandalized, but something else was peeking out at me from behind the shock.

"Are you sure she didn't make a pass at you?" I asked, remembering the women at the estate sale, remembering Jeff with his bow tie, Diana from the dinner party.

My husband is the unflappable southern gentleman. I've seen him blush only one other time, when his mother inadvertently misused the word "freak." Now I could see under the streetlights that he was red to the tips of his ears.

"No," he said, leaning his head back against the car seat.

"You're sure." The blush worried me. Protectiveness was ingrained in him. If Ellie, my oldest friend, had thrown herself at him, he'd not want to tell me.

"I'm sure," he said, staring at the ceiling of the car. "I'm embarrassed for her."

After a moment, he leaned forward, started up the car, and we drove through the dark, tree-lined streets.

At home we paid the sitter, and I went in my dressing room and put on my white flannel pajamas with the French blue monogram on the pocket and tiptoed into the nursery. My chest ached with milk, and I stared at my son in the dark, watching his breath rising and falling before I picked him up, waking him—something I never did. I settled in the rocking chair and latched him on, feeling the now-familiar tug. Some feedings I felt like a milch cow or a food port, but that night as I rocked I thought of how hard it is to help someone you love—how they never will let you close enough, or they won't listen to you, or they don't think they need help, or you don't know how to help them. Watching my infant son sleepily feed I thought, Here is someone I can help right now. Here is someone who, for this moment, will let me help.

20

The Baby Shower

Jim and I approached Viola and P. G. about being the baby's godparents, and they were touched but slightly concerned that they were only affianced. A nonmarried couple as godparents, even if they were soon to be married—was that done? Jim and I assured them it would be fine, and I began planning the small baptism.

As I knew she would, Viola took her role very seriously. "I'm throwing you a baby shower," she announced the next day on the phone.

"The baby's already here. I don't need a shower."

"Sure you do. You haven't had one."

"Vi, I have everything I need. It seems ridiculous." Truth was I hated showers, though attending them was better than having one hosted for you. I remembered my two bridal showers with a wince: one where I'd had to enthuse over dish towels and a salad spinner, the other where Jim's sister had given me a complicated set of black French lingerie that I could never bring myself to wear. The presents seemed oddly ill suited for the married life I was planning to embark on. I was going to need kitchen gadgets and underwear fit for a courtesan? Until then I'd had no use for either. Was my personality really going to change that drastically?

"Well, people can also bring a little something for the new women's shelter I'm working on if they want. But people want to give you things, you know, your friends. It's your first baby. You should let me."

There couldn't be any lurking pitfalls—could there? And I adored baby clothes. I found, much to my surprise, that I was starting to look forward to a baby shower.

I should have known Viola would be thorough, consulting me on the menu and the flowers. She'd chosen to have it at the country club her parents belonged to and e-mailed me the guest list three weeks before the party.

"Looks like fun," I said.

"Anyone I missed?" she asked.

"Well, it's up to you, but you might include Ellie Hart."

The phone went silent.

"I mean, you don't have to if you don't have space."

"No, no," Viola said with something I couldn't place in her tone. "I'm happy to send her an invitation."

"It's just that I've known her my whole life. I feel like she should be there. You know she's co-godmother with you and P. G."

Viola became all business. "So Ellie Hart. Anyone else?"

On the day of the shower, I dressed the baby in a smocked jumper and put on a smart blue dress that I'd just recently found I could fit into again.

I drove up to the country club and struggled a bit at the mechanics of getting the baby and all his gear from the car and into the club while the teenage valets watched me with a mix of disgust and amusement. But I didn't care. Though there were still patches of snow on the ground, the air held the warm promise of spring.

Viola had requested a long table for twenty in the conservatory, my favorite room in this club that I'd visited many times as a child. The back of the room showcased three huge gilt aviaries filled with turquoise and yellow budgies. The birds hopped up and down flowering cherry branches, placed there for the luncheon, no doubt, a result of Viola's attention to detail. They made a charming racket. Pale green cymbidium orchids in antique baskets were nestled in the corners of the room.

The guests' Chanel handbags hung daintily on the backs of chairs, and YSL Muses and Hermès Birkins nestled together on the floor. I was seated next to one of the energetic Miller sisters, the blond one, who was telling me about her hiking trip in New Zealand. Viola was seated on my right. My mother had begged off the invitation, stating that the shower should be a chance for me as a new mother to enjoy some time with my friends without the older generation hovering about. I'd been slightly annoyed by this. Did she think we would be talking about boys, sex, and shopping? But she'd spent a small fortune on baby clothes for Henry already, and so I'd kept my thought to myself. Betsy Dorset attended, as ambassador of the elder generation I suppose, diamonds clasped to a baby-pink cashmere sweater. Or perhaps she'd felt bad that Diana couldn't come—some important donors lunch at the museum. And so Betsy was there as representative of them both.

As I walked into the room filled with some of my oldest friends in Cleveland, I realized that as in so many things, my mother had been right. It felt cozy and like a fun time was about to begin with my friends.

Henry was passed around the guests. Genial baby that he was, he smiled and cooed until exhaustion set in. When he started to cry, I nursed him on the chaise in the ladies' room, loaded him into his stroller, and one of the waitstaff volunteered to stroll the halls with him until he fell asleep.

We sat down to lunch, which was one half of a curried chicken salad sandwich and a small green salad dotted with strawberries arranged daintily on a painted bone-china plate so thin you could see through it. As a nursing mom, there was no way this was going to be lunch for me. I wondered, not for the first time, if this small amount of food was really what my friends ate for lunch, or did they, like me, go home to a slice of cold pizza directly from the fridge? I was taking my seat when Ellie rushed into the room, late, clutching her cell phone and car keys in one hand and a slim lizard wallet and sunglasses in the other.

She kissed Viola on the cheek and was waved to the last empty chair, which was across from me. The gleaming black astrakhan around her shoulders looked Goth at this springtime soiree. I noticed the lining had come untacked and the hem was hanging out, frayed and tattered. She stank of smoke, even from across the table, and I saw her signaling the waiter for a glass of white wine. Everyone else was drinking iced tea. She smiled at me and winked, and it was then that she placed a neat stack of folded papers next to her water glass.

It was that day at the luncheon that my doubts about Ellie really started to creep in on me. I couldn't get the picture of Jim's blushing face out of my mind, and her careening appearance at lunch, the pills, and her drinking made her seem out of control. Her skin looked gray, she smelled like a bar, and she gave off the general vibe of someone on their way to a bad end.

Why I didn't embrace her, my childhood friend, and try to get her some help, I don't know. I was scared of her, exasperated, and I'll admit it, disgusted. After lunch, when I saw her coming my way, I avoided her eye, grabbed the arm of Kips Wade, turned my back on her, and headed to the living room to open my baby loot. My life right then was an embarrassment of riches. It's funny but every time I've thought my life grand, I've not failed to get a quick sucker punch in the gut. It's kept me wary and not a little pessimistic. But turning my back on Ellie then is something I'm ashamed of, even now, and something I'll always regret.

21

The News

When Ellie got the invitation to the baby shower her first thought was that Julia Trenor would be there. If she was back in Julia's good graces, if she could show her that there was nothing between her and Gus, if she could show her that Diana was spreading gossip and lies with her own agenda, maybe then Ellie could start out yet again.

Or maybe Diana would be there, though the prospect of a confrontation with her was daunting.

Ellie'd slept later than intended that morning and awoke with only a half hour to get over to the country club. Her head buzzed as if the sun outside was too bright. She decided to wear her chicest outfit—all black—knowing the sea of pastels and business gray that would be there in anticipation of spring. "Let them hate, so long as they appreciate" was her twisting of the Latin proverb. She was heading through her mother's tiny yellow kitchen. She hadn't been able to actually buy a condo in Murray Hill after her night with Gus in his former mistress's condo. She'd realized then that she'd have to cut all ties to him.

Unfortunately he still had control over the majority of her money. Her hand shook as she rifled a pile of junk mail looking for her keys. It wouldn't do to be nervous today. It wouldn't help if she looked at all frightened, and so she decided she needed a quick nip to shore her up. She poured two fingers of vodka in the bottom of a dirty coffee cup and downed it in one gulp, feeling it burn all the way down. A small drink before something this nerve-wracking—it's not like she did it often.

She was glad of the drink and her cigarette during the drive because when she walked into that luncheon room, her knees buckled ever so slightly. She caught herself and made for Betsy Dorset to kiss her cheek, but the woman waved her off to Viola, who shook her hand—that was strange—and ushered her to her chair. She scanned the room, noting Diana wasn't there, which made her feel a little relieved actually. Once seated, Ellie signaled for a glass of wine, noticing only too late that she was the only one drinking at the table.

But never mind. She arranged herself, her phone, her keys, and next to her water glass the trim stack of folded papers, a pristine packet of insurance. She'd printed out Diana's texts to Selden, complete with nude photo. She'd known they'd come in handy.

Scanning the table, she noted that Julia wasn't there either.

But when Julia arrived, Ellie would gently let her know just what a nightmare her friend Diana was, cheating on her husband and chasing so desperately after Selden. That was why she was spreading lies about Ellie. Julia wouldn't believe her. Hence the evidence—black and white, with the red bra, of course. Julia, who knew what it felt like to have a cheating husband, would not be pleased.

Barring that, Ellie thought, looking around, she might show them to Betsy Dorset, Diana's mother-in-law. That would require a deft touch, but Ellie could do it. It wouldn't be a bad thing to have Betsy Dorset in your debt. In fact it could be a marvelous thing. Ellie could only imagine the lengths to which Betsy Dorset would go to keep her son from heartache and scandal. A savvy sixty-year-old like Betsy would be familiar with enough technology to know the dangers of YouTube and Facebook in such a situation. Perhaps she'd even make Ellie chair of the next benefit she had control over. Ellie'd be back in

Cleveland's good graces—with a new platform from which she could search for love again. It'd be a difficult maneuver though. Betsy Dorset was no slouch.

But Julia still hadn't arrived. It was strange as this was Julia's natural habitat, just as the Antarctic is the natural habitat of the polar bear. Ellie turned to the Miller sister who was sitting next to her, the duller one who copied everything her energetic sister did. Conversation with her was excruciating no matter how hard one tried, and so Ellie thought she'd at least get some information.

"Isn't Julia coming?" Ellie asked.

Her end of the table fell silent.

The Miller next to her shrugged. "She should be here. I don't know where she is." There was a forced, false note in her voice, as if she were performing.

Ellie felt the tension in the silence that followed and then the low chirping of the ladies started mingling with the chirping of the budgies in their cages.

"I was shocked," someone said.

"He wiped out the McMasters. Did you know he had their money?"

"No one's seen Julia in days. They said they went to Buenos Aires, but someone saw them in New York at a midtown law office."

"I heard there'll be more indictments."

Ellie looked at the Miller sister with a frown. "What's going on?"

"Have you been living under a rock? It's all over the Internet and the front page of the paper," she said. "Gus Trenor's been indicted for securities fraud."

"No, that's not it," her dining companion on the other side said. "It's plain old fraud. It was like a Ponzi scheme or something."

"It's complicated. Apparently, people actually entrusted money to him. I always thought he just invested his own," said someone else.

"He lost it all. Spent it all. Or I should say Julia spent it."

"I heard she's up in Ellicottville. No one can get her on the phone. Not even Diana . . ."

"Shameless too. He wiped out a pension fund for one of the old steel companies."

Ellie took another sip of wine. Her first thought, the very first, was that her money was gone. After the night at the condo she didn't know how she was going to get her divorce settlement back from Gus without Julia causing more scandal. Now there might not be anything to get back.

But taking the edge off her despair at her money being lost was schadenfreude at Julia's downfall. Julia was as finished in Cleveland and as powerless as if she'd actually died. Of all the things you could do, you did not steal people's money. Making up to Julia didn't matter anymore and likely wouldn't help Ellie's situation. There was literally no coming back to Cleveland at all for Julia. Maybe she'd stay in Elli-cottville. Ellie suppressed a smile.

But her schadenfreude didn't help the problem of her money. She'd lost her job, and now she'd lost her divorce settlement. Her brain couldn't really grasp the certainty of it. Surely Gus would be made to pay her back by the courts or something. She could stay at her mother's, sure. But her mother didn't have any money to loan her beyond that. And really it was beyond pathetic, hard to even admit to herself, let alone someone chattering away at her at a cocktail party, that she was still living in her mother's house, with no security, no job, and no prospects—at her age.

When the ladies all got up to go into the other room and watch the present-opening, Ellie made for the refuge of the chintz-covered la-dies' room. The thought of the oohs and aahs over presents of smock-ing and ribbon was too much for her to take—at her age.

She was washing her hands when a flush announced the appear-ance of Betsy Dorset. She nodded at Ellie with a smile that didn't reach her eyes. "Ellie," she said coolly.

Ellie smiled back, saying nothing. She'd piled her things—her wal-let, her keys, her phone, her papers—on the marble in between the sinks, now wet with water and dripping soap.

"That's getting wet," Betsy said, nodding to the jumble with a touch of disdain. "You'll ruin it all."

There was something in Betsy's voice, thought Ellie. A voice that said that Betsy knew so much more than Ellie, that she knew so much *better,* that Ellie couldn't take care of things, that Ellie was hopeless, that she couldn't take care of herself.

Ellie dried her hands, picking up her things from the mishmashed pile. On the bottom, the edges of the papers were gray with water. Ellie decided to leave them. Perhaps it's time for Betsy Dorset to understand she doesn't know better, Ellie thought. She doesn't know at all, and there are things even she can't take care of. It was a perfect maneuver.

Ellie walked briskly then, without turning around, out of the ladies' room, past the gilt birdhouses, past the men's bar, past the waitress pushing Henry in his stroller, and out into the parking lot. She thought she heard Betsy calling her back, telling her she'd forgotten something, that she'd left something behind.

22

The Country Party

The first true weekend of spring Jim and I received an invitation to a barbecue at Cinco Van Alstyne's house in the country east of town. An offering of friendship, I thought, along with the flowers perhaps, after our talk at the museum.

During the ride to the country the baby slept soundly in his car seat amid the arsenal of toys, stroller, diaper bag, and all the other accoutrements of an infant. Jim kissed my hand, and we listened to the college radio station, the sunroof open, feeling younger than the new parents we were.

"You look nice," Jim said, eyeing my white skirt and eyelet shirt.

"You sound surprised."

"Haven't seen you in a skirt in a while," he said, something knowing right behind the sugar in his drawl.

The thing was, I'd been thinking about Cinco Van Alstyne when I'd gotten dressed. For some reason, my new-mother slovenly kit wouldn't do for seeing him.

We pulled up at the Van Alstyne estate, which must have been fashionable in its day—a 1920s faux-Cotswolds-style house with beige stucco, leaded glass windows, dark brown shutters, and a pitched roof. It was immense, I guessed at least fifteen thousand square feet, surrounded by a thousand acres of pasture now overgrown with grapevines and weed trees.

But as we drove up a driveway nearly disintegrating with weeds, I could see the stucco house was chipped and had been mended poorly with gray gashes of cement. Some leaded windows were cracked, and the shutters were peeling.

Jim whistled low. "Decomposing Tara ain't got nothin' on this."

"Didn't southerners practically invent the whole notion of shabby chic?"

"This here's a little more like shitty chic," Jim said, smiling. "Darlin'."

We parked in a soggy snowmelt field next to Detroit steel and German luxury metal that crushed the sprouting grass, dotted with newly emerging clover and rue.

He unloaded the baby. I took the diaper bag. "Leave the other stuff," he said. "I'll come get it if we need it."

"You got to love these white elephants," he said as we walked across the muddy field, the house looming in front of us. "Bleed you dry."

"Be nice," I said.

We walked into the dank front hall of the house. A cape buffalo head hung on the wall, its bullet-black eyes reflecting us, a moth-eaten bearskin rug on the floor.

Cinco smiled and came forward wearing seersucker trousers and a white shirt frayed at the cuffs and collar. His clothes had changed little since we were young, I now realized.

He smiled and kissed my cheek, shook Jim's hand, and made a great fuss over the baby. Looking over the guests, I noted that his wife, Corrine, was the only one in all black and silver chunky jewelry amid the sea of white, Lilly Pulitzer, and pearls that comprises most Clevelanders' warm-weather wear. Cinco's parents were there, as were some of their friends. Good old Cinco, I thought, always doing his duty.

"Babies agree with you," he said.

"I'm exhausted."

"Don't look it."

"That's because I'm the night nurse," Jim chimed in.

I rolled my eyes. "He lacks the proper equipment for nighttime duty."

Jim took Henry from me, put a floppy hat on the little guy's head, and went through the house out into the overgrown gardens where more guests mingled. Watching my husband in his jeans that hung loosely off his hips, with his feet in sandals firmly planted on the ground and the baby securely in his arms, I felt a moment of happiness.

"You're lucky, you know." Cinco nodded toward Jim and took a sip of his gin and tonic.

"Tell me about it."

"Not everyone gets the happy marriage."

I cocked my head at him, raising an eyebrow. "Trouble in paradise?"

He snorted. "Even I don't think this place is paradise, and I've wanted to live here my whole life."

I doubted him. This surely was *his* paradise. I wondered why he resisted admitting it.

He pecked my cheek. "Can't tell you how flattered I am about the name. Now all he needs is the right nickname."

"We didn't name him after you." I laughed.

"I know. I'm just flattered that I'm not such a disaster that you thought 'There's no way I can name a child Henry, it will remind me of that awful Cinco Van Alstyne.'"

"No one thinks of you as a Henry."

"Well, it's flattering nonetheless. It also confirms . . ."

"What?"

"That you're over me." He was joking with me, but his eyes held mine. "Can't give a child a name that will remind you of the love of your life." He grinned at me.

"We were never that way."

"No." He sighed. "I see that now. But Corrine was kind of upset."

I focused on his wife standing on the threshold of the French doors. She held a platter of vegetables in one hand; the other gestured wildly to Ellie, who stood just inside the doors.

I hadn't seen Ellie since the shower. Even from this far away her clothes looked a wrinkled mess, like she'd been on a weeklong bender.

"She shouldn't be," I said. "For all the reasons you just gave me."

"So I told her, but she's jealous of you."

I rolled my eyes. "Please. Maybe she likes to get upset about stuff like that? Adds spice—yes?"

He nodded. "There's plenty of spice."

I smiled. "Spice is a good thing."

He smiled at me, and I felt such affection for him then. I felt a shift between us. An easing back into comfort based on shared history, recent understanding, and the hope of being friends.

Ellie saw me and waved. She and Cinco's wife made their way inside the living room to me.

Corrine hugged me. "Where's little Henry?"

I waved out toward the gardens. "With Jim."

"We were just talking about Gus Trenor," Ellie said.

"It's all anyone's talking about out there," Corrine said in a whisper.

Ellie rolled her eyes. "Clevelanders and their money . . ."

"Don't hate. Anyone and their money," Cinco said. He took his wife's arm, and they set off on their hosting duties.

"So," Ellie said, turning to me. "Sorry I had to leave your shower early. I wasn't feeling well."

"That's okay," I said. Truth be told I hadn't noticed that she was missing. I tried to remember what she gave me so I could thank her now, but I couldn't.

She nodded. We were silent. The volume of the party rose around us.

"Ells," I said. "The night of the squash tournament." I needed to ask her about Jim. I don't know what I expected her to say—"Yes, I made a move on your husband"?—but she interrupted.

"Not you too."

"What do you mean?"

"So I slept with a squash player, so what?"

"Keep your voice down."

"The fuck?" she said, and turned toward the party. "I sleep with men," she announced loudly to all. "Imagine that." A man and woman getting drinks next to us smiled and quickly walked off.

She took a glass and sloshed a good inch and a half of vodka in the bottom. This alarmed me. She was already quite drunk.

I took hold of her arm and directed her into the first room we came to. Gun racks behind glass cases lined the walls, dark Turkey rugs on the floor, faded damask covering the Victorian love seat and chairs, an old-fashioned stick-and-handle telephone attached to the wall. I wondered in passing if it worked.

"Ells, what are you doing?"

"What are you doing?" she said right back. "Clevelander to your core, aren't you?" Heavy curtains were drawn against the bright spring day. But in a slant of sunlight, I saw a little pouf of dust rise as Ellie sat down in a low club chair.

"El—"

"You really give a shit that I slept with some squash player?" She set her drink down and took a crumpled pack of cigarettes out of her pocket and lit one with her silver lighter.

"I know I don't give a damn," I said, even though I actually did. "But people—"

"I am so sick of people." She slurred her S's ever so slightly, leaning back in the chair and kicking her feet over the arm. "I don't know what I was thinking coming back here."

A heavy lock of dark blond hair hung in her face, and I saw the tired wrinkles I'd first seen when I'd visited her at work.

She inhaled on her smoke. We were both silent. I was racking my brain trying to think of something to say.

"Have you noticed," she asked without looking at me, "that Cinco seems a little unhappy?"

At Cinco's name I focused in on her eyes. My breathing got quicker. "You mean his wife does? I saw you two talking," I said, hoping she didn't catch the panicky edge in my voice.

"Well, she is unhappy. She hates it out here. Can't get pregnant. Hates the country. His family's all over them." She picked up a little porcelain frog on the table next to her and hefted it in her hand. "Makes you think he would have been happier if he'd chosen the right person. Someone who could make a go of all this." Here she gestured around the room with the frog. "Instead of constantly bitching about it. Someone who enjoys house renovations, vegetable gardening."

"That's not you," I said firmly, my mind whirring. Ellie and Cinco, it made me feel sick. Cinco was mine, I thought. And then I realized he wasn't actually. He was Corrine's.

She raised an eyebrow. "But it could be."

"You don't want Cinco Van Alstyne." I felt anger at the thought of Ellie going after him—not because I felt my stomach drop at the mere thought of it. No, my instinct was one of protection. I didn't want Ellie hurting him.

"Just because you didn't want him . . . ," she said.

I rolled my eyes. "Cinco and I were never like that."

"Once when he was visiting in New York it seemed like he wanted it to be exactly like that."

Blood rushed in my ears, to my face.

"Look at this place," Ellie said, gesturing around with her cigarette. "And he was always sweet, a guy who'd take care of you. Plus, from what I gather, he likes sex—probably is a little twisted. Those perfectly mannered ones usually are."

"You don't need someone to take care of you."

She set the frog back on the table and her feet back on the floor.

I didn't want her to leave the room. I thought she might go out there and begin her campaign for Cinco right away. So I started a pep talk. "You could go back to New York."

She hesitated. I realized what I'd just said. I was suggesting she leave town. And I understood in that moment how relieved I'd feel if she did go.

"I told you, no," she said evenly.

"L.A.?"

"I don't know anyone in L.A."

"It's becoming a fashion capital."

"It's not. Besides, there are no husbands out there. All the women are young, blond, tanned . . . silicone."

"I'm talking about a job. Your career."

"I've tried. I'm not good at that."

"You haven't tried."

She shrugged.

"You're letting your life be defined by men," I finally said, desperate that she wake up, pay attention, and stop wallowing.

Smoke blew out of her nose in an angry little snort. "Look who's talking."

"What?"

"You're talking all this 'take care of yourself' crap to me. But what are you doing? Having Jim's children. Now you're a stay-at-home mom. Now you're living in service to a man and a little boy. Now you're defined by men."

I felt like I'd been slapped. "Are you drunk?" I asked, and then leaned in closer. "Or stoned?"

Ellie put her smoke out in her vodka and got up out of the chair. She didn't look at me as she straightened her crumpled clothes and walked to the door. She turned when she reached the threshold.

"Careful what you say. Some things can't be unsaid." She walked out.

I was pissed. So hypocritical given what she'd just said to me. She was the closest thing I had to a sister in Cleveland, like family, but in that moment I never wanted to speak to her again. I sank down in the chair Ellie'd been sitting in, gulping air.

When my heart calmed, I went into the front hall, but no one was there. When I walked out onto the grass, I saw Jim with an arm around Ellie, her tear-streaked face on his shirt.

I walked forward and when she saw me she broke free of his arms, turned her back, and walked toward the cars in the field.

"El," he called after her.

"Where's Henry?" I immediately asked Jim.

He pointed to the side of the house, where Cinco held my little boy.

"Go catch her," Jim said, still watching as Ellie walked in between the cars in the upper field. "She's really upset."

"I'm not catching her. You wouldn't believe what she said to me just now."

"She's in trouble." He gave a little push on the small of my back.

"Why do you suddenly care so much? You didn't want her to be godmother."

"Doesn't mean I want to see her go down the tubes like this."

"She's not going down the tubes." I turned to walk toward Cinco. "I'm getting the baby, and then I want to go."

He turned to me then. "You're being callous. She clearly needs help."

"I'm being callous?"

"She's your oldest friend."

"I've known her forever—that's different."

"She's not your friend? Three weeks ago you wanted her to be Henry's godmother."

I shrugged.

I looked in his eyes then. There was genuine pain. And as much as I loved my husband, as much as I thought he was kind, this sort of compassion was not reflexive for him.

"Jim," I said.

"Go get the baby."

"What happened that night at the club?"

"I already told you."

"What happened between you and her?"

"Nothing, I told you."

I'd already asked him if she'd made a pass at him and he'd said no. It'd be insulting to ask again. What was I saying anyway? That I didn't trust my husband?

"She did something . . ." I started.

"No."

"She does things, I know," I said.

He looked at me.

"Something happened," I said again.

He looked away off in the field, but she was out of sight now. "She kissed me," he said.

I was conscious of the sound of my breath and the sun beating down on the top of my head, heating my hair. My vision got narrow and slowed down.

"She kissed you," I said.

"Yes."

"Did you kiss her back?"

He looked at the sky. "Yes." Even as it killed me to hear him say it, I felt relief and an odd gratitude that he was being honest with me mixed with the sick feeling that he'd kept this a secret from me for months.

"Are you in love with her?" I asked, trying to keep the panic out of my voice.

"Don't be ridiculous." He looked at me then, a little angry. "We were drunk. It was nothing. She wound up sleeping with that squash player that night, remember?"

It was on the tip of my tongue to say, "And if she hadn't?" But of all things, Ellie's warning came back to me about being careful.

"You weren't going to tell me?"

"Because it doesn't matter."

It was then that Cinco reached us after making his way around the side of his house with my crying son in his arms.

"He needs a change, I think," Cinco said, unloading Henry into my arms. "Ummm, just tell me where the diapers are," he said, trying to cover, realizing he'd interrupted something tense.

"I'll get his stuff," Jim said, and walked off toward the house to fetch the baby's bag.

"You okay?" Cinco asked, looking at me.

I nuzzled Henry into my neck, which quieted him. I felt like I'd been punched in the throat, like I might throw up right there. "No, I don't think I am." Tears came to my eyes as I sniffed and blinked.

Cinco cocked his head, looking at me. "Sometimes it's an adjustment, you know. Babies and stuff." He waved a hand at us. "So I hear."

I looked at him over the baby's head. He thought I was upset because of some postpartum adjustment period. "Jim kissed Ellie," I said. It was out before I considered what I was doing. I needed to say it out loud. In retrospect Cinco was the perfect person to tell—he wouldn't judge Jim, and he wouldn't want to see me hurt. Looking back, I suppose that was the moment when we left the past, the moment when he became my friend.

His eyes got wide for a second and then were covered, almost instantly, by his innate calm. "Yeah," he said.

"You knew about this?" Tears slipped down my face then, and I quickly wiped them away.

"No," he said, backing up a step at my tone. "It's just now that you said it, I can see it."

"Can see Jim kissing Ellie?" I gulped air, trying to get control of myself. I didn't want to be seen crying at Cinco's party.

"Can see Ellie kissing Jim," he said resolutely.

My first impulse was to blame myself. I stood there silently berating myself. I'd ignored Jim, it's true, in the last months of my pregnancy and after the baby was born. What did I expect?

"What?" Cinco said, eyebrows raising as he watched me silently implode. "You've got to know she's capable of something like this."

"I've been friends with her a long time."

"Me too," he said. "That's Ellie. It's what she does. Frankly when I saw them together at the club, I thought you were a little naïve for allowing it."

"I don't allow things with Jim. That's not how we work."

"Of course you could have stopped it. Then he told me you encouraged it. Approved."

"I thought it made me look generous."

He raised an eyebrow at me. "She's jealous of you."

"Ellie? She doesn't want this." I jostled the baby. "She never has." I frowned.

"She doesn't want what you have," he said. "But *you* want what you have. You're happy." Here he paused. "She wants that." Upset though I was, I noted Cinco's clear reading of Ellie and her intentions. I'd never have to worry about her messing with him.

"She'd never be happy with Jim."

Cinco shook his head. "And from what I've seen, I don't think Jim would be happy without you."

Jim returned with the diaper bag and took Henry from me, checking my face. "I'll change him in the back of the car, and then I want to go." He looked at Cinco. "Thanks for having us," he said, extending a hand around the baby.

Cinco shook his hand. "Anytime. Come back and we'll put him on the rope swing when he's big enough."

"I'll be there in a minute," I said.

"He's a good guy," Cinco said, watching Jim's back as he walked up the field. "Go easy on him. No conditions—remember?"

"You convinced me I was wrong about that. Now you get to say 'I told you so.'"

"Wouldn't." He snorted. "Maybe you were the one who was right about conditions. Maybe all my choices were made for me a long time ago. Except one." His voice trailed off, and we turned to see his wife coming toward us—a smile on her face. He took her hand when she got to us. As always, she clung to him, silent and contained. But I saw something different this time. I saw that Cinco allowed this, encouraged it, and most of all that he'd chosen it. Whatever it looked like to me, Cinco Van Alstyne had known exactly what he was doing when he'd chosen his wife.

We downshifted then into all the polite good-byes we'd practiced at cotillions. Corrine ignored my tear-streaked face. They walked partway up the field with me to where Jim had already strapped Henry in the car seat and was waiting with the engine running.

· 23 ·

The Maserati

As she was walking through the wet field, wiping her eyes, Ellie saw Randy Leforte locking his Maserati and walking around it, heading to the party. Gone was the sharp tailoring, the flashy watch. He was wearing Nantucket Reds, new with a sharp crease; a blindingly white broadcloth shirt; and a needlepoint belt, no doubt bought online and made in China.

"Randy," she called, sniffing and hoping her eyes weren't too red.

He looked up with a smile on his face that became fixed once he saw who was calling him.

"Ellie," he said formally as she got closer. "How are you?"

"Will you do me a favor?" she asked.

Randy looked taken aback. "I thought you didn't want my favors."

"Take me for a ride," she said. "Right now."

"I just got here."

"Please," she said. "Not long. The party will still be here when you get back."

Leforte watched her for a moment and then walked around and unlocked the passenger side of his car. "Where to?"

"Anywhere. I don't care," she said, lowering herself into the curvy passenger seat.

He started up the heavy engine, and they bumped across the soggy field to the gravel farm lane. Here was ease, she thought. She wasn't troubled by the car's excesses—the outrageous curves and shiny steel.

She felt bad for kissing Jim. But being enfolded in luxury softened her self-criticism. A hug, a kiss on the cheek, a kiss on the mouth—it was still in the realm of sociability. Though she'd admit there'd been nothing polite about those kisses. What a flaming mess it would have been had things gone farther. But they hadn't. When she'd come out of the house just now, Jim had been there and seen the tears in her eyes and given her a hug. It was all very sweet, very chaste, very friendly. At the end of the lane, Leforte turned onto a paved two-lane country road and let the car go, tires squealing. Ellie leaned back and smiled. "Nice," she said.

"Seemed like you could use it," he said with his foot on the gas. The car rocketed forward.

"I suppose." Ellie dug around in one of her pockets for her crumpled pack of cigarettes.

"Please," Leforte said, knowing what she was looking for. "The leather."

"Smoke and leather go together."

"No." He shook his head. "It just smells stale."

She got a cigarette out anyway and, unable to locate her lighter, she reached for the car lighter and found it empty.

Leforte just shook his head.

"So how've you been?" Ellie asked, putting the smoke back in the pack and the pack in his door well.

He eyed her. "You're asking me how've I been?"

She nodded.

"Fine," he said. "Good. I've been doing a lot of work for the art museum recently."

"Work?"

"Volunteering. Well, fund-raising actually. It's part of getting the foundation up and running."

Ellie was impressed, though she shouldn't have been surprised. Leforte didn't have the money he had because he was stupid. The art museum was a shrewd move. You couldn't get more respectable than that in Cleveland, with a board full of heavy hitters with which to rub elbows.

She'd always suspected Leforte might be malleable, certainly a quick study. Already he was modifying himself, making himself more acceptable, and there wasn't even a wife pulling the strings. Perhaps it was all that appealing ambition.

"So you found someone to fill that position and get the foundation up and running?" Ellie asked, leaning back farther in the seat and watching the fields, hay and barley just sprouting, edged by tulip trees in bud.

"Not really," Leforte said. "I'm actually doing it all myself. It's a huge job though." He sped up. Ellie could tell he was embarrassed.

Ellie just nodded. It confirmed what she had been thinking. Leforte created that make-work foundation job to keep her in his pocket. It confirmed she'd been right to turn it down.

"The work's important," he said, as if reading her mind. "Art is. I'm a big fan."

Ellie smiled and was about to remark on his previous support of the orchestra when she thought better of making a dig at him. She realized then that there were worse things than the Randy Lefortes of the world. If she were with him, in a few years no one would even remember those billboards with his face on them.

"You know," she said sleepily, "you once asked me something."

He raised an eyebrow but kept his eyes on the road. Silence enveloped the car, and she realized that he was not going to make this easy for her.

"About us," she continued, but he was still quiet. "Being together." Was it just her or did she see his jaw tighten?

He was silent still. The car maintained a steady speed. He was listening to her flail.

"And it caught me off guard at the time and I've been thinking about it a lot—"

"Have you?" he cut her off.

"Course," she said.

He'd slowed the car now. "You have to know some things have changed," he said.

"How so?" she asked.

"Or should I say *he's* changed. Right? That's why you're talking about this with me?"

Ellie said nothing.

Leforte continued. "I try not to believe the stories about you. But I saw you with Selden that night at the museum. And now he's left. It's clear to me how you felt about him."

In that one moment Ellie could have kissed Leforte. It was strange, she knew, but she was grateful that someone else had witnessed what she felt. In recent days she'd started to think everyone thought her a cipher.

"I saw you two together, and it looked like it was all done to me. And then the rumor mill cranked up." Here he smiled at her and eased the car over to the side of the road. "I try not to listen, whether or not I believe what Diana Dorset says." He pulled over in a shady spot at the base of a hill underneath a buckeye tree that hadn't yet bloomed and next to a small creek rushing with spring rain runoff.

"I can't marry you now. You have to understand that. Last year I thought you could do better than me, but I made my play anyway. This year—"

"You think you can," she said, stopping him.

"Don't be like that." He moved toward her as if to kiss her.

She backed up. "What are you doing?"

"I thought you wanted a little more of what you've already had."

"I wanted to pick up where we left off."

"Impossible," he said, leaning back. "Unless . . ."

"Unless what?"

"You use what you have."

She leaned in close to him again, thinking he meant using her physical assets—that he wanted to be seduced. She was going to kiss him, but this time he was the one who backed off. "No," he said. "Diana's texts."

Ellie's heart quickened. "How do you know about that?"

"Betsy told me."

Ellie almost laughed at Leforte's casual reference to Betsy Dorset, like they were buddies, after her public sniping at him at the orchestra those months ago.

"She and I have become quite close since I've been shelling out for the museum," he said. "She came to see me, wanting to hire me to advise her, though libel and defamation aren't really my area."

Ellie furrowed her brow at him.

"Apparently you left copies of a set of texts between her daughter-in-law and William Selden at some luncheon, some baby shower? She asked me to talk to you."

Ellie's heart sped. That Betsy had been exploring legal options frightened the hell out of her. Maybe she'd been too hasty letting Betsy know about the texts.

"I told her it's not my area of expertise. But she wanted advice on how to stop you from making this public, if she could threaten you legally."

Ellie's stomach flipped.

"Don't worry. There's not much she can do as long as the texts are real. Though I have to say it's a little shady of Selden to be sharing them with you. What kind of man does that?"

"He didn't share them," Ellie said, her mouth suddenly dry. "I kind of found them and forwarded them to myself and made copies."

It was Leforte's turn to raise an eyebrow. "So you sort of stole them."

"It's not like I stole his phone. He left it with me." She was berating herself now for her stupidity snooping in Selden's phone, forwarding the texts, in trying to—trying to what, actually, blackmail Betsy Dorset with them? Her head swam in the heat of the car. Leforte had turned off the air when he pulled over. That wasn't who she was. She didn't blackmail people—especially over something as trivial and petty as her standing in Cleveland.

"Makes the law a little trickier, but in the end I don't think it changes your situation. If those texts make the rounds on Facebook or whatever, both Diana and Selden will look awful, regardless of how they came to be in your possession. Betsy doesn't want that."

Ellie smirked. "No."

Leforte continued. "It was a fascinating little psychological study, I have to say. Betsy started out concerned for her daughter-in-law—was she unhappy in her marriage? What had driven her to do this? But as we talked it became clear to me that her only real concern was the news being made public and her son being made the subject of gossip. Between you and me, I don't think she cares a bit for her daughter-in-law."

Ellie smirked again. "No."

"She's afraid of you, though. She doesn't know what you're going to do . . ." His voice trailed off.

"I'm not going to do anything."

"No?" Leforte was watching her intently. "Why not? Betsy certainly could smooth things out for you. She could make Diana do the same."

"Because I'm not."

"Because it's him," Leforte said. "Who knew a loser like William Selden would be so irresistible to women?"

"He's not a loser," Ellie said.

Leforte raised an eyebrow.

"I hear you're representing Gus Trenor," Ellie said, trying to change the subject away from the texts. Having Leforte advising Betsy Dorset made her nervous, like they were a team or something.

Leforte shook his head sadly. "Absolutely not."

"Why not? Biggest case of the year. Getting him off would be a coup. And I thought Gus was your friend." Ellie remembered Gus as one of Leforte's earliest champions. Though the reason for Gus's friendship wasn't mere altruism; perhaps he'd known he'd need Leforte's skills in this way.

"I find I'm starting to like Cleveland more and more." He sighed and looked toward her.

"I thought you were ready for New York."

"It's growing on me here. Cinco Van Alstyne invited me out to fish in the river behind the house last week. It made me start thinking I could be comfortable here."

Ellie knew what he was saying. With certain choices he could guarantee his position, securely ensconced in a cozy world where everyone welcomed him, where the board of the museum were his best friends, where Betsy Dorset, who'd previously ribbed him, was indebted to him. He knew it'd be a mistake to represent Gus; everyone would hate him for it if he won, and he'd be ruined professionally if he lost. But more importantly, having Ellie by his side as his wife could make things infinitely easier for him.

"But I can't marry a woman who's in love with another man." Leforte had been talking for a while and Ellie finally focused in. It was as if he'd been reading her mind.

"I'm not."

"You are. There's no other explanation for why you won't use those texts to your advantage."

"For one, it won't work."

"Well, it's true that they won't really be scared of you with just the texts unless you have something behind you." He leaned close to her across the car's console. "Someone with means behind him would scare the shit out of the Dorsets. Holding the evidence of the affair and not making a stink about it—couple that with announcing our engagement, and they'd be groveling to be in your good graces. But one without the other, I'm not sure they'd succumb so easily. Without the money, it's too easy for them to undermine you by spreading gossip to discredit you. Without the texts, perhaps they wouldn't feel so welcoming just on the basis of my fortune. But combine the two . . ." He blew out a breath. "I'm giving away money all around town."

"How much did you have to give the museum?" Ellie asked, knowing her question was sharp, but she hated where Leforte was going with all this.

Leforte looked at her, holding her eye for a beat. "Less than I'd have to give you to get what I want."

Ellie was silent, stung.

He continued. "It's one thing to get everyone back in line. But you have to keep them there. And a good-looking woman like you, it's only going to get worse if you don't marry. There'll only be more wives who don't want you taking their husbands to squash tournaments." He rolled his eyes. "I told you, I listen to the gossip, but I don't believe it all."

Leforte's view of her situation was straightforward, she had to admit that, and his solution seemed harmless—a private understanding between everyone involved, no different than a transfer of property or revising a boundary line.

"Why do you want to do all this?" she asked.

"Because I feel comfortable with you. You're like me. And you'd be able to smooth things for me in a way I can't, just like I can smooth things for you in a way you can't." He leaned across her to the glove box and opened it, pulling out a small stack of papers. He handed them to her. "Think about it."

"She gave them to you?"

"I told her I'd take care of it. I think she wants to pretend she's never seen them. Though I wouldn't be surprised if copies are stashed away in a Dorset safety-deposit box downtown in case there's ever a divorce. Really she should be thanking you."

Ellie shifted away from him then, thinking back to their afternoon at the Ritz. When she had some distance from him, it sounded like a simple enough thing to marry an attractive, rich man she didn't love. Perhaps he was right and they were two sides of the same coin. But sitting in the car with him, with the actual proposal in her lap, she couldn't imagine spending her life with this man and his starkly transactional view of the world. What else would be negotiated, bargained for—a man capable of blackmailing anyone, even her.

"But it won't work if you love someone else. I mean, you would grow to love me, but not if you're still pining for him," he was saying, and he stopped and looked at her. In that moment he must have known how unlikely his suit was. "Frankly I'll be damned if I see where he ever protected you or took care of you the way I'm offering to."

"I think I'm ready for you to take me back now," Ellie said, cutting off his rising anger.

Leforte started up the car and revved the engine.

They drove back in silence, the drive back much shorter as Leforte sped.

As the landscape blurred by, Ellie wondered at the state of Randall Leforte's heart. Could this really be what he was looking for? A social pawn and companion in getting ahead, a partner for regular sex, as well as a civilizing influence? She wondered if his heart had ever been moved. After this afternoon she doubted that was even possible.

When they arrived back in the Van Alstynes' field, Leforte dropped her at her car. The low buzz of conversations from the party drifted over the fields to them.

"Thanks," she said.

He dismissed her with a curt nod and revved the engine while he pulled forward, parked, got out, and headed for the party without looking back at her.

Ellie watched him walk into the dark front hall of the Van Alstyne house. Then she found her little red car in the field. It was time to drive home again, alone. She looked forward to the sleeping pill she'd take when she got there. Looked forward to those few woozy moments before she slipped under and everything went black.

· 24 ·

The Shaker Lakes

In the days after Cinco's party, I'd taken to bundling the baby in the stroller and taking long aimless walks around the Shaker Lakes for whole afternoons at a time, my head in a fog.

I know a double standard when I see one. And I never thought I'd be a woman scorned, but ask a woman with a cheating husband who she blames and nine times out of ten she blames the other woman, not the man. The instinct to give the man you love a pass is strong. Blame the man and everything you believed—your vows, your love, your life—is cast in doubt. It's easier to blame the other woman, whose motivations lie outside your relationship. I'd always thought it was so antifeminist, so retro, so woman hating. But now I understood why the other woman took the rap: because you still loved the man. How much more do you want to forgive him than her, a stranger?

But Ellie wasn't a stranger to me. She was one of my oldest friends. That she'd done this to me made it hurt more. How could she? I kept running through all the times she'd complimented Jim on how thoughtful he was, how kind; she'd admitted to checking out his ass.

How could I not have seen this coming? I berated myself for suggesting he take her to the club.

I'd believed Jim when he said that it had only been a kiss and nothing more. Maybe I was gullible, but he seemed sincere when he assured me. I believed that if something more had happened I would have felt it, like the aftershocks of a seismic quake shaking our marriage. I'd felt that kiss, and that's why I dragged the truth out of him.

And finally there was the question of what I was going to do. I mean, what would you do? Throw your husband out? For kissing someone? Forget the whole thing and put it behind you? Could you really? And here I was with a tiny baby. I didn't have the strength to storm out over a kiss right then. But would I ever trust him again?

What about Ellie? There was no question of her being the baby's godmother now.

So I wandered around the lakes each day. Luckily Henry loved his stroller and took long naps while I walked and tried to leave self-pity and disillusionment behind me. Migrating birds were coming up from the South and stopping in the lakes on their way to Canada.

I was in my fog one day when I saw Viola Trenor jogging toward me in her sensible exercise wear. She was covering ground fast, running flat-out really. It wasn't until she was almost in front of me that she saw me, and I could hear loud music coming from her earbuds—thrash metal. She stopped and touched her little MP3 player, turning it off.

"Don't let me stop you," I said. "You were motoring."

She smiled, trying to catch her breath. "P. G. says I'll be in the best shape of my life if I keep this up."

I was about to ask her if she was getting ready for the wedding, trying to look her best, but I bit back the words. Mere vanity would never make Viola run like that.

"How've you been?"

She shrugged. "Distracted. Thanks for the flowers."

I'd sent her a posy of violets after the shower as a thank-you. "Of course. You're amazing to have done that with the wedding planning and everything else going on . . ." I trailed off, trying to give her a way around the painful topic of her brother.

"I'm distracted with Gus." Typical Viola; she shied away from nothing. "He's been living up in Ellicottville, but the court made him come back. He can't leave the state. I've been staying with him at the house in town. He begged me because Julia's still up in New York, and he can't stand to be alone."

"I'm sorry."

She shrugged. I wondered how hard this was for someone as principled as Viola. She loved her brother, sure. But if he was guilty, and certainly in the papers and the court of public opinion he was, could she set scruple aside for him? I'd thought she would be unyielding, but it made me like her even more that she seemed to make an exception for her brother.

"How's P. G.?" I asked, hoping to lighten her mood.

"He's glad we have an excuse for a small wedding now."

I nodded, not knowing how to address this.

"He's at an artifact show in New Mexico. We're thinking of having the wedding in Boston. I think it'll be very small, like in his living room, just family."

I nodded again.

"At least that was the way we both initially wanted it, but everyone talked us out of it. We can't really see what difference it makes now."

"Vi." I was going to offer sympathy. "I'm sorry about—"

But she held up her hands; recent days must have given her a hair trigger for pity. "Please, can we talk about something else?"

She leaned down and looked at the baby then, still sleeping in his shaded stroller. A genuine smile crossed her face.

"He's getting big, not like an infant now but an actual little baby."

She cooed, and I tried to be mercifully short in relating Henry's news.

She straightened up then and looked at me. "You know, I ran into Ellie the other day."

She said this warily with a sideways glance, and I was again shown the small circumference of the Cleveland that I lived in. She already knew about the kiss.

"How's she?" I asked.

"Frankly, I'm worried about her."

This annoyed me—that Viola should be worried about the person causing me anguish. But Viola went on. "She came down to Dress for Success the other day. To meet the women." Here she smiled. "You would not believe how good she was with them." It was on my tongue to say no, I wouldn't, but actually I could see it. Ellie always had a gift for cheering people.

"She looked at résumés and talked to anyone about their aspirations. It was touching, really."

Viola's eyes clouded over at the memory. "But she looked awful. She'd clearly tried to wear the chicest thing she owned, but her clothes just hang off her now. She didn't have a stitch of makeup on, which is fine, you know. But her skin looked gray. And she reeked of smoke. She even tried to light one while she was with us, but I stopped her."

"I think she's going through a rough patch," I said, and then realized that I sounded exactly like Diana Dorset.

"Yes, but the disturbing part is that after Ellie left, the director of placement, the one who gets jobs for all my girls, came up to me. She told me that Ellie quietly snuck into her office at the end. My director had a clear sense that Ellie was trying to see if we might have a job for her."

"Like she wants to start volunteering?"

"Maybe that was it and my director got the tone of the conversation wrong, but she seemed to think that Ellie needed a paying job. Like she thought maybe we could help her find employment."

"Surely not," I said.

"Gus wiped her out," Viola said in a whisper. "I feel like I should help her."

"It can't be that bad," I said.

"She gave Gus her entire divorce settlement to manage." Viola shook her head, watching a flock of geese take flight off the lake.

"Right now it kind of kills me to even be in the same room with him. But he's my brother—you know?"

I didn't, as I didn't have siblings, but I couldn't imagine a less sympathetic brother than Gus. Viola was really too kind.

The thought of her brother put a frown back on her face. She put the earbuds back in her ears and smiled at me. "I should continue," she said. "But I think we're going to offer her something in connection with the nonprofit. Some sort of development position. Ellie's always good with people."

I nodded.

"Looking forward to the baptism," she said.

I had yet to plan any of it, and it was only a few weeks away.

She ran off then, strong and direct, with a cacophony of music in her ears.

I strolled the baby down the hill to Cedar Fairmount to pick up groceries for dinner. A uniquely midwestern type of cheerfulness must have motivated the Van Sweringen brothers to create a faux Tudor village in the 1920s in the same town as some of the largest steelyards in the nation.

I was in the produce section, wondering if the hothouse tomatoes would be hard as rocks even after I'd cooked them, when someone leaned over my shoulder.

"William Selden," I said, looking up at him. "*Quelle surprise.*"

"I warn you, my French has not improved at all." He wore a ratty linen jacket, torn jeans, and scuffed brown Church's. Tortoiseshell glasses added to the professorial effect.

I smiled. "Something tells me your French was pretty good to start with."

He made a face and quoted an aphorism about improving on perfection as he leaned down and smiled at my still-sleeping baby.

"You're back," I said.

"For the summer." He straightened. "They've extended an offer to have me return in the fall."

"And you're going?"

"They invited me to give a series of lectures."

I noted that he'd not answered my question. "Sounds good." I nodded and loaded up my tomatoes to take my leave. "Good to see you."

He tugged at my sleeve then. "Come get a cup of coffee with me."

"Now?"

"I can use some of your insights. You always know what's happening around town. I've been gone for months." This, I knew, was him wanting news of Ellie.

"I can't," I said, gesturing toward the bottom of the stroller. "I'm shopping with a ticking time-bomb."

We both looked at sleeping Henry.

"Are you walking home?" he asked.

I nodded.

"I'll walk with you then."

We paid for our purchases. He bought only a bottle of wine and a bag of pears. The bachelor life, I guess.

Once I'd settled everything, including Selden's bag, in the bottom of the stroller, we set off up the hill. We walked on Fairmount past some of the biggest houses in town, Normandy- and Palladian-style mansions built in the twenties for the haute bourgeoisie. We passed a huge Georgian manor, brick with white pillars, and saw the front half-circle drive littered with plastic children's toys and tricycles.

"I don't know if you know much about my leaving," Selden said as we turned left down one of my favorite streets. He paused, to see if I would fill in some blanks for him. I was sorry then that he was walking me home. It was one of my favorite times of day, strolling past these houses and imagining the lives that went on in them—all of the husbands and wives happy and in love. How could you not be, when you were living in that perfect Dutch colonial with the herb borders, or that Greek revival with the sunken garden on the side? I didn't want to think about Ellie anymore, and Selden kept her in my mind. Seeing I was off somewhere else, he continued on a different track. "I know you're Ellie's best friend."

"Oldest friend," I said reflexively, for I'd started thinking about her that way recently. "It's different."

He noted my check and veered off. "I suppose you're right that Ellie doesn't have that many friends, not true ones. But you're as close as they come, and I want to know how she's doing."

"You haven't been to see her yet?"

He shook his head. "I wanted to get the lay of the land first."

He seemed cowardly to me. If he had unfinished business with her, why talk to me? Then again Selden had run away. Avoidance was his default strategy.

Henry stirred, and I walked faster, hoping to make it home before he awoke.

Selden kept pace with me.

"She's not good," I said, thinking back on my meeting with Viola. "She's floundered a little while you've been gone."

This seemed to cheer him. Because it was a confirmation that she missed him, or because he wanted to see her hurt, I didn't know.

"She's had money trouble," I said.

"The Gus thing—"

"Yes," I interrupted. "He's lost a lot of people's money, including hers."

He raised an eyebrow at this; perhaps he meant something else— like her supposed liaison with Trenor.

Why I said what I said next, I'll never know. Did I want him to know the truth? Maybe I was fed up with his indecisiveness about Ellie and his romantic musings and wanted him to just cut the ties already.

And I'll admit now that in some dark part of myself I knew I was sealing Ellie's doom. That's how I think of it. You might think me overly dramatic, but I don't. For someone who had always thought herself above petty gossip, above spiteful social jockeying, when Ellie was lying in the mud, I, just as much as any of them, took my turn grinding my heel on her. I'm disgusted with myself now, but then the thrill of it egged me on. I told him that Ellie had slept with the traveling squash player. I wouldn't tell him about Jim and the kiss—that was too humiliating.

Selden's head was down, studying the pavement as we walked.

"I think she's having some issues with drinking and . . . things. I think that's what led to this," I said.

"A squash player, like a college boy . . . ?" Selden trailed off. "She's partying again?"

"She's been hanging out with Neil Vonborke and that crowd."

I knew Selden wouldn't approve of that.

Neil and Mary Vonborke were at the center of a small group of wild couples who were the subject of much scandal. Most of my friends regularly declined invitations to their parties, which were a revolving door of acquaintances and, if rumors were to be believed, offered serious drugs, ecstasy and cocaine, and swinging too, trading partners—though I'd always disbelieved this. It seemed ridiculous to me, a holdover from the seventies. Swinging in such a close social circle—really? And how did it work exactly that you slept with your friend's wife and then played eighteen holes of golf with him the next day? I'd always chalked those rumors up to bored gossip and maybe even a little envy—the Vonborke crowd was all good-looking and glitzy. But really, how different was it than the crowd Jim and I hung out with? Our friends smoked pot and a few had affairs. It was all a matter of degree—wasn't it?

Then again, lots of things in life were a matter of degree.

Jim and I had attended one Vonborke party where we'd left soon after someone suggested, in jest, wife swapping. Jim was mumbling as we got in our car.

"As if," Jim had said as we drove away.

"As if what?" I'd asked.

"As if fucking around is going to fix their existential angst and despair."

He'd taken my hand as he drove, brought it to his lips, and kissed the back of each of my fingers, lingering on the ring finger on my left hand.

It was bittersweet now to remember that he'd said that.

Selden sighed, looking at me as we turned down my street. "You think she's in trouble?"

I shrugged. "Isn't that why you're still walking with me?" What I really wanted to ask him was what, if anything, he intended to do about it, though I knew it'd sound silly. Selden, after all, wasn't her father, or her husband for that matter.

Henry stirred and started small cries of protest.

I pushed quickly down the last half block to my house, glad to have an excuse to be rid of Selden now.

"You need to get back to your day, yeah?" Selden said, nodding to the baby.

I fished Selden's bag out of the bottom of the stroller.

"It was good to see you," I said, handing the sack to him.

He nodded, turned on his heel, and started his walk back down to his car in the grocery store parking lot.

25

The Falls

A few weeks went by, fueling an uneasy détente between Jim and me. He came home early. He took the baby so I could have a bath, read a book, get out of the house, and go shopping—all without my having to beg, à la Jeff Trenor's advice. He was tiptoeing around me. Clearly he knew he'd been in the wrong. It made me feel surprisingly awful, like a battle-axe, henpecking wife, like he was cringing around me—a dog waiting to be kicked. Really, we barely spoke. This feeling of guilt made me even shorter with him. Things were rapidly spiraling out of control. And yes, all over one stupid little kiss.

Because what is a kiss really when you get down to it? A meeting of lips, a mingling of breath. Is that really so intimate, so awful? I'd started to convince myself it wasn't. Not a big deal, a small slip. And each time I was almost convinced, a small voice suggested that perhaps we were now heading down a slippery slope. That first there's a kiss, and then there's a tryst. And then I'd be mad all over again.

I was in this cycle—ruminate, rake husband over the coals, feel guilty, repeat—when I went shopping in Chagrin Falls, leaving the baby at home with the sitter. I sped on Fairmount Boulevard, heading east with the stereo loud and the windows down. Driving my car, all alone, made me feel like I was back to myself, back in my body. Still, a funny absence radiated from the backseat, from the empty car seat. So I pushed the pedal down farther and turned the radio up louder and the sun shone brighter.

I had a flash then of being carefree. Of maybe sneaking a smoke and driving to meet someone, some man, for a drink. When I was single this kind of cheerful irresponsibility often included Ellie. She'd be either by my side or meeting me. Immediately I felt tinged with sadness.

I strolled down Main Street feeling free and younger than I had in a year. In my favorite clothing boutique, I bought a little black number in chiffon and gabardine by an Italian designer for too much money. I was feeling optimistic, I guess. Maybe I'd have occasion to wear the dress with Jim as we started to put things back together. The dress looked good on me now; it'd look great after I'd lost a few more pounds.

I was waiting in line for a coffee at the shop next to the falls, with my shopping bag slung over my arm, when a familiar voice and gleaming set of eyes accosted me.

"But where is your baby?" Diana Dorset asked me before even saying hello.

"At home with the sitter." I smiled. I hadn't talked to her since her dinner party. "He's doing so well. So sweet."

She smiled at me, gripping her huge coffee. I wondered if that was why she always seemed so lively, if caffeine was the fuel for those eyes. She nodded and steered us both through the doors back out into the bright sun. "So great to run into you like this. I can't get enough of this weather, can you?" she prattled. I wondered if she'd run into Jim if she'd have asked him where his baby was. Of course not. Something about the expectations and requirements of Henry chafed today— maybe it was the sun, maybe the new dress. I knew I was being churlish, ungrateful for my gifts.

"Look at that," Diana breathed, shaking me out of my self-concern, squeezing my forearm tighter as we walked out into the sun.

Across the street in a parking lot was Ellie's old and beaten red BMW and next to it was a huge shiny Lexus SUV. The trunk of Ellie's car was open and she was showing a woman with a Bottega Veneta bag and Fiorentini and Baker boots the contents of her trunk.

"What *is* she doing?" Diana asked. But I knew exactly what I was looking at.

The woman was smiling and laughing and pointing to something in Ellie's trunk, then the woman leaned over to rummage around. Ellie smiled, her eyes hidden by her oversized sunglasses. The woman straightened up then with a pile of clothes in her arms.

Diana snorted. "Holy shit, she's selling her clothes out of the back of her car." I heard just the faintest glee in her voice, and it reminded me of her schadenfreude that night at her dinner party. Julia Trenor's warning from Ellicottville rang in my ears. It's easier to have Diana as a friend than not. I didn't want to be her friend anymore, but I certainly didn't want to be on her bad side either. I started leaning away from her, thinking of ways to make a quick departure.

It was then that Ellie turned and looked across the street, almost as if we'd called her name. I could see her blush scarlet under her glasses.

The woman loaded the clothes into her SUV, oblivious to Ellie's distress and our stares. She fished a wallet out of her bag and handed a wad of bills to Ellie. Ellie took them, furtively stuffed them into her skirt pocket, and slammed her trunk shut.

The woman drove away in her SUV, and I turned to Diana. We'd both been so enrapt watching the transaction that we'd not said anything or moved. After the SUV glided past, Ellie crossed the street with purpose.

"Shit," Diana mumbled under her breath, watching Ellie advance. She swept me up in a hug. "I've got to dash. I'm so late. Lovely to see you. Call me, okay?" She looked directly at Ellie, turned on her heel, and strode the opposite way down the street.

My first impulse was to leave like Diana, to turn and run. Ellie looked luminous in the sunlight wearing a silk halter, short skirt, and thigh-high suede boots. Every mother with a stroller on the street watched her with a combination of outrage and envy. Reports of her looking haggard were not to be believed. I was trying to remember where I parked, calculating routes to get there as quickly as possible, when she waved, effectively stopping any getaway.

I suppose I stood there frozen—the deer in the headlights, the whole thing. And then she was in front of me, reaching out a hand to pull me close and hug me. She smelled herbal-clean, like quince blossoms and birch bark—her smell that I'd known since childhood. As she let me go the underlying stink of cigarettes and burned coffee swirled out from under her hair. Her arms were freckled, and as she embraced me I had an overwhelming urge to pinch the back of her arm, hard, like I'd seen her do a few times on the playground when we were children, but I didn't.

I'd not actually seen her since Cinco's party.

"Hey," she said. Now that she was closer I could see she was wearing a thick mask of orange makeup that had settled into the lines around her nose and caked on the dark circles under her eyes. Her blouse was rayon and too shiny, her boots scuffed. Wadded money bulged in the pocket of her skirt.

"Hey." I was trying not to let her catch me doing a panicky scan out of my peripheral vision to see if anyone we knew was there, watching.

"I was just . . ." Her voice trailed off and she started again. "I've started dealing in some vintage clothes. You know, stuff I find around. New stuff too. That woman was psyched with one of Steven's dresses. He's getting so much press now. Everyone knows about him."

I nodded, mute, not knowing what to say. Here she was, Ellie, and she was selling things out of her car. I was angry at her, uncomfortable as hell, but there was a not small part of me that felt sadness.

She went on. "Of course I throw a little of my own stuff in there too." Of course she did. If anyone could convince people that her old clothes were treasures that they should buy out of a trunk in a parking lot, it was Ellie.

"How've you been?" she asked.

Our conversation at Cinco's came back to me then. I didn't know what to say to her.

"I've been meaning to call you," she said after a silence.

"Oh?"

"I felt bad about Cinco's party," she put out tentatively.

If she had done anything else, something that didn't involve Jim, if she'd kissed someone else's husband, I would have let her off the hook. That's how much I loved her, how used I was to overlooking her faults. But I was beginning to think that any friendship I thought I had with her was merely my own hero worship combined with her fear of loneliness. I would have made justifications and excuses, would have tried to make her feel better, but this time she'd hurt me.

"Ellie, I don't even know what to say to you."

The color drained out of her face. "Why?"

"You know why," I said.

We stared at each other.

She laughed, a quick fake sound. "I have no idea what you're talking about."

"Yes you do. That night at Jim's club."

"This again—the squash player?"

I was mad now. "Not the squash player."

Her mouth fell open in a little round O and her cheeks flushed as if I'd slapped her.

I didn't say anything. She would be the next to speak, not me.

"That was nothing," she said, and seeing the look on my face, she continued. I was relieved she was going to admit it. "Just silliness. We were drunk. I've known Jim as long as you have, and he's always been in love with you. It was an idiotic thing, really."

I have to admit that her explanation did make me feel better, perhaps only because I so badly wanted to believe it. She was nonchalant about it. And from the way she was talking, she didn't seem to have any plans on my husband. But I noted that she'd not apologized.

She continued. "I guess it would be upsetting if I were in your shoes. But I think I've just become desensitized to stuff like this after hanging around the Vonborkes."

I raised an eyebrow.

"Oh, the rumors are true." I could see what she was trying to do now, trying to turn this toward a cozy little gossip session. "We were all at their house the other night, and they wanted to play spin the bottle. Like from grade school. Except it must be much more exciting when your spouse is watching you kiss someone. I mean, I wouldn't know about that."

I made a face.

"I know. But you can see why the thing with Jim really meant nothing. He's such a good guy, isn't he?"

Looking at her then I realized that Ellie left chaos in her wake almost anywhere she went. I wondered if it was reflexive for her, unconscious, or if she meant to do it, if it satisfied something inside her.

"He's too good," I said.

"My experience?" she said. "There aren't a lot of them."

"So you'll take mine."

"There's no taking. Don't you know your husband at all?"

I was about to say "I know you" but thought better of it.

Ellie stepped forward as if to hug me, but I busied myself with my shopping bag and she didn't.

"I feel bad about things," she said. "I really do."

"Good to see you," I said from rote, cutting her off. It had been anything but good to see her.

"Really good to see you," she said listlessly, realizing I was blocking her out. She gave the back of my arm a significant squeeze.

On my way back to the car I stopped in a boutique and bought a hideously expensive set of clothes for Henry. I walked out of the store laden with bags. I looked at my watch, calculating whether I'd make it back in time to put Henry down for his nap. I sweated as I rushed, packages flopping around me. I saw Ellie drive past me then in her dirty battered car. And walking with my hands full, I had the feeling that the packages and the obligations weren't the worst things in the world. I felt a glimmer of gratitude.

26

The Heights

Ellie was shaking so badly when she got in the car that she had to try three times to put the key in the ignition. The kiss with Jim was a dim memory. How in the hell had this become public knowledge? No one knew about it, except Jim and herself, and he'd told—that bastard.

She pulled out of the parking space and lit a cigarette. During the drive back she was thinking that the whole town must know about this. How stupid she'd been to think it would have been an unnoticeable thing. At a Vonborke party kissing someone else's husband wouldn't have registered a blip. She wondered how bad this was. She didn't want to lose one of her oldest, and let's face it, only friend—over a kiss.

She drove too fast, stubbed out her smoke in the overflowing ashtray, and ate mints out of a tin until her mouth was numb. A more pressing issue bore down on her. What was she going to do about money? That woman with her thousand-dollar handbag had bargained her down to a hundred dollars for Steven's dress. Viola had called just yesterday offering her a job in the offices of Dress for Success. Ellie had been alarmed at this bit of charity and told her she'd think about it. The position gave Ellie the nice cover of being connected with a nonprofit, as if she were feeding her soul and not flat broke. She had her reservations though about working in a conventional office. She'd never done that before, had no skills for it, and she knew she'd be bored into a coma.

She was already looking forward to the pill she'd take when she got home. She'd sleep the rest of the afternoon, and when she woke up in the early morning at one or two o'clock when the pill wore off she'd take another one and sleep most of tomorrow morning as well.

As she entered the Heights, it all looked so serene. The mature trees, now past bloom, were hung with lush green. They cast a dim greenish light that made her feel like a fish swimming in the bottom of an aquarium or the bottom of a kelp-filtered ocean—perfect for napping.

These streets gave her a feeling of seclusion that calmed her in a way she hadn't felt since sitting in Selden's living room.

She knew he was back, knew he hadn't called her. But after her run-in in Chagrin Falls, she suddenly felt like getting all unpleasant conversations out of the way. Maybe she could wipe the slate clean today, in one day. Start over fresh, her favorite feeling—first days of school, the first days of spring.

She was determined to talk to him face-to-face. He wasn't going to run away and solve everything over e-mail. She deserved at least one conversation with him.

She felt like she hadn't talked to anyone in days besides her run-in on the sidewalk, and the loneliness of her afternoon plans of a pill and a pillow depressed her. Now that she wasn't working for Steven, time had become unreliable—dragging until she thought she'd lose her mind and then speeding up so that it seemed to be running out.

Once again she felt the desire that she'd felt quite frequently in recent days, and she turned toward Selden's house.

Selden's house. The comfort of it, the interior so hidden away and so much a part of him. She parked in front and opened the glove box, where she'd put the texts between him and Diana after Leforte had returned them. She put the papers in her pocket next to the money. He'd never seen them after all.

She was on the porch, about to slip the papers under the doormat, when she thought she heard someone inside and then the door flew open.

Selden smiled at her, barefoot in grubby jeans, glasses, and untucked T-shirt.

"Ellie," he said. "This is a surprise."

He'd caught her crouching. She straightened, putting the papers in her pocket.

He looked somehow even younger than she remembered. Maybe it was the scruff on his jaw or his glinting glasses. "You're back," she said, slightly shocked to see him in person, looking strong, put together, in spite of his usual dishevelment.

He cocked his head to one side. "Yeah, I am. What are you doing here? Come in. Come in."

"I can't," she said, turning away, suddenly wanting to disappear. She shouldn't have come. She didn't know what to say.

He furrowed his brow. "But you're here."

"I know. I was going to . . ." But she didn't finish, embarrassed.

"I'm sorry I didn't call, but I really am glad you're here. Come in," he said again, opening the door wider and trying to wave her in.

Ellie hesitated but then Selden smiled at her, and she thought she'd go in, for just a minute, just to see the interior again. It would seem strange if she left.

It was the same as she'd remembered it. Selden's books and papers littered every surface. Though not dirty, it was cluttered. He watched her surveying his living room.

"I'm working on a paper," he said. "Sorry about the mess." He looked at her for a long while. "Can I get you something?" he asked. "You look a little tired."

"You know, I never get sick of hearing that," she teased.

"I didn't mean—"

But she cut him off. "A glass of water would be great."

"Sit down or something," he said. "Seriously, I'll feel better."

While he was in the kitchen she looked at the piles of papers—letters from academic institutions, grading sheets, galleys of an article.

She glanced at his computer and couldn't help but see an open e-mail. After reading a few words, Ellie realized it was quite erotic. Glancing at the top, she saw it was from Diana and that she'd recently sent it. Diana wanted him back with all the longing and lust of the texts Ellie now carried in her pocket. The woman was dogged, that was for sure.

Selden cleared his throat behind her, and she jumped.

"Sorry," she said.

He walked quickly over to the desk, saw what she was looking at, and snapped his laptop shut.

"You and Diana . . ."

He smiled, closed his eyes, and shook his head.

"But she's writing you."

"She was, she still is, yes." He said it with a quiet resignation, leaning against the cold fireplace mantel.

"With no encouragement from you?" Ellie asked.

Selden shook his head silently. She realized then that he was holding himself awfully stiffly. And when she looked up in his face she realized why—she'd embarrassed him. By snooping through his e-mails, by bringing up the relentless Diana Dorset, possibly by even coming here today.

A tear slipped out then, partly because she was relieved he wasn't in love with Diana, partly because she realized he felt guilty around her, and partly because he hadn't called and here he was. Ellie brushed the tear away with the back of her hand.

"You're very tired," he said, alarm at the edge of his voice. "Won't you let me make you comfortable?" He took her hand and led her away from the desk to a chair.

Two more tears slipped down her cheek, though she didn't sob.

He was scrambling now that he'd seen her cry. "Won't you rest a minute?" he asked. "This chair is the best spot in the house, yeah?"

She nodded, regaining control of herself, trying to discreetly wipe her eyes.

"We need a fire," he said. "Probably the last one before summer."

He stooped down in front of the fireplace, making adjustments to the wood laid there. It gave him something to do, she knew. He was nervous. She shouldn't have cried.

"You left so quickly," she said to his back as he lit a match to the kindling. Did she see his shoulders stiffen?

"The offer required it." He stood up to face her.

"Did you like Paris?" she asked.

"Who doesn't?"

"When good Americans die . . ."

"They go to Paris," Selden said with a smile.

"Oscar Wilde," she said. "The wittiest."

Selden nodded at her.

"You didn't say good-bye," she said quietly.

Selden said nothing, looking at the floor. "I thought that best."

The smallest hum of anger rose in Ellie. "I didn't," she said.

Selden shook his head. "Ells—"

"You hurt me, you know. You reduced me to e-mails."

Selden said nothing.

Her anger rose a little farther; she felt shaky from controlling her tears. "Apparently that's what you do, I guess." She gestured toward the laptop.

"I was out of the country. It's different."

"I would have come to see you."

"Why?" he asked.

"I thought I explained why." They were silent for a few beats. "You threw me to the wolves."

She saw something flash across his face then, anger, frustration, pain? "I didn't throw you to the wolves. For God's sake, you practically killed me. And that's why I didn't want you to come. You were just trying to save your reputation. If you had visited me, it would only have been to show that you weren't having an aff—"

"You think I'm that calculating," she interrupted, her voice low. "I wanted to see you." Her voice rose. "But now that you mention it, your leaving reinforced everything."

"I believe you're saying it reinforced everything you'd already done," he said in a whiplash tone.

"What's that supposed to mean?" she asked.

"You know what I'm talking about." His voice was low.

"You're talking about a bunch of gossip?" she asked, disbelieving.

Selden pursed his lips and then said, "Randy Leforte told me himself that he fucked you on the desk in his office."

Ellie stood up.

But Selden grabbed her arm, angry now. "He told me that night at the museum, the night you showed everyone your tit. It killed me. He knew it would too. And he told me you'd been screwing around with Gus Trenor. That he was about to move you into the apartment he keeps for his . . . for his . . ."

"For his what?"

"I saw you," he breathed. "I saw you come out of there. Tell me it's not true," he said with his eyes closed.

She sat back down in the chair.

"Just tell me and I will tell them all to go to hell. The squash player, Leforte, Trenor. Just tell me it's all lies." He opened his eyes and kneeled down next to her chair.

"I wasn't dating you when I slept with Randy."

Selden let out a low groan.

"And I am not even going to dignify you thinking I'd . . . with Gus . . ."

Selden stood up and walked to a chair, flopping himself down, shaking his head. "Ellie, I can't."

"What are you saying?" She was on her feet in front of him. "You're a virgin? You only date virgins. I'm a completely grown woman. I'm not a girl."

"I'm aware."

"So I slept with someone and I regret it." She kneeled down in front of him, trying to calm herself. "Haven't you ever made a mistake?" She sounded pleading, even to her own ears, and it made her wince a bit.

Selden ran a hand through his hair. "Not like that," he said with a snort.

"Like what?" she asked sharply, on her feet again.

He looked at her, holding her eye. "It disgusts me."

"You're a snob," she said, awareness dawning, turning away from him. "I had no idea. I thought you were so free, so disdaining of . . ."

Selden said nothing and shrugged. "He taunted me with it. He told half the town."

Ellie shook her head, tears again stinging her eyes. "I cannot believe you care about my past. I can't believe you give a shit what Cleveland thinks of you."

"Don't you?" he asked.

"You taught me not to." She rose then, ready to leave. She took the folded papers from her pocket. "Here," she said, dropping the texts in his lap. "I'd hate for Cleveland to find out about these."

He let them fall on the floor, not touching them.

"I'm sorry," he whispered.

"You're a coward," she said, heading for the door, wanting to be out of his house before she started crying in earnest.

· 27 ·

The Botanical Gardens

In keeping with his contrition, one Friday night in June Jim took me down to University Circle. Friday nights the museums and the gardens stayed open late, and there were bands in the grass of Wade Oval. It stayed light until nearly nine thirty, and I think he hoped that being around a lot of people would make us feel festive.

I'd engaged the babysitter and put on my new black dress, and I was expecting a fun evening. But everything he did got on my nerves: trolling for a parking place so he wouldn't have to pay, not taking my hand when we got out of the car, complaining about the loud music, wondering about the cost of the extra police the city engaged for the evening. I was silently fuming when Jim asked me where I wanted to go first. Even this added to my ire as I imagined he hadn't sufficiently planned the evening.

We went to the botanical gardens first. I admired the herb gardens, staffed as they were by an army of volunteers who kept the beds more tidy than a Brazilian bikini wax. I was admiring the plants, trying to ignore Jim, hoping that my bad mood would pass, that my sourness would lift. And not knowing how to lift it myself, other than just waiting, I replaced Jim in my mind with Cinco. I was convinced Cinco would never have kissed Ellie. And then, as if I'd summoned them, I saw them.

Cinco and Corrine were standing away from everyone in a corner of the formal rose garden next to a huge incongruous ornamental asparagus that grew like a topiary behind a boxwood hedge. She looked down at the gravel path, arms crossed in front of her. His hand was tangled up under the hair at the nape of her neck, and she nodded frequently at something he was saying. Her eyes still gazed down as he kept murmuring, and then he tipped her face up to his and kissed her.

He looked protective. And I couldn't help but sigh a little at their intimacy. I knew then that whatever struggles they might have, and I knew there'd been some, they'd never be apart. I know it will sound strange to you, but in that moment I understood Ellie just a little. Not that I wanted to take Corrine's place. I didn't want Cinco. But I wanted what he had, what they had. What I wanted was some of his calm, his ability to make something out of where things stood. He did it, or was doing it. I wondered if I could do it too.

I saw them part and walk arm in arm out of the garden. Jim was leaning over, trying to read a sign next to a hellebore. When he saw me watching, he stood up and smiled.

"You want to get a drink?" he asked, taking my hand and steering me toward the exit. He'd not seen the Van Alstynes.

I shrugged. "Whatever you want."

"Or are you hungry? Do you want dinner?"

"No, I'm not hungry." I knew I shouldn't punish him, but I was having the worst time with it.

"Do you just want to go home?"

I shrugged again. "Whatever you want."

This was too much passivity for him, and he dropped my hand. "That's probably best then," he said, faultlessly polite, but pissed nonetheless as we got in the car.

He made a few more attempts at conversation on the way home, all met with one-word answers from me. It was an unexplainable thing, my provoking him. Perhaps I wanted to see how far I could push him after he'd pushed me as far as he had.

He paid the sitter, who was surprised we were back home so soon, while I fixed myself a bourbon and water. Jim showed her to the door and eyed me when he came back in the room.

"Since when do you drink bourbon?"

"Since now."

"Is that okay?"

"Henry's out. He won't be up 'til morning."

He looked at me, the nursing mother with the red lipstick smudged on her glass.

"It's fine," I said, drinking about half my drink and reaching again for Jim's bottle.

"Allow me," he said, sloshing a huge pour into my glass, his lips a tight line. "Are you going to talk to me?"

"Course," I said, lifting the glass slowly so it didn't spill. "What do you want to talk about?"

"Why you're so pissy."

"I'm not."

We were silent.

"So talk," I said, turning my back on him and walking slowly into our little library.

He stood on the threshold and shrugged. "This is about the squash tournament." He wasn't going to say the word "kiss," and neither was I.

"It's not."

He leaned against the doorjamb. "What then?"

"Nothing."

"You're married now," he said.

"No shit."

He winced. Southern gentleman that he was, he never liked it when I swore. "That means you have to talk to me," he said.

"That's what being married means?"

"Yes," he said patiently.

I sighed and put my glass down, sick of the liquor burn in my throat. "What do you want me to say? I'm still upset. I don't know what to do about that any more than you do."

"You're this upset about something pretty . . ."

"Pretty what?"

"Innocuous."

This angered me. "It might seem trivial to you. It's not to me."

"It's not trivial to me," he said.

"You're acting like it is."

And it was then, I guess, that he'd had enough.

"It could have gone farther, do you understand that?" He took a step toward me, his voice rising. "I'll take my beating because I kissed her, and it was wrong. If you'd done something like that I'd be out of my mind. I'd have beaten the shit out of the guy."

Some small part of me, a part I'd never admit to, thrilled to hear him say that, and another part scowled at his hypocrisy.

"But you do understand," he continued, "that it could have been worse? You can't be this naïve, this innocent. I was in a tailspin, and I pulled back. Do you know why? Because of you. Because I love you. Because in a drunken minute I leaned too far forward and kissed her. And then in that second, it only confirmed that I want you, only you."

I rolled my eyes, but I wanted to believe him.

He held my glance. "Why is that so hard to believe? I didn't want to hurt you, and I didn't want to sever us because I know that's what would have happened if I let it go farther." He saw the disbelief on my face. "I have some personal integrity. I'm not going to be sneaking in and out of someone else's bed on you." I smirked, but he kept looking at me. "You know that. At least admit you know that."

"I guess I believe that."

"Of course you do. And it could have gone farther with her, you understand? All I had to do was lead her upstairs. But I left and came home. She wound up taking that guy up to bed, seriously, almost young enough to be her son."

"Please," I protested.

"He was twenty-two."

"If she was a teenage mother—"

"She's getting to that point in her life where she's starting to look like Mrs. Robinson. That's what I'm saying." He took a step closer.

"Why did you do it?" I asked quietly. "Had you always wanted to do that?"

"Look," he said. "It was a shitty, shitty thing." He shook his head. "And I'm sorry. You have no idea how sorry I am. But you have to forgive me."

He'd not answered me. "Have you always been attracted to her?"

He crossed his arms and leaned over me. "Of course not."

This answer, I thought, was total bullshit. Then again, Jim wasn't stupid.

"Then why?" I asked.

"I haven't been pining for her, if that's what you're asking. If you think I'm a dog who slipped his leash, then why do you want me—"

"Then why?"

I waited, tensed as if for a blow. Waited for him to say he'd always loved her, or he'd never loved me, that I'd ignored him in favor of the baby, or that he wasn't attracted to me anymore.

But he didn't say any of these things. He leaned over me. "You just have to forgive me. I can't stand it if you won't. It's killing me."

Killing him, I thought. But looking in his face, I thought for an instant that he might cry.

I realized then that he'd never answer me. That I could ask, but he was never going to let me into that moment. Perhaps he was trying to protect me. And I wondered how awful the truth really was, and if I really wanted to know what led up to the kiss. Attraction, excitement at the forbidden, desire for freedom, raw lust? Hadn't I felt some of those things too since I'd been married? I'd not acted on them. Under the right set of circumstances, would I?

Why is it both the easiest thing and the hardest thing to forgive those closest to you? Easiest because you love them, hardest because it cuts deeper, I suppose.

I realized then there are things that you can choose, if you're strong enough, to not get upset about. Things you know you should be mad about, things you are justified in holding on to that you just don't want to expend energy being mad about. In the end it was just a kiss. I would never forget. It would always be there between us, that betrayal. But maybe I could let it go, just for right now.

Because in that moment I wanted my husband to kiss me the way he had before he kissed Ellie, before we had a baby, before we moved back to my hometown. The way he used to kiss me in New York when I'd walk up the block and find him waiting for me, leaning outside the door to my building on a Friday after work—his tie loosened, a wolfish smile on his face, and a bottle of Veuve Clicquot by the neck in his hand. He'd pull me toward him, his mouth at my ear; "So fucking beautiful," he'd whisper. I had a flash of Cinco and Corrine in the garden. That was what I wanted back.

It was, I suppose, how I was going to get past this thing—memory, attraction, shared history, the belief that the man I fell in love with was still in there.

So I stood up and kissed him. He was tentative, surprised I think, and then enthusiastic, with one arm around my waist pressing me to him. The thought crept in—had he kissed Ellie like this? And in keeping with my new control I pushed the thought from my mind.

So this is the work part of marriage, I thought when he released me. Until then, marriage had been easy for us. The first year that everyone says is such a huge adjustment left me feeling smug. But now I understood that the work would come. Illusions get shattered. Naïve romantic visions become too fragile to hold up under day-to-day ordinariness. I thought of Cinco then and that if I really wanted what he had, then maybe I should try to make a little of it myself.

Jim took my glass, drained the last of my drink in one gulp, put it down, grabbed my hand, and leaned his head toward the stairs. "Come with me," he said, pulling me gently, though he didn't need to.

I felt awkward following him up the stairs past the baby's room. Almost as nervous as I'd felt the first time he'd ever taken my hand and led me from the couch in his bachelor apartment back to his bed. Now he shut the door to our bedroom, and when he turned I saw determination and lust in his eyes. No nervousness or sadness, and I marveled, not for the first time, at the resilience of the male libido.

He unzipped my dress, and I tensed. My body wasn't returned from giving birth. I was scarred. I was nursing. We'd only had sex a few times, and I'd been skittering into bed wearing one of his T-shirts for weeks now. I backed up, moving to our bed. But he stopped me and shook his head, moving the dress down to my waist.

"Beautiful wife," he whispered.

Ellie came to my mind then—she, the beautiful one, not me. And I wondered if he'd whispered anything like that to her when he'd kissed her.

"Where did you go?" he breathed against my mouth. "Just now. You left me."

"I'm here," I said, wiping Ellie from my mind and focusing on the feel of his lips on my neck.

He removed my dress. His fingers dipped past an edge of lace, next to my Cesarean scar. My breath hitched.

He grabbed his hand back as if scorched. "Does it hurt?"

"It's numb," I said.

I unbuttoned his shirt, fumbled with his belt, ran my hands over the taut V of his abdomen, one of my favorite parts of him. I wondered if she'd touched him there, if she'd touched him anywhere.

He pushed me back toward the bed, taking off the rest of his clothes and mine, as I kicked off my shoes. I lay beside him, and he put his hand on my cheek, trailing down my neck.

"Come back to me," he said.

I pulled him on top of me, trying to feel his heaviness, wanting to feel the reality that this was my husband. I kissed him, willing the feel of his lips on mine to take over.

I felt his erection against my thigh, felt myself warm and opening to him. He shifted and took my face in his hands as he paused at my entrance.

"I love you, do you know?" His face was tense above me.

"I know," I said.

"Tell me you know."

"I know you love me," I said, and in that moment, I did believe.

He pushed into me then, that first moment of elemental pleasure.

"Only you," he said in my ear, picking up his rhythm, and then I set the pace until thought disappeared, and there was only the feel of my body surrounding his and the sound of his voice in my ear, whispering my name.

The Girl's Room

Sun flooded the dining room the next day as I got the house ready for Henry's baptism. The party would be here after church on Sunday, and I was laying out my mother's silver, my wedding china, my grandmother's porcelain teacups.

In recent days I'd actually started to debate going through with the baptism. Jim seemed more intent on it than I was, and so I would not call it off. But for the first time in my life, I was questioning tradition.

And this was not only because I was considering letting the whole Ellie-as-godmother thing slide. In the end, I'd invited her to the baptism, and she'd dropped off a present yesterday when I was out. That's the way things were going to stand. P. G. and Viola would be more than adequate godparents.

Not that I wanted Henry to grow up without being baptized, but at the same time, I wasn't at all sure that I thought it meant anything.

I did not think Henry was tainted by original sin. I did not believe in hell or that an infant would be sent there if it did exist. I wasn't sure the whole thing wasn't just an enormous act of voodoo.

So why was I going through with it, you ask? Well, the reasons I came up with ranged from the concrete to the ephemeral. I wanted Henry's options open should he ever decide to get married in a church or become involved in the church. Perhaps it'd mean something to him one day, and I wanted to have done my duty by him, like making sure he knew how to swim or chew with his mouth shut. Also, it was a tradition in both Jim's and my family and that also seemed a good enough reason to go on. It was an excuse to have a party, and after months of pregnancy and caring for the baby I'd been a lax hostess. And finally I thought that it at least acknowledged a spiritual side of life. It acknowledged that we're all of us more than duties and traditions and our lives as we put them together, but that there is the unknowable in every life, the part of us that needs faith in something.

I was setting out the starched linen napkins that Jim's aunt had given me when we married when the phone rang.

My mother was asking if I needed help in any way in preparing for the party. She asked who had RSVP'd and who had canceled at the last minute.

"Is Julia Trenor coming?" she asked.

"No, I heard she's still in Ellicottville. Viola and P. G. will be there of course."

"I'm just glad we never gave Gus money."

She asked if Ellie was coming.

"No, she never responded," I said, not wanting to go into the whole thing with her. "But yesterday when I was out, she dropped off a present."

"You know," my mother said, "I'm a little worried about Ellie."

"Oh?"

"Well, I know some of the things being said about her now. That she's been acting a little . . . wild." I was almost sure then that my mother hadn't heard the rumors about Ellie and Jim, because if she had there was no way she'd have described Ellie's behavior as wild. She'd have described it as outrageous, vulgar, or hateful. She was my mother after all. "And I just got off the phone with your Auntie Hart, who told me she hasn't spoken to Ellie in three weeks.

"So I was hoping that you might be able to run over there for us and check on her," my mother continued. She'd definitely not heard the rumors or else she'd never have been asking me this. "I'd go, but I'm an old lady and I don't want to look like I'm spying on her or something."

"She won't think you're spying," I said. "Why don't you go tomorrow?"

"Your Auntie Hart usually talks to her Saturday mornings. This is the third Saturday in a row they haven't spoken."

"Mom, I don't think I'm the best person to go over there right now."

"No?"

"Ellie and I, we're just . . . well, it's awkward right now."

My mother cleared her throat. "You married a man, dear, not a lapdog. They do this sometimes."

I sat there in stunned silence.

"I really don't want you to *have* to discuss this with me," she said. "You haven't mentioned it, so I figured you wanted some privacy." She sounded miffed. "But if what I heard was true, it was a small kiss. That's the extent of it?"

She waited for me to confirm.

"W-well, yes . . . ," I stammered.

"You should forgive him," she said quickly, before I could say more. "Men are wired differently than we are."

"Mom, that is the biggest bunch of bullshit. I can't believe—"

"Language."

"So they're excused from having morals?"

"They're different. That's all I'll say. There have been studies and things. Haven't you seen them? I adore Jim, you know I do. But if he ever seriously hurt you . . ." Her voice trailed off. "This is a very minor thing."

"Mom, did Dad ever—" I stopped, hoping she would fill in the rest for me, but she didn't.

"Ellie is your oldest friend," she said, ignoring my question. "And no one, as far as I can tell, has heard from her in weeks. It's very worrying."

"Well, I heard from her. I told you, she dropped off a present here yesterday for Henry. A silver frame—really heavy, and she'd had the strangest Bible quote engraved on it."

"Which one?"

"I'll go get it."

I fetched the heavy package from the front hall. The frame was sitting in the white box with the undone navy bow from the same jewelry store where we'd been looking at the brooch so many weeks ago. "Ecclesiastes 7:4," I said into the phone. "'The heart of the wise is in the house of mourning; but the heart of fools is in the house of mirth.'"

"That is odd. I've never heard of that one being associated with babies."

The phone line was silent for a moment.

"Will you just run by there?" she asked again. "Thank her for the present or something? She's clearly not herself. Do this for your old mother, and I'll feel so much better. Your Auntie Hart is beside herself down there in Florida."

I didn't say anything.

"Ellie is prone to trouble and drama, you know."

I, as much as anyone, knew that Ellie was partial to trouble and drama. "All right," I agreed.

"Call me when you get there," my mother said, and clicked off the line, no doubt calling Florida to assure Aunt Hart that I was going to check things out.

After I'd hung up, Jim came downstairs with Henry in his arms and kissed me. When I told him what I was doing, he frowned. "Your mother really thinks that necessary?"

I shrugged. "You kind of thought that yourself at Cinco's party."

"That she was in trouble?"

"Yeah, I'm going to go check."

"Today? Right now?"

I sighed. "She seemed to think it was important. I can take Henry with me," I said, reaching for him. "We need to get out for a stroll anyway."

"He can stay here with me," Jim said, holding Henry close.

I didn't know what I was going to say to her once I got over there. "Hi, just making sure you're okay"? I needed to come up with a reason to go. "I need an excuse to be over there. I thought I'd thank her for the frame. Makes sense if Henry's out walking with me."

I packed up the baby and snapped him in the stroller, and he cooed the entire walk over to the Harts' yellow colonial in Shaker Heights.

I thought about what my mother had said. My first thought was that the gossip was truly all over town now, and I suppose there was something liberating in having nothing to hide. I imagined Ellie had felt something like this when she'd come home from New York.

But my mother's cavalier justification that men are just like that saddened me—biology as destiny. Last night with Jim had seemed like a step away from mere physicality toward true connection, and here she'd brought me right back to our chemical natures. Her argument depressed me, and I wondered if someday I'd be giving a daughter the same advice. If I'd be making justifications, God help me and God willing, to a daughter-in-law for Henry's behavior. I shuddered. Progress. I did believe we were making progress, right?

When I arrived at the Harts' house, newspapers were piled on the front porch. It didn't surprise me—Ellie was sometimes sloppy—but the sight of them gave me an ominous feeling now.

I was getting Henry out of his stroller when a car pulled up behind me, William Selden at the wheel.

"Hey," he called, taking dark sunglasses off so that I got the full impact of his hazel eyes.

"Hey." I hefted the baby out of the stroller.

"Are you meeting Ellie?" he asked.

"No," I said, wary for some reason. "I'm just dropping by. Are you meeting her?"

"I came over because she won't take my calls." He ducked his head.

We were on the porch now. Selden stooped down to pick up the papers and put them under his arm.

A folded piece of paper was shoved in the door, and I took it out.

E—You can't hate me forever. Though I wish you'd leave (it's not good for you here) I promise to help, if that's what you want. Call me for campaign advice, counterattack planning, and some major battle armor (I just did a green ruched cocktail that would look amazing on you). If you won't call me, call your sponsor.
I love you—Steven

We rang the bell a few times and waited.

I tried the door; locked, and this seemed ominous to me too.

"Ells," he called so loudly that I was sure the neighbors heard.

We waited on the porch, the baby looking back and forth between our two faces as if we were playing a game.

"We could try around back," he said. "She almost never locks that one. I mean, since we're here . . . leave a note or something, yeah?" He nodded toward the piece of paper in my hand from Steven.

We walked down the driveway that ran along one side of the house and opened the gate.

"Hopefully it won't look like breaking and entering if I'm with a lady and a baby," he joked.

He climbed up the porch steps and turned the handle to the back door. When the door opened, Selden turned and flashed a weak smile at me and leaned his head inside.

"She came to visit me the other day," he said. "She was so upset, undone, and I started worrying about her." He poked his head in the door and yelled her name, throwing the newspapers in a pile on the kitchen counter, to which I added Steven's note.

There was a stillness in the house that immediately let me know something was off. It was silent, as if it'd been silent for a while.

"Ells," he called again loudly, and turned back to me. "I'm afraid I wasn't very nice to her. I kind of fucked up."

A chill shot through me when he said that.

As I've said, Ellie's father had died when she was very young. Given the absence of men in the house, the rooms were furnished in a feminine way—pink and green needlepoint in the living room, which was now swathed in white sheets to keep dust off the furniture; blue and yellow ruffles in the breakfast room, which now smelled of pine cleaner and mothballs.

We walked through the lemon-yellow kitchen, old vinyl and a scarred wooden floor.

"I came to . . ." He paused. "You know so much about us. I suppose it doesn't matter if you know more. I need to convince her to come back with me to Paris. I was awful to her. I didn't know. She showed me . . ." He trailed off and started another line of thought. "We never seem to be able to get it together. Someone's always off, or dating someone else, and I said some things that I didn't mean. I was being stupid and judgmental, hypocritical I guess. But I think now's the time. I think now she'll come. It was only a few days ago that I saw her. I know I can convince her now. Maybe it's been a week or so, but don't you think she'll come?"

He kept moving up the stairs, not waiting for an answer, chattering like a gibbon to fill the stillness—because he felt it too. I was thinking we should leave a note and go, but I also thought of Ellie's mother in Florida. So I followed him, the midday sun lighting the pictures on the walls up the dark staircase, all of Ellie—in cap and gown, on a bicycle with training wheels, as a bride at her wedding, blowing out candles on a birthday cake.

We came to her bedroom, and I was surprised to see again the frills and ribbons of her girlhood. The bedroom was still decorated in a chintz of faded pink cabbage roses with lavender stripes. Flounces and ribbons adorned the curtains and the canopy bed, which was hung in tatted crochet. Glittery stickers of kittens and turtles reflected off the chipped headboard. A stuffed lamb lay on its side on the floor.

A pair of dirty jeans lay crumpled next to the lamb. A stuffed dog sat on the window seat, underneath a neat row of identical empty vodka bottles that lined the sill above the little toy—like a display in a college frat house.

I remembered coming here when Ellie was a teenager and every surface had been littered with makeup and adornments. But they were gone now and all that remained were the vices of her adulthood and the toys of her youth.

"Ells," Selden called, walking over to her sleeping form under pink blankets edged in eyelet, though it was warm outside. "Wake up, honey."

He stirred dust motes and old glitter as he walked to her bed.

In the corner I saw a child's table with a pair of grinning blond-haired dolls sitting around an ashtray overflowing with cigarette butts. Under the table a pair of roller skates with rainbow laces—the exact skates I'd often envied Ellie for—gathered dust.

I knew then, standing in the doorway, what we were looking at—the many orange pill bottles on the nightstand next to the half-empty bottle of Grey Goose, the completely still form under the covers. A stuffed green frog grinned vacantly next to Ellie's shoulder.

All the oxygen seemed sucked out of the room. Selden said her name twice, each more loudly, verging on panic. My heart stopped. Henry stopped squirming in my arms, and I think he even held his baby breath. I couldn't think at all what to do next. Couldn't think what it was that people do in this situation.

I'd never seen a dead body before, and after a moment I walked nearer, to confirm, drawn to her.

I came around the end of the bed and saw her—skin flat and unnatural, her eyes mercifully shut. If I hadn't known this was her room, that it was my friend lying there, I wouldn't have recognized her. The white tattered ribbon had reappeared and was wrapped loosely around her left wrist. I knew for certain then that she was dead. A rhinestone tiara hung on the bedpost, "Princess" spelled out in pink paste jewels on the crown that glinted in the light, catching fire at midday.

The thought kept going through my head that I had to get the baby out of there. Somehow this was all lodging in his unconscious and would scar him.

Ellie, I thought, how are we going to get you out of this one? And I started to wonder if Selden and I shouldn't clean up the pills and the vodka bottles. As if there was some façade that she'd have wanted maintained even now that she was dead. I had the presence of mind to skim the room looking for a note. Her chipped white schoolgirl's desk still had colored pencils and stationery with kittens on it. A neat stack of envelopes with stamps, ready to be mailed, stood on the corner of her desk blotter. I picked them up and saw that they were all bills—credit cards and department stores and utilities. As if she were done now, she had paid her way.

I'd have to tell my mother, and thankfully she'd be the one to tell Aunt Hart. Even now I could hear my mother creating spin. An accident, she'd say. Ellie had been experimenting. She was always a free spirit. The thought of those two mothers, and my own son, who now squirmed in my arms, brought the reality to me. Ellie, the one I'd known my whole life, was gone.

That she'd done it to herself, brought it on herself, made it no less sad for me. It made it more agonizing. I chastised her in my head. Why hadn't she reached out for help?

As if I could have saved her. And of course she wouldn't have come to me, not after I was so mad at her for kissing Jim. It did seem trifling now. A kiss. Like the games she used to play at recess running after boys.

Of course Ellie hadn't done this because of Jim, or even because of me. But I felt a deep shame and I knew I'd been a part of her undoing.

It was then that I noticed Selden kneeling on the floor, next to the gingham dust ruffle, leaning his head against her pillow. Tears spilled down his face. He was holding her wrist, the one with the ribbon. I can't remember ever seeing my father cry. I've seen Jim cry once. I had never seen Selden cry; in fact I've never seen a man cry like that since. It took me a minute to register that he was whispering one word to her over and over, and it wasn't until I was very close to him that I realized what it was.

Love.

Acknowledgments

The peerless Edith Wharton, who would be appalled at the thought of Lily Bart in Cleveland, must be acknowledged and thanked. Her books provide me continual inspiration and an ideal to strive toward.

Gratitude and appreciation go to my stellar agent, Elizabeth Kaplan, for her belief, her advocacy, and her fine reading. Thank you.

I've been blessed by the charming Trish Todd's energy, enthusiasm, and keen eye. She and her team made this book better than it was. Thank you.

Humble thanks and love to Irina Reyn, who inspired this book with her own and then valiantly read multiple drafts and offered insights that made everything stronger and clearer. Thank you, friend.

Love and thanks to Sheila Kohler for her continual belief in my work, for her years of encouragement, for letting me know when it's done, and for providing an example of how to be a woman of letters. Thank you.

I thank the following people for providing support, love, champagne, and snacks: Jen Brian, Annie Fehrenbacher, Matt Fehrenbacher, Thomas Frontini, Kristyl Fuller, Laura Gowen, Nicole Lincoln, Halley Moore, Heather Moore, Erin Mulvaney, Joyce Quayle, Sara Schia-voni Rezaee, the women of the dinner club, the BBR ladies, and the members of the MGBC book club.

I thank my parents and my families, Fehrenbachers, Bocks, and McMillans all.

Gratitude and love in abundance to Flora and Mac, who bring meaning to each day.

And I thank Sandy—husband, love, muse, and patron—who encourages me to be unbound and think big. For that and so much more I am grateful. Thank you.